Tainted

A novel by
JD Phillips

All of the events, characters, names and places depicted herein are fictional or used fictitiously. No representation is made that any of the statements made in this novel are true or that any incident depicted in this novel actually occurred, nor is any of the same intended or should be inferred by the reader.

Tainted
Copyright © 2006 by JD Phillips

Revised Words Take Flight Books printing: 2013

ISBN 13: 978-0615946566
ISBN 10: 0615946569

Printed in the United States of America

Dedicated to all of the people who continued to love and support this story even after seven years. You are as much responsible for the resurfacing of my beautiful monster as anyone.

Special thanks to Ville Valo for kindly allowing the use of his lyrics a second time around. It means more to me now than ever.

Your love is the only thing I live for in this world.
Oh, how I wait for the day your heart burns in these heavenly flames I
have already scorched in.
I just want you to know I'll always be waiting…

-Ville Valo, "Diabolikal Rapture"

Prelude

FROM THE MOMENT I first laid eyes upon Mai Evans, I knew that he was quite possibly the most beautiful creature to have ever graced the universe – and, therefore, ought to die. Specifically, I knew that I would have to be the one to kill him. How could I have known that the exact same thought had been dancing around his pretty little head? Funny how things sometimes work out that way.

His real name, of course, was Jeremiah; but I thought that far too plain for someone with an essence such as Adonis or Dorian Gray – a dangerous beauty, a flower with poisonous pollen. I dubbed him Mai – pronounced "my" – as in mine. He *was* mine. I'd known he would be from the moment his feral eyes first locked onto mine. It was inevitable, like the passing of the seasons or a hurricane assaulting a beach house.

Everything changed when I looked into his eyes and he into mine – though it's only now that I truly appreciate the gravity of it all. I hadn't understood exactly what he'd meant to me and me to him. I hadn't fully realized who he was and what I was to become. It was all a passing storm that crept beneath our skin, a sickness, a love – I dare to call it that – that spiraled out of control. All because I stared into his smoky eyes and discovered I was staring into my own…

I know that makes little sense now, but it will in time. To explain the end one must retrace the steps of the past and relive the beginning. I want to share the story. I want someone to know what I did to Mai and understand what I'm about to do now. It all goes back to the beginning.

The start of the end.

Chapter 1

I THOROUGHLY BELIEVE it was Mai who lured me into Zarold's Bar that night, leading me in with the song that would come like one of those mesmerizing sirens in the sea. It wasn't the sort of place that I would normally feel the need to venture into, even though I'd driven past it at least a dozen times since moving to a shithole of a town called Delsby only weeks earlier. It was a small building made of red brick and covered by a dark green metal roof, a piece of history surrounded by the noise of modern businesses that had risen up around it over the decades. A true hole in the wall.

On the night in question it was raining fairly hard, hard enough to remind me how stupid it was to have put off replacing my pathetic windshield wiper blades the week before. I recall that the sky was particularly dark. No stars could be seen, the moon was clouded over and I had no place in which I needed to be. I could have stopped anywhere to get myself a drink and a bite to eat. I could have chosen any parking lot to duck into in hope of forcing the tattered blade back in place one last time. I chose Zarold's.

I learned in my college psychology class, right before I dropped out, that listening to music stimulates the same area in our brains as sex. I always found that fascinating and believed it wholeheartedly. It was, in fact, about the only thing I managed to retain from my failed college career. Listen to a song that is intolerable and the pain it inflicts runs deep; listen to a great one — one that really hits where it counts — and there's no greater rush of euphoria.

Music was much like air to me. I considered it a necessity — and yet I was incapable of creating it. Oh, I was a fairly skilled guitarist and could read music. My singing? Well, nothing was going to fix my voice. As for writing music, I hadn't a clue, nor did I even want to try: I feared it would detract from the allure of it all and demystify the magic.

As I'd soon discover, the magic is everything – and mystery is what causes the flames to burn. That night, Zarold's would burn brightly indeed.

The large wooden sign that loomed over the entrance to the parking lot in front of Zarold's boasted that a live band called Nefarious was scheduled to perform that night. I suppose that was what truly inspired me to shut off my car and enter the place, even though I rarely frequented bars of any sort during that time in my life. He knew I'd come, he knew fate's hand would guide me there. No one can convince me of anything different. I was meant to find Mai when I did. He was meant for me.

Zarold's was fairly grimy as any proper bar ought to be. It was slightly exciting for me, I'll admit, as it was exactly the sort of place my mother would have warned me to steer clear of. Dimly lit and filled with smoke, the tables covered in plaid green tablecloths that looked as though they'd not been changed for a year or more, empty bottles and old beer taps on display on the shelves overhead – it felt as though one might catch something simply by breathing the air. I sat down at one of the booths along the wall, facing the small black wooden stage at the front of the place, and hoped to disappear – something the past few years of practice had made quite easy for me to do.

I was born a blonde with dark blue eyes and slightly olive skin. I'd never been considered anything other than average, especially by myself, which had caused great pains while I was maturing. I resented it until I rather inadvertently discovered that I could use it to my advantage. Recent events had made it necessary for me to turn to colored lenses and a box of hair dye: I'd become a brunette with dark brown eyes and I liked that feeling. I liked becoming someone new, someone different that could stand out just as easily as shrink into the background. It was like being born again.

The first thing I noticed about Zarold's, other than the possible health code violations, was that no one really seemed to give a damn that I was there. At that hour, in that place, in that part of town, most of the customers were drunkards or emaciated insomniacs. Indifferent or impaired. No one so much as glanced at me. No one, in fact, noticed my presence at all other than my waitress…and him…

I could feel Mai's eyes watching from the booth across the room from mine. I could have felt them from any distance. He had eyes that were capable of physically striking their target and holding on for as long as that target could bear their pull. I never could quite settle on what color Mai's eyes were, they seemed to shift on a whim. A smoldering blue and pale green colliding. A fair watercolor gray.

Mai watched me as I ordered a soda and a cheeseburger from a frumpy waitress whose name I didn't bother to catch. I didn't realize it was Mai that was staring at me right at that moment, of course, as I'd learned to never hunt around the room when I sensed a watcher. On the off chance I met their stare it usually ended in embarrassment, with them snickering or firing off some defensive remark. *Had* I met Mai's gaze then, however, I suspect that he'd probably have offered one of his cool grins and continued devouring his current cigarette with abandon. He was always smoking, killing himself slowly, beautifully, before live audiences.

The stage was stacked with amplifiers and cords. There was a drum set and three microphones. I had my food by the time the manager started the sound check and I started scoping the area in hopes of catching a glimpse of the band. I saw mostly older men, beer-bellied husbands on retreat from their wives, and a few tired women with neon cherry lipstick and caked mascara hoping for a free drink or two. I also saw a small group of young people closer to my own age and they seemed excited, as if they had come specifically to see the show. Three women and two men; one of them was giggling obnoxiously.

What I didn't know was that the band Nefarious had become fairly well known to a select population living near Delsby. A homespun single of a song called "Clarity" had been burned off of a computer and distributed on the local college campus. A town like Delsby didn't have much of a night scene, that was true even for the college area, as it was ultra conservative and overly conscious of image. Nefarious was a secret, something the young and bored could share with one another and, as I'd soon see for myself, highly addictive. Mai had a way of pulling people to him. It was his charisma, his grace. Once bitten by one of his songs there was simply no turning back.

What the tiny rally of supporters didn't know – for there had been no pictures or press for them to refer to – was that the band

Nefarious didn't really exist yet. There was no *band* of people, only Mai acting solo. He'd written the entirety of the song, he'd played each instrument himself, and then he'd blended it all on his home computer before releasing it. Beautifully deceitful, clever and resourceful; it was Mai's nature in its purest form.

A few clapped when the manager finally called Nefarious to the stage. I would have, but I was busy taking a bite out of my burger at the time. I heard a slight murmur from the fan club of five as someone stepped onto the stage. When I raised my eyes away from my plate I saw why, though I doubt their cause for awe was the same as mine.

I saw him from behind first, fairly average in height and rail thin. He was dressed in fitted jeans that hung low on his slender hips and flared about the black and white sneakers he wore. His shirt was a vibrant indigo, sleek and long-sleeved, and unbuttoned about the wrists. He had a nice ass; funny as it sounds I remember noticing that almost right away. He didn't walk so much as swagger or glide, his arms and hips graceful in their movement. He reminded me of a feline.

The end began when he turned around and sat down upon a stool behind the center microphone, an acoustic guitar on his lap and a sly twinkle in his piercing eyes. He plugged the guitar in and then took a look around the room. He looked at me.

He was like nothing I had ever seen before. He was pretty — that's the only word I could think of — but not in a flowery, prissy sort of way. His hair was a sea of restless chocolate and hazelnut waves that fell about his shoulders in uncombed tangles. Both of his ears were pierced, fitted with small silver hoops about the lobes and a silver bar through the cartilage of the left. His lips were full and pink, his nose small, his eyes...I've already touched on the overwhelming eyes beneath sharp, brooding eyebrows. He had makeup on: eyeliner, mascara and smoky eye shadow that made him look a bit like some sleepless addict.

In my humble opinion, no guy should ever have a mascara stick in his hand, let alone know how to *use* one. At least that's what I would've said back then, anyway. All hail to equal rights and all that, but face paint? And did I mention his fingernails were also painted a dark blue? All of that equaled "fairyland" to me and I didn't go for girly guys. I was thinking queenie all the way for Mai, anticipating he would show himself to be some delicate little plaything with a voice that rivaled Michael Jackson – and then he spoke and I found myself completely enamored by him. It was the craziest thing – all part of the magic.

"Hello," he said with a goofy laugh, his voice strong and smooth, and kissed with a slight accent that I couldn't quite place at the time. "Ah…as you can see, there's not exactly a band up here. Unless, of course, you've already had yourself an excellent night of boozing and are maybe seeing two or three of me right now and wondering what the hell I'm rambling on about…"

There was sparse, but surprisingly attentive, laughter given the crowd. Mai lowered his eyes almost bashfully and caressed one of the guitar strings with his thumb just enough to provoke the faintest of replies from the instrument. He didn't appear the slightest bit nervous to be alone under the spotlight. He remained casual, completely genuine, as if speaking to a group of his closest friends, or so he made it seem. That was how he got people. Wherever he was, whatever the crowd, he always knew exactly how to best approach them and what was proper to say to earn affection and trust – not that he always followed what was best.

It explained how he'd managed to go around in an uptight, generally homophobic small town like Delsby without, thus far, getting the shit beaten out of him. He certainly didn't look like much of a challenge. He *looked* as if one strong gust of wind could knock him flat and break every bone in his slender body.

"Right. So, um, here's the thing," he continued. "I've sort of lost the rest of the band. Last I saw 'em we were at a parade in Mardi Gras. You know how it is when brewskies are tossed in with flying, sparkling beads. They may still be wandering the streets of New Orleans flashing their boobies – it's hard to say, really."

There was more laughter then and from a greater number of people. Mai had nearly everyone's attention and I suspect he enjoyed that. He was talking *to* them rather than *at* them and made it feel that way. It would have been rude for them to simply brush him aside.

"So, for better or worse, you've got li'l, ol' me and my guitar tonight. Going to give you all the acoustic treatment," he said, pausing only long enough to light up a cigarette. "If it sucks I only ask you throw the plastic cups at me rather than the glass pitchers, please."

That was it. Mai had gotten every single one of us that night, hook, line, and sinker. He knew damn well that his performance wouldn't "suck," but we'd have been too charmed to notice even if it had. The love affair began as he sang "Clarity" with the cigarette between his lips and eyes closed. He was elegance and smoke, raw vulnerability dripping with solid confidence. He loved his music as much as we did and treated it accordingly. He always wanted it to be about the music.

As for his voice…there were moments when I imagined that he was exactly what the angels above would sound like should they have come to earth to serenade us. He sang low and smooth; slightly melancholic, but uplifting nonetheless – haunting and romantic in every sense of the word.

Never in my life had I been a romantic type. Chick flicks made me squirm, I burned my mother's paperback romances and regularly mocked any sappy love song that happened to come my way over the radio. Somehow, coming from Mai's lips, words that I'd normally have found annoying or worthy of an eye roll became beautiful. I became entranced by them. Knights and their princesses. True, mad love with all of its passion and heartache and rapture…I'd come to believe that such things simply didn't exist and, if they did, I was never going to experience them. Mai represented the possibility of such things to me. That night he ignited a burning hope within me that would never fade away. I'd been struck by love for the first time.

Unanimous applause broke out once the song was finished. Mai bowed his head, smiled graciously and went on to play three others that no audience had ever had the honor of hearing before. When he was finished with the set, he unplugged his guitar and looked directly at me. I couldn't understand the flicker in his eyes…a look as if there was something that he wanted from me. But *what*, I wondered, could he want from *me*?

I think – hope – I smiled at him, but I can't be certain. Time always seemed to come to a crashing halt whenever his eyes happened to lock onto mine, that remained true throughout it all, but I think everyone tended to feel that way. The building and everyone in it could have burst into flames around me while he stared and I honestly would not have noticed.

Mai returned to his booth after taking a short little bow and had a few more beers. The manager spoke to him about doing more shows at the bar and Mai seemed quite eager to agree to that. The fan club of five surrounded him soon after, asking for autographs and taking pictures of him. Mai would later say that some people considered anyone that played on a stage important and that form of attention-seeking admiration meant little to him.

The girls and boys both flirted. There was a lot of eye batting and hair tossing, giggles and sleazy innuendo, as they tried to sort out which of them was more his type. It made me feel small and angry. I wanted to be close to him, too. I wanted to touch him, but I wasn't like that. I'd never *learned* to be like that. I'd had to fight for control, fight to be noticed, all of my life. I didn't have it in me to bounce about and cheer with wild abandon. I couldn't even get out of my booth to walk over and smile at him.

No "hello." No "loved your work." I simply sat and stared and envied. It's only now, looking back, that I realize Mai was doing the same.

Chapter 2

CURIOUS THAT WHEN I close my eyes and dare to summon any memory of Mai to my mind I see him in shades of black, white and gray. It's almost silver. It suits him. It creates a feeling of nostalgia, of something forlorn on a dreamscape. All of my favorite photographs of Mai are those done in grayscale...

I returned to Zarold's the following Friday, when Mai was due to perform again. There was really never any question as to whether I would go to see him sing one more time, I didn't have a choice. He wanted me there, I felt that he did. He called me there just as he had that first night.

I had sat in my booth for nearly two hours after Mai's first performance, sipping at numerous sodas and pretending not to stare at him. I'd sat until he'd finally decided to leave. I'd wanted to follow him then, but I hadn't. That night, after the second show, I was planning to swallow my anxiety. I was planning to speak to him.

I even tried to make myself appear slightly more presentable that night – though, for me, that's not exactly saying much. I'd combed my hair and applied ChapStick to hide how dry my bottom lip was. I'd even put on clean clothes fresh out of the dryer. The fan club of five was now a club of nine and two of the girls were sporting tight baby tees and a lot of leg. One of the guys had forgotten to button his shirt. The fascination, the curiosity about Mai's preferences in the bedroom, had already taken on a life of its own.

By then I'd done a slight reversal on my opinion of Mai. I didn't believe him to be a complete queenie – he didn't move or speak like one – and I knew several to whom to compare him; but he certainly enjoyed raising eyebrows and leaving people to wonder.

"Keep 'em guessing and they'll keep buying and paying

attention," was Mai's motto. It was his philosophy in every aspect of his life, as a matter of fact – but I'm getting ahead of myself...

Mai sat in the same booth as before, but this time he hadn't come alone. There was a bear of a man with him, a fresh drummer called Dart (don't ask me why, I never found out) who had a round, buzzed head and startling green eyes. He was dressed in jeans and chaps, and wore a black leather vest that made him look more like the leader of some biker gang than a musician. There was also a woman, dark skinned with bleached wispy hair, dressed in black leather. She had a sleeve of wild tribal tattoos down her right arm and a silver stud in her left nostril – Renna, the new bassist.

I found it fairly impressive. Only a week had passed between shows and already Mai had acquired half a band to accompany him. He was proficient enough on guitar to take the role on himself until he could find someone else, so only the keyboard and ambience were unaccounted for. No one at Zarold's really noticed, since there was no recorded album with which to compare the songs.

Mai appeared much the same as he had the previous week, except the indigo shirt had been replaced by an identical crimson one. They made for an odd-looking trio: a dark amazon, a portly biker and Mai – but they went on to play extremely well together. I've always wondered how much they'd practiced, if at all, before that show. Had they simply clicked and it all fell together perfectly, or had they gone over the songs repeatedly, racing their limited amount of time to prepare?

I don't think anyone knew that Renna and Dart were new and hardly even knew one another. *I* wouldn't have known if Mai hadn't admitted to me, not long into our relationship, that he'd made the band's first single on his own. They were accepted instantly by the patrons of Zarold's and Mai tied them to his previous tale about Mardi Gras with ease.

"So glad Dart finally sobered up enough to hide his tits away," he had playfully announced, flashing a goofy grin.

I liked it when Mai behaved like a fool. His lyrics were always so heavy, so serious and beautifully morbid, and his face naturally sad and brooding. In an instant he could transform by breaking out into an impersonation of Elvis or performing an ill-timed ass shake to an unsuspecting crowd. All of those things made him cute, light, sometimes even – forgive my lack of a better word – geeky. He could be an absolute geek at times. He liked to play – and though he more often than not intended his folly to be harmless, it did sometimes get him into trouble. That night was to be one of those times.

It started innocently enough. Mai noticed that the woman seated at the table in front of the stage was enjoying him quite a bit and blew her a kiss during the last song. He had that look on his face that I'd come to know well after he'd done it, the arched eyebrow and faint smirk. When the woman's husband became visibly angered, Mai gave him the face I'd come to know even better – the mixture of mock innocence laced with nonchalance – as if to proclaim that he'd done nothing at all out of the ordinary. I found it fairly adorable. The husband took it as a challenge and hurled his empty pitcher of beer at the stage. Mai dodged it with a startled little laugh.

The manager was quick to ask the couple to leave and everything seemed to return to normal. The fan club fussed and had more pictures taken, Mai was asked to sign napkins and coasters, and I remained huddled in my booth watching it all. Waiting. Wasting the opportunity before me. I'd not have lived up to my vow to speak to him that night, either, if I hadn't glanced outside after Renna and Dart had departed and spotted the husband lurking in the alley near the bar. He was waiting for Mai, I realized; and so when Mai finally walked out the front door, I rushed right out after him.

I can't explain what came over me – it was something I'd only felt once before in my life – but I managed to leap from my booth and run out that door so quickly that I forgot that I didn't even know his name. He'd never said it while on the stage – so I simply uttered some Neanderthal whoop. The sound startled Mai and he turned back to look at me, allowing the husband's opening punch to miss.

Mai gasped something along the lines of "Shit!" and dropped his guitar case to the ground. I'd have been laughing at how large his eyes had become – and the way he'd cursed – if not for the fact that I feared I was about to be thrashed as well. I was also a threat to the husband now and that wasn't a good sign for either of us.

I don't look much more competent of a fighter than Mai, but I've always known how to handle myself. Normally I wouldn't have gone looking for trouble, nor would I have been the aggressor; but something inside of me sort of snapped out of place that night and I went after the husband like a near lunatic. I wanted to protect Mai.

Unfortunately I wasn't all that adept at staging my offense. I ran at the guy and he threw me back flat on the ground within seconds. He got a good punch in on me before Mai struck him and managed to become the center of his attention once again.

Mai laughed throughout it all. He *laughed* – deep and goofy – chuckling between grunts and punches. He'd hurt his hand and his face was bleeding by the time I managed to mount the guy's back and began trying to pull him away. By then, the man's wife had tracked him down. He'd told her to wait in their car, she'd grown tired of waiting and once she saw what he was up to…well, I'd never heard a woman screech exactly like a howler monkey before, but it was quite funny once the ringing dissipated from my ears.

Leave it to a wife to so easily clean up a situation. The husband dropped his hands to his sides almost immediately and allowed her to drag him out of the alley. She offered apologies over her shoulder, in between angry glares at her husband. He simply grumbled in shame.

Mai was lying on his back atop a newly flattened pile of discarded cardboard boxes, his right hand lying limp at his side while he held his nose with the left. I stared down at him and he looked up at me, his eyes ablaze with playful smiles. I held out my hand and he took it. I held it for quite sometime before I helped him get to his feet. His touch was electric, pulsing. I could feel the fire burning within his veins.

Mai's right hand and wrist were fractured – he'd have a splint put on later that night – and there was a cut above his eyebrow. Blood ran in a thin stream down the right side of his face and from his nose down over his chin. He looked at me, panting and bloodied and sweating, and he grinned with such an air of satisfaction that I laughed. He had never looked so beautiful.

It turned out I was bleeding as well, from my lip, but I didn't notice until Mai reached out and wiped the blood off of my chin with his left index finger. He showed it to me and then playfully painted my lips with it, smiling as he admired his work.

"My hero, I guess I should call you," he said, tilting his head to the side. "You were at last week's show, too, weren't you?"

My face grew hot as I forced myself to nod at him and I knew that I was blushing. He *had* seen me. I'd known he had. Either that or he'd posed the question purely on a hunch. Mai was good at that. He could read people well enough to make educated guesses and assumptions, like one of those street magicians I'd seen on television. As such, nearly anyone he spoke to came away feeling special, validated…or completely freaked out because he seemed to know them so well after only a few minutes of conversation. I was the exception to that rule, though Mai wouldn't realize that for a couple of years. I believe he saw in me just what he wanted to see, what he needed to see. It should have worked out perfectly for the both of us, but life often doesn't work out as we plan it.

Still, I *had* been at the previous show and Mai could tell that I had by my reaction. "I knew I'd seen you before," he said with a hint of pride. "You had soda in a bar. Very interesting, indeed. Do you smoke?"

I shook my head.

"Well, I'm going to," he laughed. "Help me out?"

Mai was able to pull the now crumpled pack of cigarettes out of his jeans pocket on his own, but digging out a cigarette with his right hand immobilized was a feat he couldn't quite pull off. I pulled the cigarette out and placed it between his lips while he watched me carefully with those razor eyes of his. I even lit the damn thing for him.

"Assisted passive suicide," he remarked as he took his first drag. "Could they jail you for that?"

I dumbly shook my head. "Maybe you should quit," I replied. I hated how high and sweet my voice came across.

"You *can* speak," he teased, exhaling a cloud of smoke into the air with a graceful tilt of his head. "Good to know, good to know. Have you a name or am I to refer to you always as 'the noble fool that spared me a right hook to the face'?"

"I'm Blue," I said.

I had my parents to thank for that. Going through life named after a color was one of those torturous cruelties that neither Mom nor Dad had taken time to think through. Always – *always* – after introducing myself I was greeted with the confused or skeptical stare, the patronizing laugh followed by, "Don't be sad," or the all so overused question, "Seriously?"

I didn't get any of that from Mai. I *never* got quite what I expected from Mai. No, Mai simply smiled faintly, secretively, when I told him my name and then he offered a sly wink. He appreciated the irony. He *cherished* it. Mai adored all irony and contradictions in life. If something was too simple he had to muddle it up somehow. He spoke in near riddles that made perfect sense only to himself at times for no other reason than to mess with people, test their reaction – and at other times when he was dead serious and trying to express himself in his off-color way.

I often wondered what it was like inside a mind like Mai's, always bombarded by frantic thoughts and racing passions that could hardly be contained. To have so many ideas charging through the channels of the brain so swiftly that within the blink of an eye they were lost if not instantly developed.

I'd always had the opposite problem. My thoughts came slowly and everything I said or did had to be carefully premeditated. I remained silent in conversations to obsess later over what I would have liked to have said. I never acted without serious consideration to the outcome of those actions, even when the things I expected to happen were sometimes selfish whims that never came to fruition. I didn't realize right at that moment what the look in Mai's eyes truly meant as he smiled at me in his sly way.

"Do they call you 'Blue' cos of those big puppy eyes of yours?" he asked.

"It's just my name," I replied, smiling shyly and shaking my head.

"Your folks named you after a crayon?" he asked, arching an eyebrow.

Had anyone else asked a question like that I'd have surely grown defensive. I'd have certainly rolled my eyes or made some bitter reply. Coming from Mai, with his smooth voice and gently glowing eyes, it seemed perfectly harmless. Flirtatious. Complimentary.

"Yeah," I said. "They named me at the suggestion of their friend's daughter. How lucky am I to have parents that name their kid on the recommendation of a two year old?"

"Sweet. I bet you were your parents' darling, overprotected and cuddled to death until you managed to crawl your way out of the house," Mai murmured. "I was named after Jeremiah the bullfrog. You know that song? My mum heard it on the way to the hospital and since she'd had a healthy dose of wine before poppin' me out, it seemed the right pick to her."

"You're serious?" I asked; I sounded like all those people I'd hated over the years.

He nodded, inhaled on his cigarette, exhaled. His expression remained unchanged.

"Jeremiah doesn't suit you," I said. "It isn't, uh...pretty enough."

Mai laughed at me then, not mockingly, but certainly heartfelt, and tossed his cigarette to the ground. He never finished any of his cigarettes, never smoked them more than half way before reaching for a new one; it was his method of cutting back. I was already in love with him by that point and he knew it. I know he knew it. He loved it. That I'd find myself attracted to someone like *him* of all people…it seems so bizarre to me even now. He wasn't my type in any sense of the word. I suppose that's why I fell so hard.

"Shit," he said through a sigh, staring down at his right hand; it was now swollen and purple. "I've a show tomorrow. Won't be able to play like this, will I…"

"Where did your old guitarist go? For real, I mean," I said. "Surely not Mardi Gras."

It was then, with a boyish grin and devilish twinkle in his eyes, that Mai confessed what he'd done to produce the single. He was a genius, I wasn't the first to tell him that, but he didn't seem to agree. He was worried.

"I'll have no guitarist," he said, shaking his head. "How smart is that? I'll never find one before tomorrow night. I can't go out during the day and search, either. Shit, man."

"Why not? Allergic to the sun?"

I'd meant that as a joke, of course, but Mai nodded solemnly in response. It would later become part of the mystery that surrounded him, another layer of the myth, more fuel for the wild rumors discussed on Internet forums. Mai never walked out beneath the sun's light. He couldn't. He had a rare skin disease, something I'd only vaguely heard of through television shows. His skin was extremely sensitive to the sun and fluorescent lighting. Any direct exposure would be potentially devastating to his health.

"Like a vampire," he replied through a flat smile. "What about you? Are you one of those freakish day dwellers?"

I shook my head. "Not if I can help it," I replied. "I work evenings. I'm, uh, an insomniac."

"You get paid for that?" Mai asked with his goofy smile. "I don't see the appeal of rising with the sun and sleeping through the night, anyway. Night is when there's the best chance to really focus, cos you're conscious when most of the world is lost to sleep. There're so many free thoughts floating about, waiting to be grabbed like passing leaves. Our bodies are half dead when asleep, y'know? Our spirits go off to visit this giant pool or something while we're out. No one interesting is ever up during the day."

I nodded as if I understood, but I didn't. I rarely understood Mai when he started talking in his deep, enigmatic way. It wouldn't be the last time he'd mention this idea of some dead pool to me but I never got it. Not until *so* much time had passed us by. He smiled faintly, as he often did when he read total bewilderment in my eyes, and began to stare down at his hand again.

"Doesn't even hurt," he whispered. "Shouldn't it hurt?"

"I'm sure it will tomorrow," I laughed. "You'd better go to a doctor."

"Yeah, yeah, I will," he said absently. "Where do you work?"

"At…a music shop," I replied. "Embarrassing."

"Why is that embarrassing? You like being 'round music, you're earning yourself some money. *I'm* not earning any money," he was quick to say.

I'd never considered there was any bright side to working at a store in the mall at my age. I was twenty four, the age when everyone expected me to settle down, land a career and better myself in some way. I loved music, I wanted nothing more than to touch it, but somehow selling the latest "pop tart" swill to pimple-faced teens hardly seemed to be living out the dream.

"You wouldn't play guitar by any chance, would you?" he asked, mostly in jest. "Care to save my arse on stage tomorrow as well?"

"Actually, I do play – but I've only done covers, mimicking KISS and The Beatles and things like that," I replied. "I don't know how good I am."

"No shit? Please don't fuck with me now," he said, grabbing hold of my shoulder. "You can play guitar?"

"Yeah, but like I said – I'm not that good."

"Gotta be better than bloody crippled, aye?" he asked in a funny tone, slowly shaking his right arm about. "Can you read music? Could you learn a few songs by tomorrow night?"

"I-I don't know. I mean, yeah, I can read music but…I don't know if I can, uh, I mean…I wouldn't want to ruin your work."

"Ruin it? Without you I've got no guitar at all, you'll be saving it. I need you, Bluesy. I'll love ya forever, babe, I swear."

Babe. I wasn't the first nor would I be the last who Mai would call "babe," but it had certainly felt like it at the time. Men, women – old, young – he called everyone "babe" or "sweetheart" or "darling" as casually as he'd report that the moon was shining in the sky. Nonetheless, it worked. I found myself agreeing to perform with him, an act of sheer spontaneity. I took the sheet music that he thrust at me and agreed to do my best at learning it in the short time I'd been given. He seemed quite satisfied when we parted, fully confident that I'd make good on my word. I should have known it then that he was desperate. Desperation is the motivation behind nearly every act based on hope and faith.

18

Chapter 3

MAI TOLD ME once the secret to life and on the stage is to fake it. He said he didn't have a clue what he was doing when singing before a crowd, it was all smoke and mirrors and smiles. Acting on autopilot. He said no one really paid that much attention anyway because the energy took over and colored everything in a positive light. He suggested I follow that philosophy on our first night on stage together, to go with what I knew and fake the rest. It was his philosophy, always. Little did he know that it had also been mine before he and I had even met.

I was slightly terrified. Mai *should* have been terrified. Since I actually hadn't had any job at all – the music store was the job I'd left before moving to Delsby – I'd stayed up all day long working and practicing but I was far from confident and Mai still hadn't heard me play a single note. He said he had a good feeling about me and didn't need me to audition.

We were playing at a nightclub outside of town, far hipper than Zarold's and close to the campus where the Nefarious single had been making its rounds. Mai had used makeup to conceal the bruises and cuts he received from the husband, though doing so made him appear, to use his words, a bit "freakier." The shadow about his eyes was heavy and made their color appear even richer. His face appeared almost bleached.

I was with Mai as he worked to hide his battle wounds. He painted my lips black and added shadow to my eyes for the fun of it once he'd finished. I'd never worn makeup in my entire life, but I found that I actually enjoyed it. It made me look...different. Better. And it perfectly hid my busted lip.

Dart, I discovered, was an extremely funny guy. He was older than both me and Mai: a Polish fellow who talked with a genuine

Delsby twang and weighed nearly three-hundred pounds – most of which was muscle. He wore cat-rimmed sunglasses everywhere he went, along with a bandanna upon his head. He didn't own and had never even ridden a motorcycle and seemed clueless whenever someone asked him if he did. He and Mai had met at an all-night grocery store of all places and the two had bonded over a shared fascination with an unidentifiable salad on display in the deli case.

"It was mint green and it had red beans and mayonnaise in it," he told me.

"Whipped marshmallows, not mayonnaise," Mai insisted.

"Mayo!" Dart shouted.

Don't ask me which was correct – if either were. All I knew was that it was no salad spread *I'd* consider eating and neither had they.

Renna didn't want to speak to me. She wasn't much of a talker anyway, not even to Mai; but she was the sort of person who carefully chose those with whom she'd associate. She saw me as temporary; she'd expected me to be gone as soon as that show was finished, and that made me unimportant. She and Mai were old friends, I suspected that they had once been lovers, and their relationship always seemed to hang on the edge of a razor. She loved Mai, she respected him, but she didn't trust him one bit. I didn't dislike her so much as feel intimidated by her. She tended to intimidate everyone the first time they met her. Between her and Dart, I felt safe. No one would dare to lash out and attack us if they were at our side. Or so I thought.

Mai left the splint on his hand during the performance, an ugly tan thing that clung to him with Velcro and covered his hand, wrist and half his forearm. His shirt hid most of it from sight and he slipped a pair of fingerless black gloves over his hands to finish the cover up. He held the microphone in his left hand as he strolled about the stage and began introducing us to the crowd. He started with Dart and Dart started drumming when Mai said his name. Next he went to Renna and then, Lord help me, it was my turn.

I'd never had much faith in divine intervention and I thought that luck was only what each of us makes of it; but on that night I swear a miracle must have occurred. Mai was looking at me with those damned eyes of his, the secretive smile in place, and he introduced me as "Bluebee." Everyone was staring at me, waiting for me to give my guitar a voice, but Mai's was the only stare that really reached me.

He was somehow looking inside of me, as crazy as that sounds. It seems to me now that he was *giving* something to me through that long gaze; but perhaps it was the other way around and I was the one invading, snatching some of the energy that Mai's body could hardly keep contained. I took the guitar pick out of my mouth and put it to the strings. I unleashed the loudest, most outrageous shredding riff I'd ever heard and it was beyond adequate. It was superb.

Mai forgot to introduce himself. I'd begun the song with an abrupt wail and then gone into the music as Mai had written it with ease; Dart and Renna followed my lead. It took Mai a few seconds to order his mouth to close, for his jaw had dropped when I'd begun to play, and by then he had no time to announce his own name. He grinned at me, looking absolutely radiant beneath the pale blue stage lights, and then giggled his way through the opening vocals.

I had startled him, I think. I had also pleased him. He and I both knew within the span of that brief intro that we were going to be together days, years, an eternity all beneath the pallid lights of azure, throbbing amps and cheering fans. *I* was earning fans. It was all wonderfully bizarre.

There was a talent agent in the audience, a woman looking for new acts with which to forge record deals. Mai *knew* there would be an agent there that night – that gets me to this day. He knew and he'd taken a chance on someone like me to play before this agent his very career depended upon. If I didn't know how devoted he truly was to his music, I'd have thought him insane.

I played decently. I'd remained cautious for the remainder of the show and I admit to fudging a few riffs here and there. It was a lot to remember and the heat of standing before so many people was unbelievable. Anytime Mai thought I appeared to be cracking under the pressure he'd come over to where I was to sing at me or pat my back. He'd reel me back in. He'd make it feel as though he and I were alone up there and that was a euphoric rush of comfort. He made it so I could breathe again.

The audience went wild when the last song was finished and the lights over our heads dimmed. Mai had poured the same charm on them that I'd seen in Zarold's. He was witty, seductive, generous with the smiles and winks and amusing faces. He was something new, his music far removed from the mainstream pop-rock that medicated the masses with its redundancy over the radio. His vocal range was amazingly versatile, as was the sound of his songs. His music was at times rough and heavy, as unapologetic as any heavy metal band in history. It was paired with softer, sensitive ballads and always the lyrics were from his heart – emotional and real and relative. His appeal had the potential to be universal.

Mai kissed me for the first time after that show. I'd practically run off the stage once the set was finished, my arms and legs trembling as I finally allowed nerves to set in. I thought I was going to become ill, but instead I only heaved and collapsed in a corner backstage. Mai chased after me, a bright smile on his face, but I was afraid to look at him. I had messed the songs up a bit and that was suddenly all I could think about.

"You only play a li'l, ay?" he asked, bopping me on top of the head. "Bloody hell!"

"Sorry I screwed up some," I said.

"Fuck that, babe – you were *great!*" he laughed. "That intro was like…well, I didn't see it coming at all!"

"You were crazy to put me out there tonight, you know that?" I asked, sounding angry even though I didn't really feel it. "You never even *heard* whether I could play or not."

Mai shrugged in his nonchalant way. "I had your amp rigged to cut out just in case you bombed," he said coolly. "Glad we didn't have a need for that."

I can't remember if I laughed at that or not, I only remember that Mai knelt down soon after and placed a tender kiss upon my lips. His lips were soft and delicate and indescribably warm. I don't think I even kissed him back – I was too overwhelmed by everything – but he didn't seem to mind. He simply stood upright and smiled, and then Renna and Dart joined us. The agent was on her way back to speak to us.

I got to my feet and leaned against the wall to keep from falling over when Tiffany Ashcore came back to shake all of our hands. She looked like an agent, strangely enough. She was rather statuesque and annoyingly slender – probably spent much of her time with personal trainers in between regular visits to her plastic surgeon and ritualistic purges within any available restroom. She was dressed in a business suit, though the skirt was short and snug, and shirt extremely low cut on her flat chest – hardly what I'd call professional. I guessed her to be in her mid-fifties.

Tiffany had long, wavy hair that, back then, was dyed crimson, and her lovely sapphire eyes were frequently busy checking out Mai. She'd loved his voice, she liked the sound of the band. She wanted to strike up a record deal. Tiffany's father owned and operated a record label just out of state, which meant that she was quite free to round up any acts she happened to like and present them for his approval.

It was her favorite pastime, finding young artists desperate for recognition and exchanging favors with them. I imagined there were dozens of disillusioned fools out there, having been lifted by empty promises she'd only made because she wanted to have a fling with them. What she loved about Nefarious was Mai. I knew it and I'm sure Mai knew it, but the songs were good and the talent genuine. In a studio, with the proper instruments, they would be great. Tiffany wasn't so shallow that she didn't realize that.

"Are these your usual players?" I remember Tiffany asking Mai; she looked directly at me as she spoke.

"Yeah," Mai replied without hesitation. "This is the band. We're in need of a keyboardist, though. Ours was lost."

"Lost, huh?" Tiffany asked, giggling like a schoolgirl.

Dart nodded enthusiastically. "In Mardi Gras," he said with so serious a tone that Renna cracked a smile. "He bought this green spread with red beans and mayo and I just turned round and walked away from the damn fool. Crazy to eat that shit."

"Marshmallows," Mai murmured, grinning wryly.

I started to laugh. No. Giggle. I started to giggle like some giddy child on Christmas morning. I couldn't help myself. Dart's heavy accent, the deadpan way he'd delivered the tale of the lost keyboardist that never was, Mai's silly face as he'd poked at Dart one last time about the mayo…

"*Why* would they put beans and 'mallows together?!" Dart cried.

"I dunno. Probably tasted better with whatever it was making it all green," Mai replied.

Tiffany looked at Dart and then at Mai with a hint of disbelief in her eyes. She considered herself fairly important and was accustomed to unknown singers and musicians drowning her with compliments and attention – and here were Mai and Dart bickering over a deli mystery. Mai wasn't one to grovel over anything to anyone. He didn't need to. He'd already locked the record deal with Tiffany when she'd heard him sing and he knew it.

"So sorry," Mai told her, growing serious – somewhat serious, anyway. "You were saying, darling?"

"Your guitarist was off," Tiffany replied flatly. "Things like that cost the studio money during recordings."

"Blue didn't have a lot of time to prepare," Mai was quick to say, gliding closer to Tiffany and disarming her with a smile. "Completely my fault. There's no worry, Bluebee *is* our guitarist. It'll all be tip-top in the studio."

Mai's eyes remained focused upon Tiffany, until she gave into him with a submissive nod of her head. An argument with Mai could only be won if all direct eye contact was avoided, but avoiding his gaze was not as easy as it sounds. Tiffany gave Mai a time and date, the day we would be expected to lay down at least one song for her father to evaluate. Mai said he could handle filling in for the keyboardist himself and that was it. Tiffany gave us all a professional smile and called it a night.

Mai broke out into an impromptu dance once Tiffany had gone, shaking his hips from side to side with a cheerful whoop. Dart playfully bumped Mai with his butt and nearly knocked him across the room. That was when I heard Renna laugh for the first time; it was surprisingly light and feminine.

"Thanks, you guys, for playing so well," Mai said once he'd regained his balance. "It's about bloody time someone invited me into a studio."

"You're *sure* you want to keep me in the band?" I asked with a frown.

"You have to stay," Mai replied, looking quite serious. "You aren't thinking of leaving already, are you? You can't leave me."

"You can find someone better," I stated.

Mai shook his head and glanced all about the room as if suddenly disillusioned. "What are you doing to me? *Why* are you trying to ditch me? You're supposed to be my hero."

"I'm not doing anything," I said quickly, trying not to laugh as Mai sniffled childishly. "I just—"

"I want you with us. I want you with me," Mai said. "That's all there is to it."

I nodded, promised I'd never leave him and Mai instantly brightened. I wasn't certain then how seriously I should have taken his near tantrum, if he really would have thrown a fit had I refused my band membership, but why would I have refused? I was living out of a hotel, a real shithole of a place, and I'd already acquired a great deal of baggage and debt in my life. Mai wanted to hand me a free ticket into a soon-to-be-recorded band and Dart and Renna seemed to be in full agreement with him over it. Joining Nefarious was a no-brainer on my part. It was only the beginning of a daydream come to life.

"Where do you live, Blueski?" Mai asked me as we were leaving the nightclub. "Close to Zarold's?"

I nodded. "I have a room at Bargain Beds."

"That shitheap hotel?" Mai laughed.

"I couldn't afford an apartment. Don't laugh at me," I said, though I wasn't really feeling as defensive as I'd sounded.

"I'm laughing at us both, babe," he said. "I've been staying there for a near month."

I thought Mai was shitting me, but he was telling the truth. I'd been living across the hall from him, only a few doors down, since arriving in Delsby. What were the odds? I mean, really, what were the *odds* of something like that? Between Mai and me strange coincidences like that soon became a regular occurrence.

We talked a lot during the drive back to Delsby. Well, I probably did most of the talking and I didn't really say anything at all. I'm usually slow to take the initiative and begin a conversation, but once I get going I can go on for hours. Mai preferred to simply sit back and listen to people when not on stage. He preferred not to give much about himself away.

I did find out that he'd been born and raised in a small town near Liverpool, England, spending the majority of his childhood there. He'd left the country at the age of fifteen, having talked an American tourist into smuggling him to the states under the guise of a student exchange program. Once he was here, he'd found it easy enough to manage to stay. His mother had never made any reports that he was missing. Authorities never knew to care.

Mai didn't seem to miss his home much, though the often-gloomy skies of London had been far easier on his skin. He preferred rainy days and his favorite season was winter, especially after a heavy snow.

"Life is frozen in the winter," he said. "All green is buried, the flowers are tucked away, the leaves are dead and have blown away from their homes. It's also so bright, the snow. Even in the dead of night. The snow, you know — untouched, fresh snow — is a reflection of our souls if you think about it. It's the only time I enjoy being out in nature."

I tried to understand that, though I'm not sure I ever really did. Mai didn't divulge anything else to me: why he had left home, why his mother hadn't seemed concerned by his absence (I would eventually learn that she simply hadn't noticed he was missing for a few months and by then didn't know where he'd gone and didn't attempt to find out) or why he would spend long periods of time in total silence with his eyes set out far into the distance…

Mai frequently disappeared in that fashion around anyone at any give time. He'd be nearly catatonic, silent and still, yet he'd hear everything going on around him. I always wanted to go where he went during those spells of silence, to catch a glimpse of what held such a hold on him. Now I know. These days it's all I see.

Chapter 4

MAI WORKED NIGHTS as a waiter in this burger and shake restaurant that remained open twenty-four hours a day. He spent most of his time seated at the counter smoking and working on lyrics or sheets of music. Occasionally he passed the time making milkshakes for himself and his co-workers as they rarely had customers to serve.

One such co-worker was a girl called Jeanette – Mai called her Jeanie – who introduced herself to me as Mai's steady girlfriend, even though I'd never seen her at any of the shows. I met her for the first time two days after Tiffany had come to see us play, when Mai asked me to visit him at work to review the newest material he'd written.

I thought of Jeanie as a flake; most people did. She wasn't an ugly girl, but that was because her face was usually concealed by a traveling case full of cosmetics at all hours of the day. She kept her hair long and straight, and had it dyed the color of a dandelion with random streaks of black thrown in. She didn't seem to fit Mai at all and when they kissed, he always looked rather disinterested to me.

Jeanie was ever peppy as well, always giggling and bouncing about when she walked. She seemed to like me well enough, but she was the type to smile to your face and have a knife ready behind her back all the while. I didn't like her. I suppose I was jealous of her.

I'd done nothing but practice since the show and I felt pretty good about the songs Mai had already given me. but the new ones were definitely out of my league. I didn't understand his notes. I didn't think I could pull it off. Mai didn't care.

"Put your guitar out of tune," Mai stated. "Really fuck it up. Here. Give it here."

Reluctantly I handed Mai my guitar and watched as he proceeded to manually mangle all the fine tuning I'd put so much time into not that long ago. When he was finished I plucked at the strings and laughed. I could hear it. I could hear what he had in mind.

I met up with Mai at his job nearly every night for a full week after that until it was time for us to make our first trip to the studio. Jeanie tagged along with us simply because she'd always wanted to be around studio equipment. I still felt as though I didn't quite belong, but it no longer mattered. I couldn't have backed out then if I'd tried and Mai wanted me around. That was enough for me.

Tiffany was there to watch us perform, dressed in an outfit nearly identical to the suit that she'd worn before. She remained behind the glass in the control room where they had made Jeanie sit with her face pressed quite close to the window that divided us.

None of us had dressed up for the occasion, I didn't even consider that we should have, but Tiffany had stared at us as if disappointed. Mai hadn't worn any makeup and he hadn't bothered to shave when he woke that evening – a look I had become quite used to and, by this time, even preferred. His eyes appeared much darker when not surrounded by the dark shadow and eyeliner, and his face transformed from pretty to ruggedly handsome. He'd also decided to hide his hair away beneath a silly knit hat that had a pair of cat eyes on the front and pointed red and black ears on top. All of that combined with simple jeans and a black T-shirt made him seem much more ordinary and Tiffany didn't care for it at all.

She pulled Mai outside for a private talk while the rest of us adjusted our instruments and prepared to play. We all assumed she was scolding him because she'd been hoping to do a photo shoot that day – that's what Mai told us, anyway – because we were an odd bunch collectively and she was counting on Mai's appearance to sell us. She didn't want him to go out in public again looking plain, looking like himself, once our single was released nationwide. Selecting an image and sticking to it, Tiffany believed, was even more important than forming a band that could actually play with skill.

Mai was pissed when he came back in to sing, I could see that he was. It surprised me little that a serious temper lurked beneath Mai's surface even though I hadn't ever seen him angry before that day. He wasn't often physically aggressive, but he could throw daggers with his eyes and become fairly vicious with his sarcasm. That day he simply sang the way he was feeling, rough and slightly desperate. "Clarity" took on a completely different meaning because of it; it became something harsher and more powerful. Dart, Renna and I adjusted our tempo accordingly.

I wasn't sure why, exactly, Mai had become so angry, but I noticed that Tiffany winked at him as she walked away. Later, of course, Mai would tell me exactly what was said and done – much later when it was too late to really become upset over it. Had I known it was far more than a dress code issue I'd have been angry, too. I suppose that's why he didn't tell any of us.

Mai insisted on being involved in the final production of the song once we'd all played our parts. He went into the control room and became fast friends with our producer Shane. By the end of the night our single was finished and ready to be sent to Tiffany's father. I could hardly believe it. I could hardly believe that it was me playing the guitar, my work streaming from the speakers. Mai seemed to have calmed down completely. He nodded his head and mimicked playing guitar along with the song during the playback, a satisfied smile upon his lips all the while.

It was nearly time for the sun to rise when we were ready to return home. Mai didn't think he could make it back to Delsby before the sun would be upon him and that meant he'd have to stay behind. We all offered to stay with him, between the three of us we would have been able to put up for two hotel rooms, but Mai said there was no need for that. We ended up leaving Mai and Renna's car behind and taking Dart's truck back to town. Mai ended up staying the night with Tiffany.

It was fairly obvious that Mai and Tiffany had gotten together that day, but I tried my best not to think about it. Mai wasn't attracted to Tiffany, I'm not certain that he even much liked the woman, but she'd wanted to have him in her bed and so he'd gone. He saw it as taking one for the band, a duty that had to be fulfilled. She knew there was no way her father would deny a contract with Nefarious so she'd pulled the only trump card she had remaining that day in the studio: money.

What had sent Mai into such a rage that night was Tiffany's threat to charge a ridiculous sum for our session if he didn't agree to be a bit friendlier with her later on. He could have refused, called Tiffany on it and we'd probably have found ourselves deeply in debt with a company to which we didn't yet have any true commitments. We'd have been frozen, unlikely to be picked up by any other companies while the debt remained, so Mai had simply swallowed his pride and took the hit. Principles, he'd later say, are of selective importance.

"Don't kill yourself to protest the cruelty of death," he once told me. I wish I'd taken it to heart.

I didn't know the details behind Mai's decision to stay with Tiffany back then, of course, because Mai wouldn't talk about it. No one spoke about it but I think we all knew with the exception of Jeanie, who would've had to have been in the bedroom as it was all going on to gain any insight. I continued visiting Mai's work on a nightly basis while Tiffany's father worked to finalize a contract and begin preparations for the album we were going to make. Mai was withdrawn, not just from me but the world, completely absorbed in his work. Tweaking the lyrics, re-shaping notes and melodies, tossing in random sounds and then taking them back out – he was a dedicated worker, probably to a fault. I even ended up making *him* a milkshake a time or two.

Jeanie, the poor, stupid girl, took the greatest brunt of it. Mai hardly acknowledged her at all most of the time but he wasn't really cruel about it. He would nod or offer a quick kiss on the cheek or an absent smile – enough to keep Jeanie satisfied – but anyone that had a clue about Mai could see that he'd lost his romantic interest in her. I wondered when he would finally drop the axe over her head but I didn't ask. Asking would have made me sound too interested and I couldn't have that.

The studio sessions, when it came time to begin recording the album, were intense. Mai expected everyone to do their parts without any slacking but he was always hardest on himself. If he didn't hit a note as well as he thought he was capable of hitting it, he would stop and begin the verse over even when Tiffany would bang on the glass and shake her head at him. Mai refused to compromise when it came to the music and he didn't do it to be difficult – he did it because it was that important. It would earn him a lot of respect down the road. It earned me sore fingertips, Dart aching arms, and Renna a frozen scowl. In the end we all realized that it had been worth it, though. We appreciated how hard Mai had pushed us.

I never dreamed that one day he would be the one in need of a push.

Chapter 5

EXACTLY ONE WEEK after "Clarity" was released it shot to number nine on the local radio. No one knew who the hell we were, where Nefarious had come from or what we were about. All they knew is that they wanted to – and the college kids who had listened to Mai's original single were largely to thank for making that happen. They made up flyers and gave us free promotion – and Mai never forgot them. We performed a free concert in their campus courtyard that week, a tradition that Mai would insist on continuing right up to the end of it all. Fans, the real fans that shared his love for the art of music and creativity, were always dear to his heart. He said it was easy to tell the difference; the real fans never rushed out to put our autographs up on eBay.

The phone calls flooded Tiffany's office, for she'd proclaimed herself our manager and agent and no one knew how to phone Mai. We'd gotten nearly all of the album completed by this point, but we'd still neither had that photo shoot nor taken a look at the available layouts for the CD inserts. The public wanted to see us, they wanted the album and Tiffany was quick to tease the callers and make them all the more hungry. The woman was, to her credit, great at her job.

We had the photo shoot before returning to the studio to complete the last few songs. Several out-of-town clubs were interested in booking us and they needed photographs to use for promotion. I don't think I ever had as much fun as I'd had that day. Mai declared that if he had to wear makeup, so would the rest of us – though he eventually decided against that in Dart's case. A giant of a bald man with a goatee, multiple piercings, and naturally stern face simply didn't look right in glitter.

Mai was the one to give me my makeover. He straddled the chair in front of me and went to work, his face set in deep concentration as he applied foundation, shadow, lipstick and eyeliner. It was inexplicably erotic…and a bit surreal. I laughed more than once as he frowned or grunted while inspecting his handiwork.

"And *why* is it that you're so good at this?" I had to ask.

"I used to do my mum up a lot," Mai replied, gently blowing upon a blush brush. "She'd ask me to cos she'd be too bloody pissed to do it herself. Had to tart up for work and all that."

"She went to work drunk?" I asked with a giggle.

Mai smiled. "Helped in her profession, I guess," he said, moving on to combing my hair with his fingers. "Drink enough and you'd be surprised how beautiful that pole becomes."

"You mean…"

"She was a stripper," Mai said listlessly, frowning at me. "Here's how it is, Blueski – I'm gonna have to cut your hair."

"You're *what*?!" I said, defensively leaning back from him.

"I ain't gonna be the only purty baby today," he declared with a smile and a wink.

It wasn't simply a smile, either: it was *the* smile – the smile I'd come to live for – warm and tender and so incredibly inviting. I wonder now if Mai realized the irony that emanated all around him, seeing as he was a devoted fan of such things. Someone forced to live in the darkness, hidden in the night, yet capable of lighting up rooms as brightly as a ray of the sun with one simple smile. I doubt he did. Mai never seemed to see himself the way everyone else did.

I sat fidgeting in my chair as Mai took a pair of scissors and a razorblade to my hair. I trusted him, though I'm not sure why – considering he'd never taken a razor to anyone's hair in all his life; but I didn't like the uncertainty of change. Mai loved my hair because it was so fine and straight. He could do things with it that his naturally rebellious, wavy hair refused to allow. He cut mine short in the back and let it fall longer the closer it came to my face. It fell about my chin in the front and he used styling wax to give it a sleek polish.

I looked unreal when all was said and done, almost like a wraith or some strange porcelain doll. My face was so white that my hair appeared nearly as black as my lips and the eye shadow was a rich gold and silver blend. It was like I'd evolved into a living mask, living art, and it was liberating. I'd gotten in the habit of trying to hide away from everyone, but now I wanted to be seen. It felt *safe* to be seen. Empowering. Mai gave that to me. I think that had been the reason he'd asked me to play for him to begin with.

"*Let* them see you," he whispered in my ear. "Because I shouldn't be the only one that does."

"Mai…"

There were so many things I wanted to say to him, but I couldn't. I couldn't grab hold of anything intelligent to say and then Mai was gone, off to check on Dart, Renna and his own wardrobe. I was left alone to change into the suit that was waiting for me. It took me several seconds to regain the feeling in my legs and get to my feet. My ear was still tingling from where Mai's breath had danced upon it.

We remained an odd, eclectic looking bunch as we stepped before the lens. Our photographer was named Mitch and he really didn't know what to do with us at first. There was a couch, upholstered with red velvet, for us to use as well as an elegant floor lamp that had been sculpted to appear as though it had wings about the glowing bulb.

Mai liked the lamp. He gravitated toward it almost immediately and lightly ran his hand down its spine. The lamp matched him in a way. Mai was dressed in a sleek black jacket with no shirt on underneath – he left the first four buttons unfastened – and fitted black jeans along with his trusty black and white sneakers. He turned his head and took a long drag off of his cigarette; Mitch snapped his first photo.

Someone started the music, a good instrumental rock album, and Mai loosened up. We piled onto the couch together and Mai made a few silly faces while Renna and I decided to play things straight in all the shots. About half an hour in, after Mai had already downed a few beers, he decided to remove his jacket. In one picture Mitch captured Mai kissing Renna on the neck while he was caught kissing the top of Dart's head in another. Mai climbed up behind me on the couch for the final shot and wrapped his arms around my chest. He rested his chin on my shoulder, touched his cheek to mine, and offered the camera a cross between a hungry scowl and an alluring pout – a glare soon to become infamous.

Once developed I was able to see the beauty of it all – the lighting, the pose, the sensuality the two of us had created. Mai's gray eyes were dazzlingly sharp and seemed able to cut through the limitations of celluloid. It was as if he could see right through it all, as if he was staring directly at anyone who happened to be gazing upon his picture. It wasn't simply the color of his eyes alone that held such beauty, either, but rather what could be seen lurking behind them. I'd had my eyes cast downward, my face turned away from the lens. I appeared slightly fragile, again like some delicate doll, and Mai was the wolf lurking over my shoulder.

Renna and Dart were in that picture as well. Dart was against the wall behind us with his arms crossed, dressed in his biker gear with a rather intimidating expression on his face. Renna was on the opposite end of the couch, sitting sideways with one leg pulled close to her body and one hand dangling over the couch cushion. She was staring at the ceiling, looking almost like a goddess in her snug leather and golden fiery mane. We all looked our best, fresh and comfortable and real. I believe that was the best group photo to ever be taken of us.

When the shoot was over Mai and Dart decided that we should all go to the first bar we could find to celebrate. We sat at a round table atop green vinyl stools. Renna had a Bloody Mary while Mai and Dart devoured a couple of pitchers of beer. I had a diet soda – much to everyone else's amusement.

"Don't you ever drink?" Mai asked. "Booze, I mean. Don't you drink booze, Blues?"

I shook my head and decided to tell him I'd never been drunk in all my life as that answer seemed to please him.

"You don't drink, don't smoke – what *do* you do?" Dart asked.

I shrugged and sipped at my soda. "I go to the movies," I eventually replied. "I like to be alone there."

"Jesus, the excitement," Renna murmured, shaking her head.

"You a virgin, too?" Dart asked with a cackle. "Goodie-goodie."

"Ay! There's nufin' wrong wif that," Mai was quick to say, his words slow and beginning to slur. "Blue's not like most of us."

"You mean normal?" Renna asked.

"Who's nor-normal here?" Mai questioned, sloppily lighting a cigarette. "Not you. Not me for sure. Normal's for the shocial zombies and I'd rather shoot m'shelf than be like them. I certainly wouldn't kish one of 'em."

"You sure?" Renna asked, sounding bitter. "Your lips have never been choosy as far as I can recall."

"You callin' me a whore?" Mai questioned, chuckling under his breath.

Renna simply shrugged and shot Mai a skewed smile. It was

insinuating and more than a little insulting. Mai's face became solemn, his eyes sharp, and when Renna started to laugh at him he slammed his glass down upon the table with such force that it cracked. Renna's smile remained, obviously pleased she'd managed to throw salt in unhealed wounds. Dart made a drunken grumble of bewilderment.

"You got sumthin' to say, you say it," Mai said. "I don't give a shit. You takin' a dig at my mum? I don't give a shit!"

"It ain't me you're mad at," Renna laughed. "*She's* the one who pimped you backstage at her nudey bar."

I'd never seen Mai move so quickly. He leapt out of his chair and shot across the table as if about to strike but Renna was out of her seat and out of his reach within seconds. The beer pitchers and glasses hit the floor and shattered; I moved my soda out of the way just in time.

Renna patted Mai upon the head and then helped Dart maintain his balance as he rose from his seat and started toward the exit. They left me to "deal" with Mai (who by then was simply lying across the table and silently staring at the floor) but I honestly didn't mind. I wanted to be the one to pick him up. I wanted to be the one to mend the broken pieces. Vain, I know, and horribly unrealistic that I believed I was capable of such a feat.

"Well," Mai murmured a good five minutes after Renna and Dart had left us. "I've made an utter arse of m'self."

"Maybe a little," I said with a small laugh.

"I'm...lyin' on the table...aren't I," he stated rather than asked, lifting his head jerkily in order to stare at his own reflection on the tabletop.

"Yep."

"My eyes look like a raccoon," he remarked. "And I've spilt the brewskies..."

"I don't think you need anymore anyway," I said, patting him on the back.

"No?"

"No," I replied. "I think you're drunk enough as it is."

"Yeah?"

I nodded.

"Blueski...I don't think I can get down from here," he said through a goofy giggle. "I fink I'm shtuck."

"Shtuck?"

"Shtuck," he repeated, giggling again. "Oh! Oh...sumthing's

pokin' me. I'm lyin' on…on…oh! Why is there a bloody fork on the table? Help me, baby, won't you?"

It took quite an effort to help Mai safely get back to his chair, especially since I couldn't quite lift him up and the flimsy table threatened to topple over any time he shifted his weight too much one way or another.

The manager chased us out, angry over the broken glasses and pitchers. I practically carried Mai as he stumbled and giggled away from the mess he'd made. I attempted to hail a taxi, but we weren't having any luck. The euphoric warmth of the liquor began to wind down about the time Mai and I approached the front steps of our hotel. He allowed his head to fall upon my shoulder as he sang – slurred, but still perfectly in tune – tightly clutching my arm in both of his hands. He nearly tripped as we passed through the main doors.

Our rooms were both located on the third floor and there was no working elevator in the building so we had to take the stairs. Mai continued to cling to me until we'd reached the last turn in the narrow staircase and then he stumbled off to the side, fell against the railing and nearly tumbled right over. I grabbed him in time and pulled him back, startled, but Mai simply laughed and fell to his knees. Such a fall could have killed him – he knew that as well as I did.

There was a distant, wistful air about Mai as he gazed through the bars in the railing at the darkened floor below he'd nearly fallen to meet. He stared hard as if searching for something, as if he expected something to rise up to greet him. It seems to me now that he was contemplating leaping down to embrace it.

"It slipped away," he whispered, pressing his face against the bars. "Did you see it?"

I shook my head. "What? Did you lose something?"

"Death. The dead pool," he replied. "It was here and passed me by. Why does it do that, Blueski? Why does it pass me by?"

That was the first time Mai scared me. It wasn't like a terror, it wasn't the kind of fear that evoked a scream so much as a subtle panic that crept beneath my skin and made me feel hollow inside. I shivered when Mai's pale eyes rose languidly to meet mine. I couldn't quite make out his expression. I didn't realize what it meant for the both of us.

"What are you saying, Mai?" I asked, leaning forward to brush the wild waves of tangled hair away from his face.

Mai swallowed hard and stared, his bottom lip trembling slightly. "You won't leave me, will you? Blueski? I'm always…always waking up alone. You won't leave me alone, will you? It's always worse when…when I'm by myself."

I had no clue what was going on inside Mai's mind, I dismissed it then as being brought on by all the booze and no food inside his system, but I made the promise. I promised him that I'd never leave him regardless of the circumstances. He seemed relieved, comforted. He allowed me to lure him away from the railing. It was a promise that I'd truly intended to keep even if I hadn't fully understood the ramifications of it at the time.

"Don't…I don't wanna go home, Blue," he said softly. "Okay? I can't stand the quiet. The noise hurts my head."

"I've got some aspirin," I said.

That made Mai laugh but the laughter was weak. Hesitant. Faded. I took him to my room and sat him down upon the rocking chair near the door. He sat silently staring at nothing in particular, his lips fixed in a pout. I unbuttoned his jacket and offered him one of my T-shirts to change into, a worn and stretched out old thing that would inevitably be far too large for him.

As I slid the jacket off his narrow shoulders and pulled his arms out of the sleeves I spotted a silver hoop through his left nipple and a solid black ankh tattooed upon the underside of his right forearm. He called it the greatest irony in the making, a symbol of life permanently etched upon a body that was in constant decay and would one day be no more. I admired it, even ran my finger over it, and then I noticed the blood upon his side.

Mai hadn't been kidding when he'd claimed to have been speared by a fork back at the bar. I found four deep holes, each the size of prongs, in his side. A small trail of blood ran down from each of them.

"You hurt yourself," I said.

"Look at that," Mai marveled, staring at me rather than at his injury.

I ran warm water over a washcloth and lathered it up with a bar of soap. I brought it to Mai and ran it over the wound, noticing a strange indention in his ribcage as I gently wiped the blood away. His ribs had been broken at some point in his life, I assumed, and hadn't properly mended. He watched me as I washed and dried the injury and then he took my hand in his and gently caressed my flesh with his thumb.

"Do you know how beautiful you are?" he asked.

I shook my head, well aware I'd begun to blush, and quickly pulled away from him. "You don't have to say crap like that," I mumbled.

"You don't believe me? Hasn't anyone ever said it to you before? They haven't, have they. Of course they haven't. You don't stand out in the crowd. You *try* not to stand out. Like at my shows. You sat there and enjoyed the music and you didn't...you didn't come fuss over me just to be close cos I'd been on a stage and that's sumthin' to do. I saw you, you know," he whispered, staring straight into my eyes. "I saw you. You couldn't hide from me. You're on a dif'rent track from everyone else."

"That's the nicest way anyone's ever called me a freak," I said with a short smile, pulling away even further. "Put this shirt on. Scrawny as you are, you can't sit around this place without one."

"You're only a freak if that's an acronym for beautiful," Mai said firmly. "I see myself in your eyes. What I'd like to be."

"Acronym? You are *so* drunk you're talking out of your head. I don't even know what you're talking about," I laughed.

"I know you don't," he said with a smile. "You're so... simple..."

"Great. Now I'm stupid, too?" I asked, shaking my head.

That wasn't at all what Mai meant when he'd picked the word "simple" and I knew that despite what I'd said. Whatever he *had* meant, it prompted him to stumble up out of his chair and put his arms around me. He hung on my back and nibbled at my shoulder as his hands crept up over my chest.

I could see him through the mirror that hung on the wall before us, breathing down my neck and staring with hungry anticipation. Had I allowed it to occur, Mai and I would have gone to bed together right then and there. We'd have stripped one another down and we'd have had sex and I'm sure it would have been spectacular. It would have also been empty, almost abusive on my part to take advantage of Mai in such a way. On that night I decided not to violate him. I think I may have been the first person he'd encountered that hadn't.

I laid Mai down on my bed and covered him with a blanket. I planted a warm kiss on his lips before he fell asleep and then studied his face. With eyes closed and lips in a relaxed pout he looked somewhat like an angel, his hair a tangled web across the pillow. My pillow. I liked the way Mai looked upon it.

Mai slept restlessly, poised upon the pillow as if he knew he was being watched, muttering and frowning and flinching. He slept like someone that had been in a lot of unsavory, unsafe locations throughout his life and had learned to sleep lightly.

I caught sight of another tattoo after he'd wrestled his way out from under the blanket and turned his back to me. He had it across his lower back, at the location I'd seen a lot of young girls place cutesy butterflies and flowers. Mai's was a beautiful gothic cross with sharp, curved points. There were two hearts intertwined, one whole and the other broken, at the base of it and a grim-faced angel with feathery wings hovering up above; her face and hands were skeletal, boney and ashen. It was eerie but also lovely in a macabre sort of way. I wondered what it meant.

I covered Mai with the blanket once again and eventually laid down beside him on top of the covers. I cautiously stroked his hair, twirled a strand of it around my finger, and then I ended up drifting off to sleep alongside him.

40

Chapter 6

MAI HAD A long running fascination with old, decaying objects. Cemeteries, houses, buildings, inventions.

When I woke that afternoon he was sitting on the bed beside me, smoking and watching a documentary on how the Vikings had built their ships. It was enough to send me right back to sleep, but Mai appeared thoroughly engrossed in the program – so much so that he didn't even notice I was awake and staring at him for a minute or two.

"Amazing how the more we develop technology, the dumber we all become as a society," he remarked, shaking his head. "We look at the pyramids, we look at these ships and we can't imagine how they managed to build them with their oh-so-primitive tools when we can't seem to replicate them with our advanced ones. Did you know we've still no idea how Machu Picchu was built or what it was used for? There's no mystery at all these days. Centuries from now they'll find our remains and our buildings and they'll say, 'They all looked the same.' It's a tragedy. Cookie-cutter houses. Sleepwalking souls."

Given the fact that I'd only been awake a grand total of five or six minutes I stared up at Mai, rubbed my eyes and made a wonderfully thought provoking reply along the lines of, "Uh-huh."

At least Mai was talking like his usual self again; I considered that a good thing.

Mai had woke, slightly surprised to find himself in my bed with his pants still fastened. He said it had been the best sleep he'd had in years. He'd been awake for quite awhile and had been careful not to wake me. He said he'd considered going back to his place, but didn't want to leave until he got the chance to thank me.

"There's nothing to thank me for," I said, sitting up with a yawn.

"Oh, don't do that," Mai said through an exhalation of smoke. "There is and we both know it. I've no idea what I might've said or did, but I apologize just in case. I've, um, been known to dive pretty deep into the crazy pool once enough alcohol has set in."

I couldn't help but smile. "It's okay," I said and meant it. "It was fun – except for when you nearly fell over the stair rail."

"Did I?" he laughed. "That's almost as good as when I played chicken with a double-decker bus back home. Some bloke knocked me out of its way right in time."

I shook my head. I wasn't sure if Mai was serious or not. He seemed to be, but I didn't like the image he'd placed in my head. He gave so much of himself away in so many ways and seemed to attempt to only damage himself in return.

"Mai…"

"Let's not talk about it anymore, ay?" he asked, smiling around the cigarette in his mouth. "It's daft, really. Isn't it? Over and done and all that."

"Yeah," I replied. "Sure."

"What're you doing tonight, Blueski?" he asked. "Anything you can't get out of?"

I shook my head again. I told Mai I'd quit my job – what else would I have to do? "I'm the one who doesn't do anything, remember?"

Mai shrugged. "Well, I dunno, now, do I? What *do* you normally do? A movie or something?"

Mai stroked my hair as he spoke, mild amusement flickering in his eyes. He'd never really done anything ordinary, never really hung around someone as plain and simple as me. He saw it as some sort of adventure, I guess. A fresh conquest. I decided to give him what he wanted.

"I can't picture you going to dinner and a movie," I said with a grin.

"Why not?" he asked sincerely. "I've gone to movies, I love movies. Who doesn't? I'm not that far out, am I? I shit like everyone else and put pants on and all that."

"Put pants on?" I asked. "Isn't it that you put your pants on one leg at a time?"

"What? You mean people don't just jump in both legs at once like I do?" he questioned with mock surprise.

"You would."

"So are we on, then?" he asked, hopping off the bed. "Can I come round for you tonight?"

"You're serious? What about your work?"

"I quit," he said with a shrug. "We're band mates, right? We're friends. Don't tell me you're already so sick of me that we can't just hang out for a night."

I certainly wasn't sick of Mai and he damn well knew it – it wasn't anything that I needed to say out loud. I told him to come by around eight and he returned to his place to shower and do whatever it was that Mai did when no one else was around.

I can't explain why I felt so nervous waiting for Mai's knock upon my door that night. He hadn't referred to the outing as a date and I was certainly not about to think of it as one. I wouldn't have been able to function normally if I had. I showered and dressed and did my best to style my hair as Mai had fixed it for the photo shoot. It wasn't all that difficult; Mai had cut it to fall into place with little prompting.

Mai showed up ten minutes early in a long-sleeved black shirt, jeans and about five inches cut from his hair. It was still damp, shorter in the front and combed back like some teddy boy from the fifties. He appeared quite proud of himself.

"Nice," I said. "Tiffany's going to throw a fit."

"I know," he said with a fiendish grin. "I can't wait to see her face when she first sets eyes on me. You ready to go?"

I nodded. Mai took me by the wrist and yanked me out of the room, moving as if he was about to burst with energy. We ran out onto the street and Mai hailed a cab by lifting his shirt and sticking out his tongue. It worked on the first try.

We went to a horror flick, some cheesy mainstream title with virtually no plot and airhead teens running, flashing skin and falling down amongst gallons of fake blood. Mai made a sport of it, making funny noises and unleashing fake screams and occasionally throwing himself against me as if terrified. He threw more popcorn than he ate. I don't think I'd ever laughed so hard during a movie in all my life.

Afterward we found a nice Italian restaurant to eat at, a quiet and dimly lit place with live music and homemade bread. We attracted more than a few stares as we sat down across from one another in a booth for two. It appeared quite romantic to them, I suppose, but Mai attracted stares regardless of where he went or what he was doing. Male or female, there wasn't any soul that didn't do a double take for whatever reason when he passed them by. He couldn't escape it.

"Not just me gettin' the eye," Mai nearly hummed under his breath, smiling at me. "I might have to get jealous."

"Not enough attention for you?" I teased.

Mai shook his head. "Not what I meant," he replied, arching an eyebrow and reaching across the table to stroke my hand with his finger.

"You're the jealous type?" I asked.

"Horribly," he confessed with a sheepish smile.

"Me, too," I said. "Doesn't it bother you the way everyone stares at you?"

Mai shook his head. "I don't notice," he said sincerely. "I don't think they do. I think you imagine it, Blue. See? No one's looking now."

I gazed about the area. No one was looking because no one else was seated in the bar section with us at that moment. Mai had a smile on his face when I looked back at him; he was simply being sarcastic and I'd fallen right into it.

When the waiter came around I ordered a diet soda and Mai opted for a regular soda. I didn't say anything to him but it did please me that he was laying off booze for the night. I liked him better sober, coherent, when his odd ramblings were so often poetic rather than unnerving.

"I like this place," he decided. "It's dark in here. Cool."

"I've never been here before," I stated.

Mai shrugged. "Neither have I. I'm going for ravioli. Wanna split it, babe?"

We ended up sharing the meal and then we split a massive slice of cheesecake after that. I noticed them about halfway through the dessert, two girls and a boy that were pointing and giggling in our direction. It turned out that they'd recognized us from an online ad for The Razor – the club we were scheduled to perform at in a few days – and they were gleefully watching our every move. That photo, that pose with Mai peering over my shoulder, had already sparked rumors.

"Are they still there?" Mai asked. "They've been hanging 'round since we ordered."

"They have?"

He nodded. "They're wondering if we're an item," he replied, poking at the crust of the cheesecake. "We should toy with 'em."

I laughed. "What do you want to do?"

Mai smiled, flicked his wrist effeminately, and then lightly stroked my arm. I couldn't help but shake my head helplessly and laugh. It didn't matter to me at all that we'd become some sort of display, I couldn't take my eyes off of him. That was all Mai wanted to offer to them, though. A limp wrist and flirtatious brushing of hands – he knew how to play them.

After dinner we ended up going away from the business district and to a horribly neglected old building that had at one time been a church and later a townhouse shut down for illegal drug activity. It was made of red brick, several stories high, with a round window at the very top and arched windows of stained glass along the second and first floors. The trim was in bad need of repainting. The yard was overgrown and riddled with thorny bushes.

Mai was in love with the dump and especially fond of a window on the second floor that had a cross painted upon it. He wasn't religious, not even overly spiritual, but he had an inexplicable love of crosses all the same. Celtic, Christian, any and all in between – Mai adored and collected them. He'd stumbled across the place while wandering about when he'd first moved to Delsby and admitted to breaking inside of it on more than one occasion.

The interior, I found, was far worse than the exterior had been. The previous owners had not been kind and hadn't seemed at all concerned with keeping its historical value in tact. We had to use flashlights to navigate throughout the gutted building, stepping over fallen debris and clutter as we walked along the chipped walls patched in numerous places by shoddy dry wood. Many walls had been knocked down to create larger rooms. The high ceiling had been sectioned off in a sloppy fashion with warped beams covered by wooden slabs. I noticed plastic sheets hanging practically everywhere as we carefully ascended the narrow white staircase, all sagging under the weight of gathered leaves and – odd as it sounds – dead pigeons and their discarded feathers.

The top floor of the building had been made inaccessible. The second floor was covered with a ratty brown carpet that smelled of mildew, dust and pigeon stool. Every room was dark save for one – the one with the window that Mai loved most – at the end of the hall. The room appeared orange as we approached it, a trick created by the street lamp outside hitting the colored glass of the window. I could see a shadow of Mai's cross through the opened door that loomed before us.

"It looks like it's filled with sunlight, don't you think?" he asked. "Orange glow, soft hues. Sometimes I stay here all night and watch the real sun rise through that window there, through the cross. There's a lot of energy in this place. A lot of souls have come and gone, prayed and laughed and cried, but it's especially strong in here. When it's quiet…if you listen hard…the walls breathe. C'mere. Here. Quiet. Do you hear it?"

Mai placed his finger over my lips and pulled me into the center of the room. He kept his finger there and gazed toward the ceiling expectantly. I listened as he'd asked me to and waited. I didn't know what I was listening for, wasn't sure what to think, and then it came. A slight rustle in the plastic that started out light and gentle and then rose to a near crackle as it drew nearer to us. I felt a subtle breeze and then Mai's lips were upon mine, gently aggressive and unyielding. I couldn't have resisted kissing him back even if I'd tried.

The plastic continued to flutter up above and all around us. I suppose it might sound strange to some people, he and I finding romance in some derelict shell of a once grand structure while surrounded by the smell of decay and the sounds of pigeons pecking and fluttering their wings. Faded walls, spongy carpet, discarded feathers, the pulsing plastic sheets…and love.

I refuse to believe what we shared was anything less than love. It wasn't about physical attraction though we both found one another pleasing to the eye. It wasn't tainted by lust. Mai kissed me for a few seconds, maybe minutes – though it felt like an eternity – and that was all. I took the feeling of that kiss and allowed it to enter my veins. Something that had always been dormant inside of me, for better or worse, was awakened that night because of it.

After that we ended up walking to the park – really more of a glorified walking track with a manmade lake in the center of it – so Mai could look at the stars. He never liked to remain in one place for very long, he could never do one activity without yearning to drop it for another. I suppose that's why he could easily fire out so many songs. The lyrics were really only short poems set to music, they had clear beginnings and distinct endings. He could write one and then another and so on for as long as words came to him within seconds, switching gears between their varying moods and tones with ease.

He had lived in almost every state, even if some of his visits had been for no more than a single night. He'd slept in a number of curious places. He'd gone for days without sleeping just to see if he could. He'd studied a number of religions and cultures only to come to the conclusion: "It's all the same bullshit. Different words, different places, different extremes, but all the same shit."

I really had no argument with that. If everyone wages war in the name of their God, either one of the gods is asleep or the fools are killing each other for the same dude and he doesn't see any reason to intervene. I told Mai that and it made him laugh.

"Don't drag me into the middle of your bloody land division, I gave it to the primates for a good reason," he mused, imitating God. "He may well be cheering for our civilization to eat itself."

"I wouldn't say that."

"You just don't want to think about it," Mai said. "What good do we do? What purpose do we have? Blow things up, tear each other down. He set free will out to be a trap, man. We're damned if we use it to disagree – that's how we're taught.

"Sure, sure, we've got freedom of choice but only so long as what we choose is the safe, mainstream ideal. Step outside and you're going to hell. If I'd gotten a pound for every time Sister Mary told me my lovely li'l face would one day keep Satan company, I'd be one rich bastard right now. Just cos I said God sucked for putting his son on earth to be nailed. Admittedly, that sounds worse to me now; but I was seven then and it was a perfectly innocent observation. I was damned before I could even cross the street unattended. All downhill from there."

"Who's Sister Mary?" I asked with a laugh.

Sister Mary was one of the nuns that taught Sunday school where Mai had spent nearly ten years of his life. Mai's mother never attended church, but she often dumped Mai off for the evening sermons and school to get him off her hands for a few hours. Sunday, Mai told me, was the only day the kinky club where his mother worked remained closed and so it was her time to enjoy herself. She couldn't, apparently, enjoy herself with Mai in her presence.

"She had been leaving me with neighbors, but they got tired of that fast," Mai told me. "If she left me alone, they threatened to report her. Church seemed the best option. Once you're in those nuns bolt the door, man. I didn't really mind, except for when I got myself paddled for talking too much. It was fun pissing off those bitches, it really was."

"Always a good reason to attend church," I murmured, shaking my head.

"Wasn't ever any point in trying to fit in with 'em," Mai said in a distant voice. "Sister Mary made it quite clear that I was the son of an unwed whore, I was tainted with her sin while prenatal. I wasn't baptized – still not – and I spent most my nights backstage with women wearing glitter and not much else by the end of the evening. I was the class example of what *not* to be.

"I never realized being at mum's club was unusual until then. Never knew I wasn't like any other kid. We've all got that moment, I guess, when the blinders are snatched off us and then there's no turning back. I liked it backstage at that place, far better than being home alone with mum and her latest twat. The women always fussed and took turns tucking me in…gave me candy and kisses. Mum's money always went into powder or booze, her boys paid our rent. When she hit dry spells, we'd have to cut out and move and I hated it. Now look at me. I still don't stay in one place for more than a year."

We'd given up on walking and found a picnic table that faced the lake to sit upon by the time Mai had started rambling on about his childhood. It felt as though I was the first he had ever confided so much in. It certainly seemed that way as the words simply poured from his lips with absolutely no pauses or hesitations, as if Mai had dared to finally pull a plug and it all came racing forth on its own volition.

I didn't know much about Marina Evans, but the more Mai spoke of her, the greater my disdain for the woman grew. I was actually quite angry by the time Mai realized how much he'd been talking and closed his lips tightly with a startled gasp. His eyes were focused upon the lake, the reflection of tall street lamps and an elevated bridge flickering over its calm surface. In his mind he was wondering how deep the water was. In his mind he pictured himself diving into it from the bridge above.

Mai didn't believe it in my nature to act on anger – he'd never even known me to *become* angry – but I'd begun clenching my fists and shaking my head almost involuntarily. I wasn't upset with Mai's mother alone: I was fairly ticked off at this Sister Mary as well. True, I didn't know the woman, I didn't expect I'd ever see her face, but I'd known her type. Half of my insecurities as an adult had been planted by teachers or other "role models" shoving seeds of inadequacy and intolerance down my throat while I struggled through puberty. I'd never been angry at them, I still wasn't, but I felt angry for Mai.

"What's got you seething?" Mai asked, having snapped back into the present.

He was smiling. How could he smile? *Why* was he smiling, as if he wasn't feeling the least bit bothered? I hadn't caught on to his tricks yet. I didn't know how to sniff out the warning signs, the truth of his character. Mai could make anyone believe everything was perfectly all right even if he was holding a gun to his head and about to pull the trigger – a dangerous beauty, as I said before, and not solely to those around him.

"I'm not really in trouble until the vein's been torn open," he'd later tell me; I know now I should have smacked him for it.

Getting back to that night, though, I found I couldn't keep my mouth shut. No grown woman had the right to tell any child that he was doomed because of the choices made by his mother, nor should she discourage him from voicing his opinions. Mai believed I was one of those children who had come from a loving home with an easy life, but other children hadn't. Other children were bombarded by negativity and airbrushed expectations, they were taught indifference and insecurity. Don't stand out, don't ask questions, don't do or believe in anything the masses don't approve of. Be self conscious to a fault, be as uninformed and blissfully ignorant as possible.

"It's not right," I said. "That nun had no right to do that to you. You were seven."

Mai shrugged. "People do it still and so would she. Things don't change. It's not something we can ever outgrow, societal judgments. They'll always be there with every generation that comes and goes."

"You must have felt so alone."

"We're all screaming in a crowded room and no one ever hears," Mai said softly. "I want people to hear, you know? I want people to shake off those potato sacks, believe in things for the right reasons and not because that's just what they've been told to believe. I want them to *really* believe in something."

"You can make people do that," I said. "With your songs."

"Our next single can be 'Fuck the Man'," Mai laughed.

Mai already had a good start as far as I was concerned. He'd managed to win over a portion of Delsby natives. Farm boys and true "manly" men had clapped and cheered for him in his glitter and lipstick and that was no small feat. I understood Mai's admiration of androgyny, why he loved to go out painted up and flirt indiscriminately with all genders and races. He always presented himself as rather playful, harmless, but he did have more in mind than simple shock value. He wanted to make people think and possibly reconsider old prejudices. The world will always be in a constant state of change. Some move with or against those changes with signs and legislations and protests and then there are people like Mai: blatant and blunt and daring.

"We'll never be a truly equal society, complete equality would cause death by assimilation," Mai said. "Rights ought to be universal, though. I don't believe that some people are created to be damned because of the way they are or who they fancy. I refuse to believe that."

"They argue it's all a lifestyle, not the way we're created."

"Pish," Mai muttered. "Did you honestly wake up this morning and consciously *decide* that today you'd find men hot cos you went after chicks the day before? Stupidest load of swill I've ever heard and that's saying a lot. You like one or the other – or both – but that's true *all* the time, it's not a hat you wear on Saturdays. The same's true for boys who feel they're really girls or vice versa. The choice, the only choice, is whether to live a lie. That's true for everyone. To live a lie is the same as bein' dead no matter who you are."

All those things Mai said to me that night would eventually be put into print over the years in interviews and to support both protestors and supporters alike. It never occurred to me there, in the park, how powerful those words were or how great an impact they had the potential to make. I'd simply listened and nodded and enjoyed how animated Mai had become. He was simply being honest. He actually truly *cared* about something and most people I'd known up to that point hadn't.

Some people, however, would come to see him as a threat.

Chapter 7

MUSIC ALONE CAN'T sell albums these days. It's sad but undeniably true that artists who choose to keep their clothes on or aren't extremely pleasing to the eye are much less likely to succeed unless they have a gimmick to fall back on. In that sense, Mai was a true rarity in the business. He had the looks and – unlike many of his counterparts – was actually capable of singing beautifully without the aide of machines and electronic enhancers. He was always singing… on the street, in the shower, in his room…

Mai called our first album *Deciduous Garden* and decided to use the newest song he'd written, "Blue Nights," as the closing track. I hadn't asked if the title had anything to do with me, the subtle wink from Mai had told me all I'd needed to know, and the lyrics were the loveliest I'd ever read by far. It was an appeal to all the burned and weary hearts to continue on, to turn their backs on the darkness, and look to the souls in the sky.

"There's always light to be found," the last line read. "Even if it's simply in another's eyes."

Mai even incorporated a fairly lengthy guitar solo for me to indulge in. I was thrilled.

Stores could hardly keep *Deciduous* stocked on their shelves, mostly because it only shipped from two distributors and trickled in at about four copies at a time. Tiffany did that on purpose and it was fairly smart of her as it made people all the more eager to get their hands on it. Had the locals not respected Mai so much, however, they would have simply burned copies for one another and called it a day. It was the first of many calculated gambles that Tiffany would make.

The album sold well and our show at The Razor had gone as smoothly as it possibly could have. Singing and playing keyboard wasn't going to work for Mai, however. His voice was harder for the audience to hear and it was difficult to truly connect with the crowd while seated in the back. Minnie Cross was Tiffany's solution.

Minnie Cross – where to begin? Minnie was a near light pole of a man – he stood nearly seven feet tall – and he was even thinner than Mai. His face was long and dominated completely by a sloped nose beneath queer, ice blue eyes that always left me feeling cold. He kept his fine, limp hair dyed black and allowed it to hang about his eyes in listless strands. He came to us in black lipstick and white paint upon his face. I never saw the man in anything that wasn't black.

He'd gone by Minnie since hitting his growth spurt early in middle school and threatened to cut open any person foolish enough to speak his given name of Dudley out loud. I couldn't help but think of a foghorn whenever he spoke, for his voice was deep and rattled the inside of my ribcage, but when he moved…whoa. Considering he was all arms and legs Minnie possessed incredible grace, sort of like a panther on the prowl. When he sat down to speak to someone it was always with spidery legs crossed and an unlit, hand-rolled cigarette perched between his skeletal fingers. Every time he wore a suit Mai teased that he was imitating the animated skeleton from that Tim Burton flick about Christmas.

Minnie was more than qualified to join us. He'd done plenty of shows with a number of groups that had all disbanded before any major successes could be claimed. He'd had classical training, formal schooling and he genuinely enjoyed the songs we'd already released. He brought with him his personal keyboard – a real mother of a wonder – as well as a traveling drug buffet. He had uppers, downers, injectibles and suppositories. He had things to evoke trips or to make the user feel, and I quote, "like a veggie." Pep up or fall flat – Minnie had the cure or poison for any type of user.

I loathed the drug buffet. Minnie tried to bring it everywhere we went. Mai wouldn't allow him to keep it out in the open backstage as a lot of young fans and policemen tended to pass by during our shows for one reason or another. I never touched any of the treats during that first tour, I had no interest in them whatsoever, but Renna enjoyed valium and Dart wasn't at all opposed to marijuana and the occasional ecstasy tablet.

Mai swore to me that he'd never indulge in any of it either because he didn't like having his thoughts filtered by chemicals. As I'd learn soon enough, though, any time Mai swore it usually meant that he was lying. He enjoyed liquor, he shared a joint with Dart on more than one occasion, and I know he became dependent on pills to force sleep to come while we traveled from location to location that year. Otherwise he'd remain awake for hours, pacing the floor of our hotel room or the tour bus. A new town, a new hotel, a new crowd, performing at concerts and shooting music videos – it left him restless.

Despite my disdain for Minnie and the occasional chaos that came along with him, our first tour was the best we would ever have. Our debut album had hit the states hard. It went platinum. It went triple platinum. Every major venue across the US suddenly wanted to book us. We were featured in magazines and Mai's pictures were constantly popping up inside the pages of those teen heartthrob issues Mai liked to call bundles of glossy toilet paper. The press begged for interviews – most of which Mai declined. The ones that he did give usually played out more like practical jokes that only Mai was in on. Charming sarcasm and meticulously vague replies became his trademarks.

We toured on, unaware of most of the hype, playing for screaming fans that cried and girls that threw their bras and panties at us. I always wondered what on earth they thought we'd do with such things and Mai laughed at me and said I was missing the point. I never wanted to touch them.

Mai frequently crept into tiny bars and low-key clubs with his acoustic guitar and played for free between the major stops. I always went along simply to watch him. It was particularly entertaining when he'd pick an amateur night to venture up on the stage as I could only imagine the horror of the person that had to go on after him…

Tiffany had an official website started that included a forum through which our fans could communicate with us and a tour diary. She hired Basil Hallford to tour along with us to snap photos and film our live performances. I liked Basil the first moment he introduced himself to me. He was from Alabama and came to us in blue jeans and a white t-shirt that fit snug against his muscular chest. His dark brown hair was cut short and combed back, his cheekbones chiseled, his eyes a misty shade of green; he looked like his living should have been in front of a lens rather than behind it.

Mai didn't tell any of us that he and Basil already knew one another, let alone that they greatly disliked each other. That was something I'd only learn quite later, as they'd both remained nothing less than professional around one another at that time.

The tour was fun. Magical. It was flooded with all sorts of firsts and the kind of euphoria that can never be re-created again regardless of circumstances. Mai played with the audience, he'd make silly faces while he sang and shout at them to sing along. Once he even tossed his microphone out to them and challenged them to finish the song on their own while he clapped and smiled. He would frequently yank his shirt off and throw it to whichever fan seemed to be yelling the loudest, keeping his expression playfully deadpan and demeanor nonchalant all the while. If they whooped loud enough, he'd shake his ass at them or blow kisses or look over at me and simply start to giggle. If we happened to have some hecklers in the crowd he'd smile sweetly and flip them off or – with great pleasure – also blow *them* kisses.

We made history for having the highest grossing tour of any freshman band, especially since we'd done most shows as the headlining act alongside another unknown band called Frothe – a band destined to fail, though we would see their lead singer Arieal again years later, frigid as ever and part of another doomed quartet.

Mai's sweet face, smoky eyes and smooth voice seemed to seduce and snare nearly everyone we encountered, and Basil was there documenting every bit of it. Basil knew how to capture the beauty in things, especially people. He knew to be patient and wait for those moments when his subjects would be caught unaware. Mai and I with our heads together, Dart in a bellowing laugh, Renna in a private sulk, Minnie sprawled out on a couch that came a near foot too short for his spidery legs to fit upon. He took several of me while I was playing on the stage. It was the first time I saw photographs of myself and actually thought I was beautiful.

Basil captured a black and white shot of Mai just after one of our last shows on the tour, a picture that would go on to become rather iconic. He'd snuck up on Mai during one of his absences, when Mai's mind had disconnected and his dazzling eyes were focused on something no one else was able to see.

He'd been sitting on one of the speaker cases, dressed in black jeans and the jacket from our first photo shoot, his eyes smudged with black shadow like a raccoon. His hands were folded in his lap, a nearly spent cigarette clutched limply between two fingers. The side of his head was resting against the wall and he stared straight ahead at darkness. The lighting and the frozen shroud of cigarette smoke combined to create an ethereal effect. It was to later become the cover for our single "Fallen from Grace." It was later to be flashed on all the newscasts when Mai was believed by the world to be dead.

We'd been happy on that tour. There were photos of us smiling, laughing, clowning around and all were genuine. Mai's time was increasingly snatched up by reporters Tiffany insisted that he speak with, but he'd never felt right about being the sole spokesman for Nefarious. The rest of us didn't really *want* to speak – I certainly didn't – but Mai was always trying to get us to join him in front of the camera.

I couldn't have been more content in those days. As silly as it may sound, Mai was my drug. I didn't need to get into Minnie's buffet so long as I had Mai near me, smiling at me, joking with me. Mai frequently slept in my bed, wherever we happened to be, snuggled up against me as if I made it feel safer for him to close his eyes. No matter how he flirted with fans or press, always he would find a way to wink at me and I knew it was all harmless...a part of the game. Then the tour had finished and we found ourselves hunted down by a nearly forgotten face: Jeanie.

The fact that Mai had failed to mention that he and Jeanie were engaged to be married wasn't nearly as disconcerting as the fact that he greeted her with an embrace as if nothing was amiss when she just suddenly popped up at our hotel. Worse than that, I found out that Mai had been writing letters to her the entire time we'd been on the road – something he'd managed to keep a secret.

We were in New York, staying in the executive suite. We had a music video to shoot, part of which was scheduled to be shot in the morning in the lobby downstairs and in one of the available conference rooms so no natural light could reach Mai. Basil was working on the project, building the sets and getting the lights adjusted properly. Once the sun fell outside we'd be moving to our next locations, a bridge and a small cemetery right outside the city. If all went as planned, we were expected to get the entire thing filmed in one day.

Jeanie was her usual self, bubbly and dim and rattling on and on about what all of her friends were saying about Nefarious and how much she wished she'd traveled with us. She pranced about the room as she spoke, unpacking her things, snooping in cabinets. Mai lay stretched out on his side on the bed, smoking and listlessly rolling his eyes at me. He wasn't listening to a thing Jeanie was saying. I could hear nothing else.

"Can we talk?" I asked abruptly. "Outside? Alone."

"Sure, Bluebee," Mai replied, rolling off the bed with graceful ease. "Back in a few, babe."

Jeanie smiled and went on about her business as Mai and I shut the door behind us. The hall outside our room was as wide as my old bedroom back home, all gold and red and pristine. It offered plenty of space to pace.

"Please don't give me silence," Mai said. "If you're angry, say you're angry."

"Why didn't you ever tell me that you and Jeanie were so serious?" I asked.

"We aren't serious," Mai replied with a shrug, his eyes pools of projected innocence. "I haven't missed the girl one bit this past year, you know that."

"You're *engaged* to be married. That's not serious?"

"Not to me, no," he said lightly. "Jeanie says that we're engaged, she started tellin' people that after our third date. Jeanie also says that eating ground up eggshells makes her fingernails grow faster."

"Does it?" I had to ask, fighting the urge to smile.

"Of course not but I told her she was right," Mai confessed with a smirk. "Make an omelet and she'll come at the shells with a hammer and a straw."

I shook my head. "If you aren't engaged, why does she still tell people you are?"

"Same reason she eats the eggshells, Blueski, she's not the sharpest needle," Mai said through a chuckle. "I never made a proposal and neither did she. I've bought her no ring. When she asks what our wedding date is I tell her the end of time or, once, I told her it was the day after my funeral but that just confused her. I can't make it any clearer, can I?"

"You can get rid of her," I replied, my voice trembling slightly. "Why keep her around?"

Mai shrugged. "She's funny sometimes," he said. "Good for a laugh. Don't worry, Bluesy, I'll tell her off soon. It's been in the mail long enough, ay?"

"Are you going to make love to her first?"

Mai blinked as if temporarily caught off guard, as if I'd invaded his privacy, and then he shook his head and laughed at me.

"Honestly, Blues, you ought to know better than that. I've never made love to anyone in all my life. I'll see you on the set, babe. I have to hurry back before she starts trying on my lipstick. Too damn expensive to let her waste it."

With that Mai gave me a warm kiss on the cheek and then he disappeared into our room with Jeanie. I'd been left alone and I didn't understand what I was feeling. I went downstairs to look for Dart and Renna. Hell, I'd even have considered sitting down to talk with Minnie at that point.

I ended up with Basil.

58

Chapter 8

THE SET WAS impressive considering the small area Basil had to work with. The curved stairwell in the lobby had been lined with white candles that rested in crystal dishes. Strings of elegant white lights like one would wrap around a Christmas tree hung down in individual strands from the banister above in front of a dark midnight backdrop. They created the illusion of a sparkling curtain, a sea of stars.

The stairwell and walkway above had been closed off especially for us, all guests and employees were being asked to use the elevator exclusively. A genuine grand piano had been brought in for Minnie to use and he was gently fondling its ivory keys when I came off of the elevator.

Mirrors were being set along the wall behind Minnie to enhance the effect of the sparkling curtain. I have to give Minnie credit. I found him crude and sometimes even repulsive but he became something else while seated at a piano. The skeletal fingers found an inner grace and moved breezily, creating some of the most beautiful melodies I'd ever heard. He was playing Mozart that day, a rolled cigarette in his mouth despite the numerous signs about the lobby clearly outlawing smoking in the building. No one was going to say anything to him, no one ever did. He was built like a tree and had dead eyes – amazing the doors such a combination can open.

"Hey, bitch," he greeted, not looking up from the keys; he tended to greet everyone that way. "Free from Mai's hip for the morning? Oh. That's right. He's got company."

So much for grace.

"Get used to it," I heard Renna say. "He never settles. There's always someone else he'll find to call a muse. He jumps from one to another to another. All his pets become disposable once he's gotten whatever he wanted from them."

I'd not even noticed that Renna was there, seated on the floor next to the piano with her hand on Minnie's thigh. She and Minnie had developed a bit of a romance that the rest of us had become aware of near the tour's end. They were a bizarre duo, mismatched in every way as far as I could see, but I didn't consider it my business how things played out in their bedroom. As long as it didn't interfere with work Mai had said that he had no reason to care, either.

"I'm not a pet," I said, rolling my eyes. "Mai's a friend like the rest of you. That's it."

"We don't sleep in your bed during the day when an 'itty bitty stawm scawes us,'" Minnie said, peering at me out the corner of his eye. "No wonder Mai's seemed more tired lately."

"Sleep is *all* we do," I stated.

Neither one believed me and I don't know why I'd grown so agitated with them for that. Of course they didn't believe me: I'd sounded thoroughly defensive and that's what they expected of Mai. He got that reputation, but it wasn't true. I want people to know that. Mai flirted, he kissed, he touched; but I don't think he had sex with all that many people – certainly not as many as he could have. He never did anything to dispel the rumors, though, and even I had my share of doubts during our time together. All I knew for certain then was that what he and I had was pure, almost innocent. Two words no one would ever associate with Mai's name during my lifetime.

I didn't have a clue where Dart was, I suspected he was in the hotel's bar, so I decided to head over to the conference room. It's amazing how paint, plastic, foam and fabric can transform a spacious room into a completely different world.

Basil was lying on the floor on top of a large sheet of plastic covered with sand, white and fine. On the wall behind him was a painting of the sun shining down on an empty beach. Across the room, divided by a simple sheet of plastic, was a mock hospital room. Green tile walls, white linoleum floor, a standard issue bed and realistic equipment all stolen – according to Basil – from the set of *ER*.

"Nice," I commended.

"I think it's the best we can do," Basil said. "It had better please his highness."

I didn't really appreciate the way Basil had said that...the thickness of the words...the unintentional condescension. Somehow the idea that Mai was domineering, a control freak, had begun to trickle into the public mind. A few reporters – those Mai had refused to do interviews for – were stating that he was vain and arrogant. He was, after all, the one photographed most often and pretty much the sole speaker for the band. It was his picture on our albums, in the magazines, and he would get most of the screen time in this video as well. Reporters could think whatever they liked but, unaware that he had a past grievance with Mai, I'd expected Basil to know better.

"It's not like that at all," I said.

"One day it will be," he replied. "It always happens. You guys are great, I'd hate to see resentments get in the way. You're too good for that, Blue."

"Me?" I laughed; I'd begun to blush.

"Maybe I shouldn't say anything," he said, lowering his eyes. "Just remember there are people out there calling your name, too."

I had never even thought about that, that anyone would be noticing me while we were on the stage. Basil left his assistant in charge of the set and took me to a guest computer with Internet access upstairs. It was true. Fan sites had pictures of me, they had posts devoted to me on their message boards. I'd become a celebrity and I hadn't even known it.

I didn't know at the time what Basil's intentions were when he took me online and gave me that moment of self-realization. I didn't even notice then that he'd done anything to change my state of mind but a seed had been planted. I was *in* a band – I was a part of it – it wasn't only about faking things anymore. I was important to the group as a whole and not just to Mai. I was important to the fans.

"You should play for me sometime," Basil said. "I like to toy around in my studio. You could call me if you ever feel like just going wild. The bigger the solo, the better. No rules. I could produce you or something."

"You have your own studio?"

"It's where I do private photo shoots, but I've got a corner for recording," he replied. "Extremely humble, don't be picturing anything grand, but it gets the job done."

"Sounds fun," I said, and I meant that. "Maybe I will call you."

Basil smiled, smooth and serpentine. "I'll slip you my number later. You'd better hit makeup now – the shoot starts soon."

"Hitting" makeup to me normally meant going to Mai, he

was always the one to paint my face, but with Jeanie around I didn't want to bother him. The lipstick I found easy to do, black liner and dark burgundy. The eye pencil made me nervous, however, so I skipped it and went straight to the metallic gray shadow. I smeared it on the top lid with my finger and then below the eye. I looked slightly wicked, like some sort of addict. I loved it.

We all ended up with dark smudged eyes before the shooting began. We were all slightly washed out, emaciated, gritty – the perfect look for Mai's concept of the video we were about to make. It was for "Clarity."

The song was about not being able to find the light, of being lost in the world. Mai had written it partly about himself and his inability to walk outside beneath the rays of the sun. The tagline said as much, only being seen by the light on his way into the grave, but by this time it had proven itself to be much more.

It was the first song Mai had released. It was the song the blooming fans had listened to and identified with. It was a bit of an anthem for all the underdogs and outcasts – those of us ignored and tossed aside and overlooked.

Everyone wants to find the light – acceptance, love, warmth. Some only receive it when no longer living on the earth. It's one of life's most enduring and tragic ironies and Mai had penned it beautifully. He'd waited to bring the song to a video. He'd wanted to make certain it was made correctly.

Drug addicts seemed another source of fascination for Mai, I think because his mother had been one and he recognized how easily he could become one if ever he gave in to the temptation. Some people killed themselves with the drugs for the pleasure of it all, a high worth their lives, while others did it to dull the pain inside that nothing else could mend. It was those people that Mai most identified with. It was those people the world seemed to shun most, condemning them after failing to catch the warning signs and help them before it all went amiss.

Basil filmed shots of Mai walking throughout the hotel, passing hired extras and a few volunteers, stumbling and shaking as if ill. No one was to so much as glance at him as he passed by. He mouthed the words to the song, occasionally, as he walked and stumbled his way to the main staircase where we all stood waiting.

We became actors, too, the four of us. We stood talking to one another while Mai took a strategic stumble down the stairs and landed at our feet. Renna was a natural at appearing cold and indifferent, she simply stepped over him and laughed. Minnie followed her. I was the only one who acknowledged Mai, doing so only because he grabbed my ankle, and then – as directed – Dart swatted my shoulder and I shook my head at Mai before walking away.

Basil called for a break after that. He wanted to quickly review the footage and, if he liked what he saw, we'd be finished with the lobby. We had attracted quite an audience during the filming and Mai motioned for all of us to greet the onlookers while we waited on Basil. There were signings and photos taken, everyone seemed to want a piece of us. I don't know why no one noticed the angry man near the back of the crowd, I suppose we were all too distracted by the flashbulbs and chatty boys and girls. No one realized that he wasn't a fan, that there was a cause for concern, until a woman screamed and Mai was suddenly gone from my side.

The man turned out to be Ronald Grantz, a disgruntled parent whose son had been hanging pictures of Mai up on his bedroom wall instead of the swimsuit models that he'd expected to see. I saw him shove Mai to the ground, yelling something about "fag," and then he pinned Mai down and took a swing at him.

The fans were on top of the situation before any of us could react. Imagine a dozen teenage girls and their mothers screaming and attacking a heavy-set man in his forties with their purses and fists. The man's son was there, too, attempting to hide his face with his hands. When the women pulled Mr. Grantz away, it was the son that helped Mai get back on his feet.

"Pathetic!" Minnie laughed, shaking his head at Mai. "You went down like a noodle."

"He sat on me!" Mai cried, playfully defensive. "He cheated."

"I am *so* sorry," the son whispered. "He's not taking my coming out very well at all. I followed you here and I guess he followed me. Oh, but I'm not a stalker or anything. Honest."

"This is *his* fault!" Mr. Grantz yelled, pointing at Mai. "Prancing around and telling kids to do the same."

"I only tell them to be themselves," Mai said, holding his eye. "Everyone should at least be honest with themselves and live according to what they believe is right for them. You ought to support your son for having the guts to tell you how he feels, man. Now, does someone have some eyewash or something? My eye is burning like a mother. I think there's mascara in it."

By then hotel security had taken hold of Mr. Grantz and were preparing to escort him out of the building. I asked Mai what he wanted done before Basil's makeup crew ran off with him and he told me to do nothing. Security wouldn't allow the man back inside the building and that was good enough for Mai. He wasn't angry.

"Find out the boy's name, though, if he's still around," Mai said. "We'll give him a backstage pass to our show coming up."

"We have a show?" I asked, frowning.

"The campus anniversary," Mai replied, smiling before inhaling sharply in pain. "All right, now I'm seriously blind. Where's the saline?"

The free show at the campus that helped us on our way wasn't on any of our schedules. Turned out Tiffany had told Mai that we'd not be doing it and Mai, in his defiant wisdom, decided we would regardless of what she said. I set out to find the son, not knowing what doing so would mean. A late-teenaged boy with milky skin, nearly white hair and odd brown eyes that carried an occasional red tint – he was an albino, the first I'd ever seen, and his name was Hazel. Irony Mai could truly appreciate, though I suspected it was a name the boy had simply decided to give himself.

When I explained to him that Mai wanted his name and number to invite him to one of our shows, he hugged me. He reminded me of a little puppy, so eager to show affection, always upbeat and energetic. I should have known right then and there that he was trouble.

Mai's eye wasn't burning because of makeup. They had cleared his skin of the powders by the time I returned to the backroom and were holding a bag of ice to his face. He'd been hit hard just below the eyebrow. His eye was red and the skin around it was already beginning to swell and bruise. Basil was furious.

"We only have the bridge and cemetery for one evening!" he was shouting. "And you! You look like you were stung by a bee!"

"It's fine," Mai said coolly. "I did just take a tumble down the stairs. This'll add to the realism."

"You shouldn't put powder on your eye with it like that," I said. "Should you?"

Mai shrugged. "Probably not; but we are on a tight schedule, ay? It'll be fine."

And it was. On Mai's insistence, they blended the injury with powders to hide some of the bruising and make the swelling less evident. Mai's face became even more black and white and gray, like a movie star from an old silent film, and he was ready to shoot the scenes in the conference room. Laying on the sand beneath the artificial sun, being placed in the hospital bed and evaluated by a doctor (Minnie in a lab coat with his back to the camera) and, finally, "dying" as evidenced by the flat green line on a heart monitor that actually wasn't hooked up to anything. All the needed shots inside of the hotel were complete.

"I'm starving!" Mai cried as soon as his death scene was filmed. "Lyin' still is hard work."

"I'd think it less of a workout than what you normally get in a bed," Minnie said with a sneer.

Mai playfully punched him for that. I could have wrung his neck.

We had only just sat down for a bite to eat when Tiffany phoned Mai's cell phone and insisted on talking to him. Somehow she had already found out about the attack and seemed to have plenty to say about it. She was, on one hand, pleased that the incident had been captured by Basil's film crew; but she wanted someone fired for the apparent lack of security all the same. Mai, especially Mai's face, was her top commodity and it wouldn't be worth much to her if permanently damaged by an "angry soccer dad."

Tiffany was preparing to leave her office and come to our hotel even as she harped at Mai over the phone; we were all grateful that we would be filming at Tolsta Bridge by the time she arrived. I wondered if being yelled at by Mr. Grantz had bothered Mai at all, he claimed it hadn't when I'd asked, but it had bothered me. It was frightening how quickly things had turned from pleasant to dangerous. Mai could have been seriously hurt. Any of us could have been grabbed and thrown down as he had been. I hadn't been prepared for that side of it all. I don't think that Mai was, either.

"Give me an official quote about the attack to post on the website," I heard Tiffany say over the phone; Mai rolled his eyes at me as she said it. "Make it clever."

"A man threw me down and bitch slapped me, Tif. I'm not feeling too clever," Mai replied dryly. "Blueski…what'd I do with my cigs?"

"Give me a quote or I'll make it up myself," Tiffany threatened.

"The man was clearly worried about his kid and I respect that," Mai said with a sigh. "He was also disappointed his child doesn't fit his narrow ideal of normality – and if he's so insecure that he blames me for toting some eye powder and kissing a few gents now and then, well, he should get his head out of his arse. Satisfied?"

"Hardly. You know–"

"Sorry, babe. I'm losin' my connection!" Mai shouted, slamming the cell phone against the edge of the table violently. "Damn vulture. Honestly. *Where* are my cigs?!"

I pointed to the pack lurking behind Mai's glass of water and he laughed, stating the fact he was "half-blind" as his excuse for not having noticed them on his own. It was hard to look at him in the makeup, made to appear cold and gaunt like a corpse. Harder still to imagine that one day he would look that way to me without any makeup involved. Even one of his dashing smiles hardly lessened the effect. I told him that he looked like death and his eyes darkened.

"You've never seen what death looks like, then," he whispered.

I was soon to discover that Mai was right. I hadn't seen death yet, but I was about to.

In time we all would.

Chapter 9

IT'S HARD TO say when Mai's obsession with death and his idea of some grand dead pool where souls congregated when hovering in between began, but I eventually came to understand his infatuation. The media would go on to call him cursed and maybe he was – *he* certainly believed he was – but not in the way they thought. Looking back it was something that had always been present, but it didn't show itself in a way the rest of us could see until that night. Not that any of us had a clue what it was at the time, of course. Mai was the only one who immediately recognized it for what it was.

The sun had only surrendered its throne a half hour or so before we arrived at Tolsta Bridge, so Basil still had a bit of natural light with which to work. Tolsta was the perfect location, as it was no longer an active bridge for motorists. It was old: its green frame brown with rust and neglect, and its original foundations had long ago been removed.

It stood fairly low to the ground and was only used now as a massive bench – for photography or as a stop on the architectural tours that were held every weekend. When filmed at the proper angle, however, with Mai perched carefully upon its railing, no one would be able to tell it wasn't as tall as any other bridge. They had placed safety nets down below as a precaution. All Mai had to do was shuffle across the bridge, looking cold and dejected, climb onto the railing and fall. Simple. Or so it should have been.

We had a drink while waiting on the lighting. No one would be in the bridge scenes except for Mai and me, though we wouldn't be on screen together. Renna, Dart and Minnie had simply come along to hide from Tiffany. It was a good thing that they did, too, because only minutes into his work a member of the lighting crew nearly got himself killed.

His name was Matt and he'd climbed on top of the bridge in order to hang a few lights. We all felt a cold gust of air brush over us and then Matt flipped as if he'd been knocked over by some unseen hand. No one knew if falling from the peak of Tolsta would have killed him or not, but he was in the wrong place to hit the safety net below at any rate. Minnie, as tall as he was, managed to reach up and grab Matt's ankle. He shook Matt down from the beam he had fallen onto and Dart was able to catch him before he hit the ground. One potential disaster resolved with ease.

Then we discovered that no one had actually checked the safety net to ensure that it was secure. Mai did his job. He crossed the bridge, looked over his shoulder, climbed the rail, and gracefully fell back into dead air. When he hit the net we all heard a snap, followed by a short groan. The net had collapsed beneath Mai – he'd hit some rocks below and he was far too slight for anyone to even *try* to blame the breakage on his weight.

Mai wasn't badly hurt, of course, only scraped here and there during his struggle to untangle himself atop the rocky ground beneath him. He even laughed about it once he was back on his feet. When we packed up and moved on to shoot in the cemetery we were hit with another mishap and, well, Mai stopped laughing.

Basil did the funeral scene first, in which I stood alone before a freshly covered grave looking as solemn as I possibly could. I'd even managed to produce a few tears as I tossed two roses down on the dirt. All that was left was for Mai to lie down with his eyes closed in the casket that Basil had rented so that they could get a shot of the lid being lowered over his face.

Renna found the casket "creepy" and refused to so much as look at it. She even lost her normally stoic front and shrieked when Minnie playfully tried to shove her up against it. Mai didn't fear it in the slightest. He lovingly ran his hand over its side before crawling inside. This cemetery, or at least the coffin, seemed compelled to return his affection. It locked itself when the lid was shut and none of us could get it open again.

"Break out, man! Like that chick in the old ghost story," Minnie laughed. "Bloodied her fingers and tore her fingernails all to shit, but she made it home again. Right?"

"Man, shut the hell up," Dart said, slapping Minnie upside the head.

"I don't think he can even hear us in there," Minnie stated

with a chuckle.

"I *hear* you!" Mai shouted, his voice muffled and breathless. "Open this damn thing!"

It's hard to say how long Mai was actually stuck in there – it seemed an eternity at the time. We all kept at it, prying and smacking and kicking. The lights were flickering as if on the verge of burning out, threatening to leave us in darkness. More than a few members of the crew were spooked by it all. Ten minutes...fifteen...maybe more...then Renna announced she was going to break the hinges off with a hammer. Basil stopped her.

"They'll charge out the ass for that!" he said. "There's enough air left in there for a while yet. We'll call a–"

Mai started beating on the lid like a madman, cutting Basil off, and Renna hit the hinges with the hammer anyway. She knocked them loose and Dart pried them away. I quickly lifted the lid up and tossed it aside.

Mai popped up like a spring toy in a box and immediately threw his arms around me. He was hot, covered with sweat and breathing hard. He'd busted a few of his knuckles.

"Where's our love?" Dart teased. "We helped, too."

Mai smiled brightly and got to his feet before jumping onto Dart's back and kissing the top of his head. Dart playfully shook him off and then Mai turned toward Renna with a mischievous glimmer in his eyes.

"You're welcome," Renna said flatly, holding up her hand to keep him at bay. "No hug and kiss crap, 'kay?"

"No, no, no. You get a kiss," Mai proclaimed, chasing after her. "You and that hammer."

"I'll *help* you kiss the hammer," Renna replied, though a smile had come to her lips.

The ride back to the hotel was quiet. Mai had grown solemn – still – and when he saw Tiffany in the lobby waiting to pounce he charged right on by her. He was going up to our room to be with Jeanie. All he gave me was a flippant smile as he dashed up the stairs and I was left alone. Again. Again I ended up with Basil.

He actually came to me this time around. I'd snuck away from Tiffany and slipped into the conference room where the painting of the false sun still hung upon the wall. I was stroking it, running a finger over the painted rays, when Basil cleared his throat and startled me half to death. He was smiling.

"Crazy night, huh?" he asked, shaking the camera he was holding in his hand.

I nodded. "That's one word for it."

"I'm probably going to work into the morning, editing and all that. I think I've got all the footage I need. Care to keep me company?"

I started to shake my head but something stopped me. Mai was gone, off in our room with *her*. What was I hanging around for? My only option was to bunk with Dart because Renna and Minnie were busy in their own room and Dart snored like a pig. Besides, I'd never seen film editing up close and personal and I loved films.

So, I went. Basil's studio wasn't far from the hotel: a spacious, hollow building with no windows and a strong front door made of reinforced oak. Rooms were formed by simple dividers, large pieces of standing wood that Basil had painted himself, instead of solid walls. One look at the place was enough to know it was home to an artist.

Basil hadn't been lying about the furnishings within. There was a painting studio, a section cluttered with paints and brushes and canvases. There was the small sound board and recording equipment near the bedroom. The darkroom for photographs was downstairs and monitors and computers made up the film editing station. I couldn't imagine having so much, partaking in so many things. I almost envied him.

I wasn't the only one to think all the trouble during the filming had been worth it. The video played out perfectly. Mai wandered the hotel in clear need of help and found himself ignored by everyone. He fell at my feet and I turned away. He stumbled his way to the bridge and leapt off seconds before I came walking by. At the hospital he pictures himself on the beach while the doctor quickly looks him over. He dies and gets shut in the coffin. I stand over his grave and shed a few tears. Shots of us playing our instruments and an actual coffin being lowered into a hole in the ground would be added later but I basically got to watch the video in its unpolished entirety before anyone else that night. I felt honored.

"Love born in death, that's what he should have made the title," Basil remarked. "What the hell has 'Clarity' got to do with it?"

"It's giving clarity to the listeners," I said; that sounded right to me. "A warning, I guess. I like it as is."

"You have to. Not like he'd change it if you suggested

otherwise."

"I told you before, he's not like that," I said. "You toured with us, you've seen how we work."

"I saw all of you working your asses off to glorify him," Basil replied. "The whole behind the scenes thing is basically finished and ready for your tour DVD. You don't speak on it even once."

"I don't *want* to talk."

"You should," he was quick to say. "Mai could easily cut and run on all of you, take all of the songs with him and you'd be shit out of luck. You deserve better than that."

I said that Mai would never do something like that and I'm fairly certain that I believed it at the time. It was all about planting ideas with Basil. He slipped them in like whispers in the dark and they settled somewhere in the pit of my stomach. He couldn't come right out and blast Mai, he couldn't make it seem personal. I didn't realize how subtle he really was.

"Mai wouldn't leave me hanging like that," I said.

"Sure he wouldn't," Basil murmured. "Who's he with as we speak? I can see that you're all tangled up by him. You should smarten up and leave him first. That'd be a real kick in his ass."

"You talk like you hate Mai or something," I said.

"I just really like you. I think you deserve better is all. Sorry if I ran my mouth too much."

"S'ok," I whispered, smiling faintly; I couldn't help but feel flattered.

Basil kissed me that night and I returned it. Then I laid down upon his bed. I don't know what came over me when he asked to take my picture but I agreed. The next thing I knew I'd removed my clothing and posed for a near dozen photos shielded only by a thin sheet or, once or twice, my guitar. I'd never really gotten so much attention before and I knew the pictures would turn out fantastic. It never occurred to me to ask what purpose Basil had in mind for them at the time. I was too preoccupied with thoughts of Mai sharing a bed with Jeanie when he could have been having me.

Chapter 10

MAI'S EYE WAS encased by a solid purple ring the next morning and the eyelid appeared heavy. It was late in the afternoon when I returned to the hotel wearing the same clothes I'd been wearing the day before. I walked into our room to find Mai pacing restlessly. He practically pounced on me as I started through the door, jittery and wide-eyed. He said he'd been worrying about me.

"I woke up and tried to find you. No one knew where the hell you'd gone," he said. "I needed you."

I nearly rolled my eyes at that. "I was out with Basil," I said. "I saw the finished video, it's really terrific."

"You were alone with Basil?" he asked. "All day?"

"Yeah. So?"

One would have thought it the end of the world. Mai threw his hands up into the air and started grumbling under his breath and then he looked at me as if he expected something to be out of place. He asked me if I was all right – a silly question, I thought – and I laughed at him.

"Why wouldn't I be?" I asked.

Mai shook his head. "Never mind. Just, ah, just keep clear of Basil, okay? Don't spend time alone with him anymore."

I admit I took Mai's words the wrong way, as if he'd been telling me what to do – which, to be fair, he was – for all the wrong reasons. How arrogant was he to tell me who to spend time with when he had a fiancée on the side? A fiancée that he'd allowed to waltz in and take over the room we had been sharing.

"I'll sleep with whomever I please, you damn hypocrite!" I snapped. "If I want to hang out with Basil, I will."

"Why are you yelling at me?" Mai asked, his voice remaining soft and collected. "Don't shout at me, I can't take it."

"Where's Jeanie? Huh?" I asked, crossing my arms. "Why the hell did you need *me* with her around, anyway?"

"Jeanie's gone," Mai replied with a small smile. "You were right, Blueski, I needed to break away for good. I had to put it in terms she could understand."

Talk about night and day. When I'd entered the room I was ready to smack Mai and now I was ready to throw myself at him and beg for a kiss from those sharp lips of his. He knew it, too. Make no mistake about that. Mai always knew when he was making himself irresistible to those around him, that's why his flirtations always seemed so effortless. I started to laugh.

"So you explained it to her using finger puppets as visual aids?" I asked through my laughter; I couldn't resist.

Mai, remaining completely deadpan, nodded without hesitation. "I owe you a new set of gloves," he replied. "And a boot. She, uh, threw one of yours out the window and nearly killed an elderly woman scootin' by below on her hover chair."

That made me laugh even harder and I fell against Mai in order to keep from falling to the floor altogether. He wasn't wearing a shirt, only his jeans, and his hair was damp as if he'd just stepped out of the shower. I'd never wanted him so badly as I did at that moment and my hands started venturing downward, down his back, near the belt loops of his low-riding jeans. Jeanie was gone. Mai was free for the taking.

"She nearly killed me when she threw back that curtain," Mai continued, slinking away from me in order to light up a cigarette. "Bloody bright day it is today. I had to hide in the bath for a few hours."

I snatched the cigarette away from Mai and took a quick puff off of it. The look of utter astonishment on his face was priceless. He blinked absently with his lips slightly parted and stared as I exhaled a puff of smoke. He'd never known me to ever want a cigarette.

"Joint suicide," I remarked with a wink.

"Technically a murder and a suicide," Mai corrected. "Second hand smoke and all that."

I nodded thoughtfully. "Who will they say is killing who, I wonder," I said, arching an eyebrow.

"That is the question," he asked, shaking his head at me, "isn't it?"

Chapter 11

SOMEWHERE, IN SOME city, I'm quite certain that Hazel Grantz would have been classified as a stalker and prosecuted accordingly. At least, he would have been had his object of desire been anyone other than Mai. Mai was the champion of strays and underdogs. and Hazel Grantz was a bit of both – an unfortunate puppy in need of a new home.

I told myself that it was only because Tiffany was so dead set against the idea that Mai invited Hazel to stay with us when the boy reappeared in our hotel lobby, but what I ended up believing was that Mai was trying to spite me for having gone with Basil. Hazel showed up with all of his belongings shoved in a backpack and a tattered guitar case in his hand, pleading with the hotel manager to call Mai's room for him. Mai just happened to be coming down the stairs and spotted Tiffany attempting to shove the boy out the front doors. If he hadn't interrupted her, Hazel would probably have been gone for good.

"You stop pushing that kid right now or I'll fling myself out the door after him and die a sunny death," Mai threatened, only half in jest.

People rarely called Mai out when he made threats like that because he'd been known to attempt to carry them out on more than one occasion. That was, I eventually discovered, the real reason he'd nearly ended up flattened by that double-decker in London. He was obsessed with death, as I said before, but he had no fear of it. I think he was in love with it and perhaps it with him. It *did* seem to follow him.

At any rate, Mai invited Hazel to sit down to dinner with us in the hotel's restaurant and for once I was as unhappy with his decision as Tiffany. She still hadn't had a chance to go over the incidents that had occurred the day and evening before, and I'd been looking forward to talking to him in private for a change. Instead, the meal's conversation revolved around Hazel.

Hazel was an odd looking boy, I thought. I hadn't really noticed him the day before, but I did at the dinner. Round face and eyes deeply set above a petite nose, lips so thin that he reminded me of a Muppet when he spoke. He never seemed to sit still, either. He was always smiling and bouncing about in his seat. He was shorter than I was, dainty like a doll, with wrists that appeared weak and scrawny arms. His hair appeared even brighter beneath the light hanging down above our table, making him shine like a little beam of sunshine. I loathed him.

Hazel had ran from the airport to our hotel because his father had arranged to send him to military school the instant the plane landed back in their hometown in Wyoming.

"I didn't know what to do," he said. "You always say we're dead if we go against our true selves and I never have. Military school will kill me, you know? I can't do it. I know you're a big star and all…I don't know *why* I even came here to see you, but…well, I only need to hide out for a while. Maybe my dad will give up and fly back without me."

"I'm sure he will after a few hours," Mai said with a thoughtful nod. "A day at most. He didn't seem like a patient man to me, but…are you sure you really want him to? Most likely he'll not let you in should you want to go back home."

Hazel nodded. "I know that. But I can't be who he thinks I should be," he replied with a sigh. "I can play. Maybe I can land some session work or find a band with an opening."

"I'll ask around for you," Mai said. "Smoke?"

Hazel quickly shook his head. "I didn't come for a handout. God! I totally sounded like I did, didn't I? Oh, man. I'm so sorry! I wasn't at all trying to…"

Mai smiled – he gave Hazel *that* smile – and flicked his lighter to life. "I'm offering because I want to, don't worry so much," he said breezily. "What else can you do in the meantime? You look like you know computers."

Of course, Hazel knew *all* about computers – Mai was never wrong about things like that. Mai decided that Hazel would be the new administrator of our official website, as well as a tech at all of our shows. In the course of a meal, Hazel had gone from homeless and distraught to securely employed as Mai's new darling. Tiffany offered no arguments about it; the sooner Mai was finished with Hazel, the sooner she could sink her claws into his back.

Hazel was so overcome with gratitude that he gave Mai an embrace powerful enough to nearly knock Mai out of his chair. Hazel was big on hugging people, always with his bright grins and giggles. He was honest to a fault, even if answering a question truthfully might possibly earn him a punch to the gut. He never drank nor smoked nor took any drugs – not even aspirin, for God's sake – and he totally worshipped the ground Mai walked on regardless of how hard Mai tried to break him of that habit. He was the sweet golden boy, a dim-witted sunbeam. He made me feel nauseous.

Hazel flew back with us when it was time to give our show on campus. Mai sat in between us, headphones over his ears and eyes closed because he still hadn't learned to enjoy flying. I read. Hazel sat giggling and making friends with the strangers seated across the aisle from him.

The other guys seemed to like Hazel, though I maintain that was because he was so easy to pick on. Dart enjoyed tackling him and mercilessly ruffling his hair. Renna often tested how stale the bread rolls backstage had become by bouncing them off of his head. Minnie never stopped trying to talk the boy into taking one of his druggie treats. Minnie said Hazel was a tough sale, excellent practice for his business.

The crowd we attracted was so large that the campus couldn't accommodate everyone. It was Mai's idea that we set up our gear on the roof of the university's tallest building to give everyone an equal view of us. It was a wildly windy day, downcast and drizzling. We were all frozen solid by the end of the night. Mai sang himself hoarse and I lost all feeling in my fingertips, but we loved every minute of it. The screams of the fans below climbed up to us and the energy they projected was as warm as the sun. This was what Mai played for – genuine appreciation, the feeling that he was giving something to people he'd never even meet. It was the strongest and safest kind of love to share.

Unfortunately, the authorities at the university hadn't been quite so appreciative. We hadn't gotten permission to use the rooftop and we'd created a total disruption to their regular schedule. Mai almost got himself arrested for mouthing off to the headmaster, but Tiffany successfully intervened and managed to calm everyone down. She was absolutely furious afterwards, especially since she'd told Mai not to hold the show in the first place. Mai had never been more ecstatic.

Chapter 12

COMPLETING OUR SECOND album was a trip. It coincided with a slew of award shows, public protests and the abrupt end of Renna and Minnie's relationship. We'd been nominated for a number of awards – best new artist, best video, best single, best album – and everyone wanted us to give live performances.

Mai didn't consider the awards to be a priority whatsoever. He had no faith in the ceremonies, he thought of them as mere popularity contests where those that played the game and ran the mainstream gambit cashed in and true artists were overlooked. The only show he agreed to perform was that put on specifically for fans, where the fans dictated the winners. It was always about his audience.

Unfortunately, we'd lost our bass player. Three songs recorded on the album and the awards show around the corner and Renna simply walked out of the band. Minnie was glad she'd gone and Dart – who'd started smoking marijuana regularly – was indifferent. Mai considered Renna a "no call, no show" and declined my suggestion to phone her and ask her to return. He replaced her with Hazel. Stupid, annoying, talented little Hazel.

Hazel wasn't good with the guitar – he was genius. I truly hate admitting that. He *should* have been good given that he practiced five hours a day like a compulsive freak. He could write, too. He and Mai shared credit on two of the songs on the new album before all was said and done, and they were good songs. Our sound became a touch darker, richer. Mai's lyrics became even more warped, sincere and relative to its listeners. It was going to be a good album, even better than the first, and Mai opted to perform one of the new songs at the awards show before it had even been released as a single.

I suppose I should mention another collision during all of this – one that centered around those photos that Basil had taken of me. Nefarious was becoming more and more recognizable so what better time to feature my bare ass in a magazine? I'd attempted to hide the whole thing from Mai and I did – until the day we were to perform during the ceremony. Minnie was to thank for that. He'd gotten a copy of the magazine on his own and left it open where he knew Mai would see it.

It was only a prank as far as Minnie was concerned, but Mai took it far more seriously. He seemed to think I'd been violated, which I had since I'd not given Basil permission to release the images, but I'd consented to the shoot. I made certain Mai was aware of that. Mai wanted to know if they had been taken before or after he'd warned me to stay away from Basil. I told him the truth.

"Right, well, I'll handle this," he said, a cigarette hanging between his lips as he studied my image.

"What's to handle?" I asked. "It's over and done."

"He's capitalized on you without your permission," Mai replied, frowning at me. "If someone's gonna use you, at least get paid for it."

I smiled and borrowed the cigarette, taking a quick hit off of it. "Next time," I said playfully.

Mai shook his head, eyeing the pictures one last time. "You've a lovely bum, my dear," he commended, a wicked smile crossing his lips. "Just don't drop your pants for Basil again, ay? Tif told me he came round asking for you the other day."

Nice how no one had told *me* that Basil had been asking for me but isn't that the way it always goes? He was to be at the show, photographing for the press as awards were won and performances given. Part of me hoped to run into him. Fan mail had been more than favorable about those pictures of me, it didn't seem I really had much reason to be mad at Basil when looking at the grand scope of it all.

Hazel had a panic attack before we went on the stage. I'd never seen anyone have such an attack though I'd heard enough about them to recognize what was up. He collapsed in a corner of the dressing room and drew his knees up to his chest. He trembled, began to sweat and could hardly catch his breath. Minnie said he looked like someone in withdrawal, but we all knew Hazel never touched that sort of stuff. The little shit was simply terrified to go out and play before so many people.

We'd already won our awards for the night, three of the four we'd been nominated for, but Hazel had remained backstage during the acceptance speeches. Now the time had come for him to stop hiding. It was a bit like coming out all over again.

Of course, it was Mai that talked Hazel back to a peaceful state of mind. He whispered softly into the boy's ear, patted his arm, stroked his hair. He gave Hazel his guitar and told him to think of it as a shield. No one could touch him so long as he was playing.

"Don't think of the other people," Mai told him. "Play for me. You go out and play just for you and me, baby. Okay? Play for me."

Hazel nodded and slowly got to his feet after that and Mai gave him a kiss on the cheek as if to thank him. Mai was pretty that night, made up as he much as he could stand. A gentleman backstage offered to hold the door open for him as we left the backstage area; he seemed greatly confused when Mai thanked him with his deep voice. A hush fell over the crowd when Mai stepped on the stage. He had them in the palm of his hand before he'd even opened his mouth.

"Don't be alarmed," he told the audience with a snicker. "Ren has indeed turned into a young white boy this evening. No need to adjust the color on your telly at home."

Laughter arose from the darkened seats.

"Seriously, in case you've not heard, dear Renna decided to leave us to pursue…whatever it is she's doing now, so we've asked Hazel here to join our clan," Mai continued. "Welcome him warmly, his place is certainly a deserved one."

I don't think anyone knew what Mai planned to do at the awards show as he gave his playful banter. It's quite possible that *he* didn't even know what he would end up doing – he certainly couldn't have been prepared for the aftermath. Live television is always the greatest test, the most unforgiving form of media.

We began the song during Hazel's applause. Hazel was anxious, he rushed things at first, but soon it all fell into place. People were on their feet, jumping around and bopping their heads. High heels were kicked off, sequined gowns disregarded and stomped upon. They loved us, all of us. It felt as if we'd reached the top of a mountain.

I knew Mai was up to something when he gave me that slick grin of his and winked toward the camera. He brushed up against me during my solo and stuck his tongue out near my ear. Then he stalked over to the opposite side of the stage and moved in close to Hazel.

I spotted Basil in the pit below right when it happened, his camera tracking Mai but his eyes focused upon me. Mai motioned for Hazel to come closer to him, as if he wanted to whisper something in his ear. When Hazel leaned forward, Mai planted one of the longest, most passionate kisses I'd ever seen upon the boy's lips. Tongues collided. The audience screamed – cheered – their applause rising to a near deafening roar; Mai turned toward them and laughed playfully before beginning the next verse. Hazel appeared to be in a slight daze but he continued playing without missing a note.

At the time it was perfectly innocent, a way of living up to the expectations and jerking around unprepared censors. Mai was having fun and it certainly hadn't hurt Hazel any. The audience went with it, recognizing the spirit in which it had been intended. The "kiss incident," as it would go on to be called, would bite us all in the ass, however, and sooner than one might have thought. The network didn't even allow the end of our song to air, they'd cut to commercials as quickly as possible once Mai's lips had touched Hazel's. Mai later called it discriminatory, claiming they'd have raised no such objection if it had been two women doing the same thing.

It didn't seem all that big of a deal to us. We'd been banned from live television because of it, sure – but that bothered Mai little. The problem was Mr. Grantz. Hazel's father was shown a clip of Mai locking lips with his boy and he exploded in front of the first reporter he could find. Hazel was a few weeks short of his eighteenth birthday. Not only had Mai "perverted a family oriented (clearly the man never *watched* music award shows) program" but he was also the "molester of an underage and gullible child."

Of course, none of this would hit for a day or two. That night we went off to one of the after parties where Mai had invited a select few of the fans from our website to join us. He was surrounded the second we arrived, able to move only when the crowd allowed him to. He smiled and laughed, gracious and charming. He kept Hazel at his side, his arm around his shoulder, and motioned for me to join them but I declined. I was busy signing autographs for a couple of girls.

Minnie and Dart settled in a corner of the room and started challenging people to drinking contests despite Mai's reminder that we had studio work in the morning. They were smashed within an hour. I was busy for much of the night, playing guitar for people and spying on Mai as he kissed and flirted with one fan after another. No one could resist him and it made me angry. I wanted to be different. I wanted Mai to chase after me.

Basil approached me about an hour into the party and pulled me off to the side to speak privately. He wanted to know if I'd seen the photos and, of course, I told him that I had. A few people had even requested I sign copies of the magazine that very night. Basil wanted me to meet him at his hotel room so he could explain how my pictures had been released. He claimed that it was an accident. In all honesty, I wasn't interested in anything he had to say; but when I caught Mai watching the two of us together with alarm in his eyes, I agreed to leave with Basil at once.

Basil and I didn't speak much during the cab ride and when it arrived at the address he'd given the driver, it was not a hotel that we came to a stop in front of. I thought it was a mistake until Basil handed the man money and told me to get out. I suppose I should have refused but I didn't. Instead I only asked where we were.

"This is my temporary studio," Basil replied. "I've rented it to last while I'm in town here. Better than a hotel, don't you think? More intimate and I can show you some of my latest work."

With a shrug I got out of the taxi and watched it pull away from the curb and out of sight around the corner. I wasn't feeling nervous, not for the reasons I should have been. It was almost like running away from home all over again. The rush I felt walking with Basil was quite similar to how I'd felt when night turned to day and I knew my parents had discovered I was gone. I'd never regretted that decision, to leave my home and become someone else. The decision to follow Basil wouldn't turn out quite as satisfying – it didn't take me long to realize that. I made the mistake of losing control of the situation.

The studio was a bit of a sham, I knew that as soon as we entered the building and Basil let me into a nearly empty studio apartment. An unfolded futon, a tripod fitted with a camera, and a small refrigerator plugged in the opposite corner were the only furnishings to speak of. It didn't take a genius to know what Basil had in mind. Take more photos, maybe have a fling on the bed, or a combination of both. I was in the mood for neither.

Basil shut and locked the door behind us – the kind of lock that required a key even from the inside – and asked me to have a seat. Given that the bed was the only furniture available I simply stood in place, crossed my arms, and stared at him.

"Playing hard to get?" Basil laughed. "Why bother? You didn't have a problem stripping down for me before."

"And now I'm in a damn magazine," I replied, sounding angrier than I actually was. "Thanks for that."

"I'm going to choose to take that sincerely," Basil said through a smirk, quickly raiding his refrigerator. "It's hardly done you any harm, has it? You looked fantastic, Blue. Lemme guess...you're only bothered because King Mai didn't approve?"

"Mai doesn't have anything to do with this," I said.

"The hell he doesn't. Here. Have a drink," Basil insisted, shoving a glass in my hand. "I saw your face when he pulled his stunt tonight. Shameless. He thinks he can get away with anything and then he spends his time judging everyone else. His luck will run out, you know. Flames always burn out eventually, after they've consumed all they can."

I remained quiet and sipped at my drink as Basil fidgeted with his camera. He really expected that I'd give him another photo shoot, for no one ever turned Basil down; but he never came right out and asked me. He didn't need to. Despite what I'd told Mai early in our relationship I knew how to hold my alcohol – I'd taken Basil's drink with little worry of becoming totally smashed – but I hadn't anticipated that he would slip something in it. I was ready to fall on my ass by the time the glass had ran dry.

Basil made his move after the glass fell out of my hand. He moved with rehearsed speed and accuracy, tearing at the buttons on my shirt. I started laughing, laughing at his nerve, and he took that as acceptance. When he'd completely unbuttoned my shirt, however, I started shaking my head. Rejection cuts like a knife, especially from a drugged out fool, and Basil decided to simply throw me down on the bed. I punched at him, of course, but I wasn't in any shape to fight him off by that point. He had me.

"You can't refuse after you've already posed once," he said, his normally suave voice now a growl. "Everyone's seen those pictures. Who'd believe I forced you this time? The public tends to think all you Nefarious people are free and easy as it is."

I'd never been on this end of things before. Basil had me pinned down and it was getting ugly – I was getting desperate – when he came bursting in. Mai. I didn't know how he'd found us at that moment but he literally knocked Basil's door down and went after him like a rabid dog.

It's funny. Until that day I'd assumed Mai wasn't much of a fighter, but he had Basil off of me and onto the floor in no time at all. There was a quality to Mai's eyes I'd never seen before, sharp and wild. He knocked Basil flat and struck him with the tripod, panting and cursing under his breath. I simply remained on the mattress and stared with wide eyes, more than slightly in awe of him.

"Are you hurt?" he asked me, quickly running his hands over his face. "Huh?"

I dumbly shook my head.

"I'll have you arrested!" Basil said, cowering on the floor. "Breaking in and assaulting me...You know what'd happen to someone like *you* in a jail?!"

"You ought to consider the same, you sick bastard," Mai was quick to say. "I warned you. I warned you Jeri would be the last you did this to. Want to come at me? Come at me and I'll shove this tripod up your arse!"

Basil didn't move. I'm fairly certain he was too afraid to. No one ever pushed Mai when he was fired up like that. Mai held his hand out to me and I took it. He led me to the doorway and told me to fasten my shirt and then he pointed at Basil one final time.

"Never speak to, look, or touch Blue again," he said. "Next time you won't be able to get up if you do."

Basil gave no reply.

Mai had to fasten my shirt for me before we managed to hail a cab outside seeing as I didn't have the coordination to do it myself. He didn't say a word to me all the way back to our hotel, he simply sat and smoked and stared out the window at the passing blurs of light and people. I didn't say anything, either. I was lost in a fog, unsure of what to say or do. Should I have thanked Mai? Should I have gotten angry at his intrusion? I ended up, eventually, asking him who Jeri was.

"A girl I dated once," he replied.

Surprise, surprise.

"Basil asked her out first, she went with me instead. He got a stick up his arse and tried to swoon her away with promises of a modeling career," Mai continued. "She did a photo shoot for him, he moved in on her. She said no and he slipped her a treat just as he did you. I wasn't around to stop him then and I couldn't prove what he'd done. Jeri kept mum about it to get her pictures published. I could only spread the word, ruin his chances for work whenever possible. Had I known Tif'd hired him, he would never have worked on our shit but once he was there…I guess I'd hoped maybe he'd changed."

"Why didn't you tell me all this before?" I asked.

"I didn't know you'd dropped your pants for him," Mai replied shortly. "And you said you'd steer clear of him so I believed you."

"I say a lot of things," I murmured. "You really believe all of it?"

"Of course I do. Why? Do you lie to me?" he asked with a soft laugh.

"Everything is a lie."

I said nothing further, ignoring Mai's burning gaze. Mai let the matter go, only because of what had happened that night and the fact that I was only half coherent as it was, I'm sure. It was a relief that he didn't push things. He could smell the vodka on me, I know he could, but he didn't say anything about that, either. So much for my claims of not being a drinker.

When we finally arrived back at the hotel Mai gave me a hug, a long and powerful embrace that I felt was truly sincere, and smiled sadly. "We've work tomorrow morning," he said. "You'll be good to go?"

I nodded.

"G'night, then," he whispered, lowering his eyes.

Mai waited for me to unlock the door to my room, his hands shoved deep in his pockets. As I walked through the doorway I heard him thinking out loud, speaking under his breath. He asked who I really was. I pretended I hadn't heard him.

Chapter 13

IT BEGAN WITH a quiet wave. Mr. Grantz inadvertently became the driving force behind the record-breaking sales of *Aberration* – the second of the three albums Nefarious would release. When he realized that Hazel was too old for the law to intervene over the kissing incident, he started bellowing out for parents to protect their children and their values from the poison Mai tried to infect them with.

It's never hard to start the banning of something. Encouraging people to burn merchandise, destroy albums – it's nothing new. It happened to The Beatles after Lennon's infamous remark about Jesus and probably a half-dozen rockers before or after them. Naturally, it happened to us as well.

Uninformed or spiteful parents, uptight conservatives, religious zealots always in need of something new to demonize, jealous boyfriends and those simply wanting to be a part of something and land on television all joined Mr. Grantz's cause. History had already proven that those with true talent and a real connection with fans outlive such fits of damnation. Mai would do the same. To Mr. Grantz's great dismay, Mai would actually take hold of it and fly.

Aberration was released a week before Hazel's birthday and it had been well publicized that Mr. Grantz's army of protestors were planning to surround the store where we had a scheduled signing to urge everyone to avoid us like the plague.

It goes without saying that Mr. Grantz hadn't cost us any fans up to this point. He'd succeeded only in provoking a few parents to snatch all things associated with us away from their children and, to those children, Mai had a special message which he posted on our website: come to the signing and be compensated for the loss.

No one knew exactly what Mai had in mind. Not me, not

Hazel, not Tiffany. Tiffany was afraid he was planning to give away copies of *Aberration* free of charge – the horror on her face was priceless – and Mai only smiled at her in response.

The signing was set to start at nine in the evening, but crowds began to gather as early as six in anticipation of the great shouting match they were expecting to occur. Television crews, entertainment reporters, supporters and protestors alike all lined the streets behind the metal gates set up by security. Tiffany instructed Mai not to allow anyone to get as close to him as he had the day Mr. Grantz had attacked him, she had to protect her assets, and Mai had sworn he would keep his distance. She should have known that meant he was lying. Mai never swore to anything unless he intended not to follow through with it. He only told the truth in subtle ways when no one was paying much attention.

It was an act of incredible genius and stupidity on Mai's part to place himself dead center in the sea of angry parents and disgruntled individuals with an acoustic guitar as his only potential means of defense – but that was Mai in a nutshell. He sat amongst his enemies and started to play an acoustic rendition of one of the songs from *Aberration*, slowly capturing everyone's attention as he sang.

It helped that Mai didn't look a thing like the image all the fans and haters had come to know. He'd showed up that night completely free of makeup – breaking another of Tiffany's rules in the process – dressed in worn jeans, sneakers and a simple black sweater that was too big for him. His eyes appeared darker without the surrounding powder and the slight stubble about his chin and jaw and mouth added maturity to his boyish face.

No one, not even the most loyal of fans, would have recognized him and it was nearly impossible to determine where his voice was coming from as he had chosen to sing out of their line of sight. As such, the fans believed they'd been listening to a recording and the protesters that had watched the performance took him as one of their own singing a wholesome tune to peacefully support the cause. Mr. Grantz even shook his hand and commended him on the beauty of the song when he'd finished.

Mai picked up his guitar as nine o'clock drew near and discretely slipped beyond the metal gate. He turned and winked at the fans and, once they saw his smile and realized who he was and what he'd done, they began to cheer madly. Behind a mask of makeup or not, Mai's smile – goofy, devilish, alluring – could never be mistaken.

"A smile that lures the lemmings off the cliff and how happy they are to go," one reporter would write.

We all sat at a white rectangular table near the back of the store with black markers and silver gel ink pens in hand, waiting for people to bring their recently purchased copies of *Aberration* back for us to sign. Mai sat in between Hazel and I, having placed a bit of shadow about his eyes and color on his lips. We actually didn't know at that time what he'd done, but I knew he had done *something*; he had that air of mock innocence within his eyes and the subtle smirk upon his lips that I'd come to know so well.

The sales were excellent. They played the album on the overhead speakers as people went down our row, sometimes gushing while other times silent. Fans, I'd noticed, tended to go only one of three ways. "Gushers" are those that flail about like morons and throw things and usually attempt to climb up on stage to grab at us. Minnie adored them, he always boasted after receiving "Gusher sex" to whoever found themselves unable to avoid him.

"Lukewarms" enjoy the music, but never get into it deeply. They nod their heads and give brief, asinine smiles meant to appear cool because they can't allow themselves to come across as gushers. Lastly, there are the "Rocks," those so lost in shyness or subdued lust that they become awestruck or stoic, silent shells hardly even capable of establishing eye contact. They are petrified at concerts and mute at signings. Blank, staring eyes.

I preferred the Rocks. It was amusing to see them stutter and squirm. I liked them because I knew that every single one of them would surely be the craziest freaks known to man in bed once their shells were cracked and their hold on restraint lessened. We rarely had Lukewarms: it was always one extreme or the other, and that night was no exception. I found myself kissed, fondled, groped, nervously giggled and screeched at, glared at and ignored altogether by timid men and women with CDs in their hands. It was the best.

Most people opted to hang around after getting their albums signed by the five of us. They peeked in through the store windows and giggled and waved. Minnie and Dart were both eager to leave, vultures anxious to snatch one or two fans up for the remainder of the evening as always, but we still had the press to contend with. And Mr. Grantz.

Mai colored in a few hearts by his signature when a couple members of Mr. Grantz's army, having officially gone AWOL, purchased *Aberration* and requested an autograph. Mai could have spurned them as Minnie had, but he remained perfectly gracious. He hadn't gone undercover, so to speak, to humiliate anyone – only to force them to reevaluate their purpose for protesting. Mr. Grantz's campaign had begun over pride, over being embarrassed by his child, but now it had branched out to an attack on Mai's words and music – songs many outside hadn't bothered to actually *listen* to. He never intended for his lyrics to be offensive, he didn't use foul language or attempt to evoke anger or hate. A few people there that night got that and, naturally, after speaking to Mai, became charmed – new members of our "cult," to use their own words.

We were being interviewed by a reporter called Tara when Mr. Grantz quietly stepped into the store. She was asking Mai about the controversy around the kiss he'd planted on Hazel – who hadn't? – and Mai was actually offering a somewhat sincere reply when I noticed Grantz approaching.

"I don't understand the big fuss that happened cos of it," Mai was telling Tara, staring thoughtfully at the tabletop. "I mean, I did it because I hadn't kissed Hazel before and I tend to kiss everyone I meet. No one raises any fusses when I kiss girls, no one accuses me of encouraging heterosexuality. It's all the same to me. I'm really quite harmless."

"Harmless," Tara repeated with a giggle. "I somehow doubt that."

"Damn straight you should doubt that," Grantz said. "This is all a joke to you, isn't it? How easy life must be for your kind."

I had visions of Mr. Grantz pulling out a heavy shotgun from beneath his trench coat and blasting us all to hell. I'd even begun to contemplate whether I should duck beneath the table or move over to cover Mai. Of course, Mr. Grantz had no gun. He created all wounds with words alone.

"You poison everyone you touch and drag them down to your level," Grantz continued. "You confuse innocent kids and smile as if you've done nothing."

"You give me a lot of credit," Mai said through a demur smile. "Why not just call me Satan and be done with it?"

"You'll get yours, son. You can only play games for so long," Grantz replied.

"Whoa! That sounded like a threat," Tara said quickly; she sounded excited. "Here on camera you're making a threat?"

Mr. Grantz scowled in Mai's direction for several excruciating seconds and Mai took it, seemingly undaunted by the weight of the glare. He'd faced people like Hazel's father his entire life, people like Sister Mary. He never let them see his fear but I felt it. I knew he was terrified right then because his arm was touching mine and I could feel it shaking.

"Ain't gonna get by with no threat while I'm here," Dart said in a tone that would have intimidated anyone who didn't know him well enough to see through it, clenching his hands into fists.

"Man warps and kidnaps a child and no one gives a damn because he has a nice smile," Grantz scoffed. "It isn't right. It just isn't right!"

"Stop it, already!" Hazel shouted, rising suddenly from his chair.

It had taken me a few seconds to register Hazel's voice, it had come out so unexpectedly confident and commanding that it sounded like it belonged to someone else. I'd grown to think of the boy as the stupid pup that yaps and trots along with the bigger dogs in hopes of finding acceptance and protection. Soft-spoken ever so sweet dopey Hazel had a spine, after all.

"No one kidnapped me and you know it," Hazel said. "You said I couldn't come home with you unless I went to military school and I'd have died there. Mai was nice enough to take me in, give me a job and I'm happy now. I'm happy for the first time in my life."

"As his playmate?" Grantz nearly spat.

That made Minnie giggle; Dart smacked him upside the head accordingly.

"As his friend," Hazel replied. "You never understood what it was like growing up being and feeling different from everyone else. I couldn't play out in the sun the same way other kids could, I didn't look like they did and I hated myself for it. Then I saw Mai in a magazine and when he said he knew what it was like not to fit in and he wore paint just to play around and take control of things, that we're dead if we aren't true to ourselves…well, something clicked, Dad. I'm just me, who I always was but didn't show. I still look different but I'm able to use it. People stare at me and I smile. *That's* what Mai did for me and if you think it's so wrong, I don't really give a shit."

There had never been a heavier silence, not in all of history and certainly not in a music store. Mai's mouth was literally hanging open, his eyes focused on the now flushed Hazel, truly rendered speechless for perhaps the first time in his life. A heavy ash fell from his neglected cigarette onto the table below.

I don't believe I'd ever heard a more sincere and spontaneous speech in person in all of my life. Hazel had cut the matter to its core in a matter of minutes and he'd been firm, but hardly cruel. He'd finally stood up for and asserted himself, and he'd be quoted many times over in the next day's papers and news reels. He'd done beautifully and swept Mai off his feet a bit. My disdain for the boy rose to hate.

It's hard to know if Mr. Grantz was at all moved. He kept his expression unchanged and shook his head before walking out of the store. Hazel started shaking as if about to have another attack and Mai demanded that all cameras be shut down. Surprisingly, on that day, the press respected his wishes and allowed Hazel to weep without being documented. Mai kept his arms around him throughout it all, whispering comforting words the rest of us were unable to hear like a father calming the aftermath of a nightmare.

Cha[ter 14

MAI WANTED TO do something huge for Hazel's birthday. He'd already planned on a small party of sorts, of course, but then he got it in his pretty head that a mere dinner and some cake simply wasn't good enough. Not for the golden boy who had so skillfully kissed his ass in front of an entire store full of people and a television crew. He kept asking me what he should buy the kid and I didn't have any suggestions. He'd already given Hazel more than his fair share as far as I was concerned.

In the end, Mai would opt for a quieter dinner back in the studio, out of the public eye, and he insisted we all attend. When he called me an hour before the event was to happen, freaking out because the caterers had fallen through, I admit to taking a twisted pleasure from it. They had apparently gotten the dates mixed up when I'd phoned to book them earlier as a favor to Mai. An honest mistake.

Then Mai told me that he intended to make the meal himself and I'd laughed at him. He didn't know a thing about cooking: his livelihood came from his smokes and any packaged foods he could find lying around. Somehow he talked me into coming over to assist him.

We had a great time that night, the two of us making a total mess of our studio's kitchenette. Mai had already placed a sheet of dinner rolls in the oven by the time I arrived – a foolish decision, given that he'd not yet started the actual meal. He forgot all about them while he worked on preparing the salad and ended up leaving them in for far too long. I knew he was in serious trouble when I found him poking at a pan in the smoking oven and was greeted by: "They aren't meant to be black like this…are they?"

Somehow we managed to pull it off. Pasta with a red meat

sauce, salad and makeshift (by that I mean buttered toast sprinkled with garlic salt) garlic bread. Not a complex meal, sure: but don't mock the challenged. Mai hadn't even been certain what, exactly, needed to go into the salad for heaven's sake. The kitchen was the one room Mai's mother hadn't known her way around and no one else had been there to teach him.

Tiffany even came to the party that night, though I've always suspected that she invited herself. She brought along her current fling of the week, a hopeful young singer named Marshall with pretty blue eyes and an expression that reminded me of a stoned duck. There wasn't much going on in Marshall's buzzed head; but, on the bright side, all of the extra space allowed him to more clearly hear himself sing. Hey, Marshall told me that himself, I swear, though not in so many words. I don't believe he *knew* that many words.

The "hit" single Marshall had only just recorded was – and I am not making this up – a techno tune that consisted solely of the line, "Mmm, baby you be shakin' it like Jell-O," repeated in various ways. Sadly, it did receive a nice chunk of airtime for a week or so. I *wish* I was making that up.

Anyway, to get back on track, Marshall left us early because he had a photo shoot to attend in the morning and needed extra time to find his hotel (in case he got lost along the way) and we moved on to presents. Dart had purchased a Playstation game and Hazel practically squeaked with joy. They loved those damn games: it was what they'd found to bond over. Mai loved to watch the two play, but he wasn't any good himself. I'll never forget the day Dart tried to teach him how to play and he got "killed" in battle because he was repeatedly pressing the wrong button.

"Five minutes," Dart had teased. "You lasted a whole *five* minutes."

"He wouldn't stop jumping," Mai said defensively. "I think it's broken."

Minnie, true to his nature, gave Hazel a dark purple bong with Indian symbols and deities painted upon it knowing damn well that we'd use it more than Hazel. He thought it looked cool. Who puts a bong on a shelf for decoration? Well, who else other than Hazel, I should say.

My grand contribution was a box of guitar picks. A guitarist's best friend is a pick and I'd been telling Hazel to switch the kind he used for months. Sure, the gift seemed small – it *was* small – but it went hand in hand with Mai's gift and Mai allowed it to seem planned that way.

Mai pulled some serious strings – I can imagine exactly what he'd done the persuading with – to get a local guitar shop to name its latest prototype after Hazel. It was a new model – sleek and light and capable of creating fresh sounds – and it had "Hazel" engraved down its neck. The Hazel bass guitar would prove to be a great success, of course. I hadn't thought it possible to feel mocked by a carved slab of wood until that night.

"Well, guys, I didn't bring a gift but I do have exciting news," Tiffany said brightly. "*Aberration* has set new records. Anyone questioning whether you had staying power has gotten their answer now. This tour is sure to go down in history. It's going international."

"International?" Mai asked. "We're skipping up to Canada?"

"Don't be smart," Tiffany said. "*Deciduous* was just released in France, Germany and the UK – you're huge there right now. They want us to play at a couple of their stadiums and I've agreed. You can only go up from here."

I had a sinking suspicion that Tiffany was running her foot up and down Mai's leg then, because he jumped suddenly in his seat and hastily lit a cigarette. We were all thrilled with the idea of going abroad, but Mai seemed perturbed. I guess the reason should have been obvious: he didn't want to return home.

Mai didn't allow the change of plans to dampen things any. He kept the mood light for Hazel's sake and himself tipsy to ensure that he'd remain jovial. Hazel broke in the new guitar using – imagine my pride – one of the picks I'd bought him, while Minnie, Dart and I broke in the bong. Tiffany left us to our idiocy. Mai stepped out on the small terrace to be alone with his.

Dart and Minnie were sprawled across the floor giggling hysterically when Hazel quietly rose to his feet and stepped outside to find Mai. I spied on them from a distance, watching as they shared a warm embrace. Mai gently patted and stroked Hazel's back. Hazel rested his head on Mai's shoulder and then they smiled at each other.

"Thanks," Hazel said sweetly. "This was the best day I've ever had. You have no idea."

"I think I do," Mai said, keeping his eyes focused on the sky above. "You remind me a lot of myself."

"Really?"

Mai nodded. "But you're brave," he whispered with a

bittersweet smile. "You're blessed. You should be blessed, you deserve it."

Hazel shook his head in a dopey way that made me want to shove him right over that terrace and laughed. He was so simple. So empty. He didn't understand what Mai had really said to him. He couldn't grasp the gravity of it. It seemed such a waste.

"You give me hope, Hazel," Mai said. "What you said last week…that was really something."

"I was just tellin' the truth," Hazel replied.

Mai nodded solemnly. "I know. That's what's precious about you."

Again Hazel shook his head. He was like a chicken or a bobble head on a spring. "When's your birthday, Mai? I wanna do something real big for you."

Finally the kid asked an intelligent question – a relevant question – because I didn't know when Mai's birthday was, either. He'd never told me and I'd never bothered to ask; Mai and I never talked about such trivial things. I could plan the mother of all bashes, make certain that I completely beat Hazel to the punch and steal back Mai's attention…

"Two months ago," Mai replied. "Two months ago tomorrow, actually."

Another idea put to shit. I couldn't wait a near year to rip Hazel out of Mai's heart. It'd be far too late by then.

"Why didn't anyone tell me?!" Hazel cried, genuinely despondent. "God! I must've seemed horrible to not even give you a card or…or…"

"Calm down," Mai laughed, playfully covering Hazel's mouth. "No one knew. I wanted it that way. Recording the songs was more important."

"I still wish I'd known," Hazel said with a pout.

Mai simply smiled and leaned forward to place a light kiss upon Hazel's lips. "You're sweet," he said. "Don't ever change."

"Why would I?" Hazel asked, looking confused.

"You'd better sleep," Mai replied, shaking his head. "We have a long flight tomorrow. I may need to borrow your bong before we take off."

Hazel laughed and followed Mai back inside the building. I think Mai knew that I'd been watching them, I'm sure he glanced in my direction as they passed the rack I was hiding behind, but he never said anything to me about it. It was to become a trend between us, things being left unspoken, but we both knew. We always understood one another, he and I. He knew as well as I did that Hazel was getting in our way.

Chapter 15

THE TOUR WAS an unbelievable ride. Never had so much success come linked with such misfortune. We were booked to play in arenas at least twice the size of those in which we'd played the first time around and tickets were selling out as soon as they went on the market. Mai bought several of the tickets himself to give away to some of the loyal webfans, because they were disappearing before some of them could get home from school to order. The extra media, the hype, the way Mai had handled himself around the protestors…*everyone* wanted to be at our shows.

First we toured the states. Nearly all of our protestors had disappeared. It did them no good to stand outside of the stadiums – they kept losing people to our music during their speeches – so they veered over to written articles and pamphlets. The seats were always filled, though the fans never actually *sat* in them, and the Rocks were a minority amongst the Gushers.

We were having fun, all of us, playing games of all sorts on the tour bus. Mai was lost in a compulsive fit, ceaselessly writing like a man possessed by the pen. Some days, he didn't lift his head from his notebook or open his mouth to speak for hours on end, he simply scribbled and hummed and shook his finger about in mid-air now and then. He was always the brightest, the most cheerful, when the writing was coming easily. Not even halfway through our tour he had enough material for a third album and then some. I always loved to watch him work. How dark his eyes would become, how intense his face would become. He truly did go somewhere else when he wrote. I wished I could go there, too.

Angie Deveroux was onboard to take photos and film our performances this time around. She was a friend of Dart's sister and therefore came highly recommended. I liked Angie immensely, she did a great job of capturing all of us during the shows – something Mai also appreciated. It was a shame what happened to her. A new chapter to build on the growing rumors that Nefarious was cursed.

Angie wasn't the only person who died that day in October, but she was the only one who we personally knew. The arena had been overbooked, too many tickets were sold or too many managed to sneak in for free – details mean little now – but there simply wasn't enough space for every body in the audience. Security had done a poor job with the barricades as well, putting up shoddy slabs of wood covered with plastic trash bags instead of proper railing. They were like easels or two playing cards stacked in a teepee. They were begging for disaster.

It happened during "Immortal Death." Audiences always pepped up during that song – I never knew anyone able to resist at *least* bopping their head along with it; and since all we really had in the audience were Gushers to begin with…well, one can imagine the euphoric pandemonium that erupted. Shirts and bras were off before the first verse had even ended and were being hurled toward the stage while the crowd whooped and sang along. They almost overpowered our amps. Mai was eating it up, smiling slyly in my direction as he sauntered back and forth. He always became most alive when he knew people were screaming at him, getting off on music that he'd written…getting off on him. I suppose it was the only form of admiration he knew how to accept.

We'd be criticized later for continuing to play, but people have to understand that we had no way of knowing what was going down until it was far too late. Disaster came in waves, starting at the back and charging forward in rolling domino fashion with unstoppable swiftness. We could hardly see one another amongst the lights and fog. We never saw the flimsy barricades. We certainly never saw them fall.

The barricades, propped up on cinder blocks, stood around four feet high. They fell in the back first, crushing those directly beneath them and knocking everyone else forward. Watching the footage of it later was much like watching a war flick at the theater, the way all of the people were knocked down row by row like soldiers caught in the aftershock of a bomb – or blades of prairie grass flattened by the wind. Dominoes. Screaming, frightened dominoes.

To his credit, Mai noticed the unfolding horror before the

rest of us. He never moved around as much as Hazel and I, and he made it a point to eye the audience as often as possible. I usually watched my hands while Hazel thrashed about like a frog being electrocuted; I doubt he ever saw much of *anything* while on stage.

Mai saw the bodies falling and stopped singing, a rather perplexed expression on his face. He motioned for all of us to cut the music and we did. That's when we heard the screams...the bodies falling, one after another. It was like the revolving whoosh of fan blades.

"Angie, move!" Mai shouted before throwing the microphone down.

It was too late. We all saw that it was. I don't know what Mai thought he could do, but I was grateful that Dart managed to lock his arms about Mai's waist before could jump off of the stage. We could only watch as the last row of people fell forward and brought the front wall of wood and plastic down with them. The wall landed directly on top of Angie, as well as several security guards.

Mai looked like a rag doll hanging limp in Dart's arms, his feet hoisted off the ground and arms loose at his sides. He'd stopped struggling – but still Dart held on, too stunned to think to let go. None of us were sure what to do.

Once Mai was back on the ground he ran down to the audience and did what he could to help those that had fallen, yelling for someone to phone some ambulances all the while. We all helped. Dart lifted the barricades and tossed them aside, Hazel helped those uninjured back to their feet. Minnie even carried a few who were injured off to the side.

Nine died at that concert, including Angie, and several more were injured. Mai didn't want to continue with the tour, but we were set to fly overseas next and Tiffany wouldn't allow him to back out of it. He issued a statement on behalf of all of us, via video, to be played on televisions all across the US expressing our regret and sympathy. He refused to recite the written speech Tiffany gave him and instead simply rambled on for a bit. I believe that's why he came across as so thoroughly sincere. He *was* sincere. He kept trying to blame himself for not noticing the problem sooner, as if stopping the song earlier could have prevented it all. I tried to tell him how silly that was, but I still found traces of guilt in his eyes.

Fortunately, our schedule allowed for two days to freely wander Paris before our next scheduled show and we didn't allow Mai to squander the time away moping. We lost Dart and Minnie almost right away, probably because Minnie didn't know French and answered "oui" to everything. I would have liked to have had Mai to myself, but five is an odd number and I certainly couldn't have convinced him to make poor baby Hazel explore a foreign country alone.

The three of us became inseparable during that trip because Hazel never went away and I refused to leave Mai alone with him. We toured, took photos, got thrown out of a cinema by an angry, chubby man that was screaming French at us and flirted freely with the natives. Someone like Mai hardly raised an eyebrow in Paris – the people didn't give a shit. I enjoyed my time there.

Nothing quite screamed that I'd "made it" as loudly as the massive billboard with my face on it near our concert arena. We were all five on that sign with "Nefarious" printed in gold letters over Mai's head. It was a good picture of us, too. Minnie smirking behind huge black sunglasses, Dart with one eyebrow arched inquisitively, Hazel staring at the floor with vacant innocence, and me gazing directly at the camera in a sultry way while Mai blew smoke in my ear through a playful grin. I took a picture of the billboard.

When we finally went back to our hotel, we found that Minnie had been having quite a celebration during our absence. Men and women of all ages were laying about the suite, passed out or well on their way to oblivion – and for once Tiffany wouldn't be able to scold him for it. We spotted her in a far corner with an aspiring French guitarist, as wasted as everyone else. The silly buzz that the world might come to an end once the calendar switched to 2000 in a couple of months had given everyone the perfect excuse to behave as badly as possible.

Mai wasn't much interested in gratuitous sex or drugs, he was still feeling badly about the concert mishap, and he'd never given enough credence to the apocalypse gossip to allow it to interfere with his work. He took Hazel into his bedroom so they could work on their latest song and I found myself alone. Again. In retrospect, I'm sure that all the two of them did was work on the song but I spent a fair share of that evening imagining all sorts of lurid happenings behind that closed door.

"Cheer up, buckeye," Minnie told me, a mocking gleam visible in his icy eyes. "Sniff yourself some joy."

"Hazel should," I muttered.

"Little 'Goody Goody' says drugs are bad," Minnie snickered.

"I can get him to do it," I said, taking a line. "Give me something to give him."

So Minnie did. Of course Minnie did, I knew he would. He didn't understand anyone not interested in drugs, he didn't care to even talk to them since he had nothing to talk *about* if they didn't use. He and I had spent more time together over the second tour, bonding over the occasional midnight treat. Mai was always busy working and I had nothing else to do.

"And I thought you were a goody goody, too," Minnie remarked.

"You were supposed to," I said. "What good did it do?"

"You sound like…like a secret agent," he laughed.

"You have no idea. The things I could tell you would scare the shit out of you."

Minnie only frowned. Fortunately, he'd prove too out of touch to later recall that particular conversation.

I held on to the gift, a small hit of acid, until we finished our show in Paris and then I told Hazel it was a stamp. He put his tongue to it like the naïve dope that he was and he was on his way. Anyone that stupid, that unassuming, is asking for trouble. I maintain that my tricking him was really the greatest thing I could have done for him. He needed to smarten up a bit. He needed to open his eyes.

At first, it seemed nothing was going to happen. We packed up our stuff and returned to the hotel, planning to fly out to London the next evening, and Hazel was acting like his normal self as far as I could tell.

Later I'd find out that he'd started feeling strange during the ride back, but didn't think a whole lot of it given his history with occasional panic attacks. I hadn't taken that into consideration, by the way. I hadn't thought about Hazel's problem with anxiety because he hadn't had an episode for months. I learned an important lesson that night: never give someone like that acid – especially without their knowledge. It isn't pretty when hallucinations and exaggerated fear collide.

The shit hit the fan after we'd settled down for the evening. We were all exhausted, the show had gone on long and we'd put a lot of energy into it. We'd decided to turn in early (early for us, anyway) when Hazel started yelling. He yelled – no distinct words, no reason, no explanation – and then locked himself in the bathroom so no one could look in on him.

Minnie slept through it all. There was no waking him once he'd popped a few of his sedatives. I wish I'd done the same. I imagine that Dart did as well. We heard glass shattering once, twice – and then Hazel's screams became weaker...more like feeble whimpering.

Dart helped Mai break the door down while I stood back, next to where Minnie slept, watching with a twisted kind of fascination. Hazel sounded like a monkey, howling and whining. It was a sound we'd all remember forever.

Mai found Hazel huddled in a tight ball in the bathtub, bleeding and starting to hyperventilate. The mirror over the sink was shattered, as was the shower door that had once stood before the tub. Slivers of glass were on the floor, in the sink, in the tub, in Hazel.

Dart guarded the doorway as Mai cautiously approached Hazel and attempted to climb into the tub alongside him, waiting to grab the boy should he try to flee. I watched over Dart's shoulder as Hazel fearfully smacked at Mai. He even attempted to attack Mai with a jagged piece of glass before allowing him to slip down beside him.

"Give me a wet cloth," Mai said softly, gently. "I need to get this blood off him."

"Mai," Hazel whimpered. "I thought...I saw...I thought..."

Mai tenderly silenced Hazel and told him to close his eyes. Hazel calmed down considerably, stopped his whining, and managed to regulate his breathing enough that he didn't pass out while Mai cleaned his wounds. They weren't serious, mostly only gashes about his knuckles and palms, but any injury to a guitarist's hands are potentially dangerous.

"What's he on, anyway?" Dart eventually asked.

Mai shook his head, too angry to speak. He knew. I thought for sure he knew what I'd done, but I had to test it. "Can I help?" I asked.

"You can kick Minnie's fucking arse for this," Mai said, working hard to keep his voice level for Hazel's sake. "I know he's behind this."

"Bugs! Where do they keep coming from?!" Hazel suddenly cried, slapping violently at the edge of the tub. "Everywhere!"

"Close your eyes, baby boy," Mai whispered. "Nothing's going to hurt you while I'm here."

Hazel squirmed at first when Mai put him in a hold of sorts

to prevent him from flailing his arms about, but he soon gave in to it. He'd continue to whimper for a near two hours but he was much more subdued. Mai's firm hold gave him security, a sense of control despite the chaos he thought was all around him.

Dart went to bed, but I remained outside the bathroom door, out of sight, listening as Mai whispered or softly hummed in Hazel's ear all through the night and into the morning. What a disaster I'd caused. Mai was like a knight rescuing a delusional damsel, calm and knowledgeable and far too sympathetic. He'd spent many long nights like this with his mother as a child. He'd always been there to mend the broken pieces she came home in and so riding out such a storm came quite naturally. He harbored no resentment toward Hazel – *that* was the disaster. It only brought them closer. Mai knew the boy had been tricked and he'd never forget or forgive it.

Hazel would kiss Mai before the day was done, right before exhaustion threw him into a deep sleep that would cause them to delay their flight. He kissed Mai on the lips and told him that he was in love with him. *In* love, understand – far more severe than proclaiming only to love him.

"I know," Mai said. "But I can't love you quite like that, baby doll. I've never gone with a man."

Hazel started giggling. "Liar!"

"It's true," Mai laughed. "All kiss and no stick. I just like to play around, y'know. I'm a boob man all the way."

"I could get implants," Hazel said through a yawn.

"True," Mai said, still laughing softly. "I don't care much for silicone, though. Besides…you can do better than a fool like me. You'll find him one day."

Hazel hadn't heard a word of that, he'd already fallen asleep, but I doubt he'd have retained Mai's words even if he had been awake. I peered around the corner briefly then and saw that Mai appeared to have tears rolling down his cheek. The sight only made my determination to drive them apart that much stronger.

Chapter 16

WE WERE LATE arriving in London. Minnie, Dart and I flew together with Tiffany to confirm our hotel reservations and prepare to save face should Mai and Hazel not make it in time for our show. Mai considered ditching us, I know he did. If one of us went AWOL we probably could have been easily replaced by a session player – but there was no replacing Mai. Piss him off and the danger of having no show at all arose. We got his message loud and clear.

Fortunately Mai was too driven by guilt to spite us at the expense of his fans. They had paid to watch him sing and he wasn't capable of disappointing them. Hazel came ready to play as well, though he looked like hell. Jittery, plagued by dark circles under his eyes, bandaged hands and when he and I made eye contact before stepping out onto the stage I knew that he knew. He fired accusations with his dark little eyes. An unspoken war had begun and the fact that he'd not mentioned the stamp to Mai was proof that he wanted it kept between the two of us. That was fine by me.

Hazel didn't flop about quite as much that night, he didn't have it in him, but I doubt anyone else really noticed. The crowd was smaller than what we had been playing to, but Mai actually preferred it that way. He'd grown to miss those quiet clubs and bars like Zarold's.

There were two people in the audience of particular interest that night, one of which would choose to remain elusive while the other was an instant leech waiting to latch onto Mai the near instant the curtain closed: his mother.

Strangely enough, Marina Evans looked exactly as I'd always pictured her in my mind: a woman in her fifties with a fairly rocking body and skin like leather. Face caked by heavy makeup, hair sprayed stiff, clothes appropriate for a sixteen year old and half bombed out of her mind – she was Minnie's dream come true. He was the one who allowed her into our dressing room backstage without realizing who she was hoping to have some fun.

Mai didn't look a thing like his mother, but I knew she'd had a few surgeries in her day so that made it harder to judge. Her hair was like dirty dishwater, her eyes a vacant olive, her nose and chin long and chiseled. I'd likely have mistaken her for a gifted drag queen had I simply passed her on the street.

One would have thought Mai had been shot when he stepped into the room and saw her standing there. He gulped, choked on his cigarette smoke and stumbled back a few steps. He'd just returned from sending Tiffany and Hazel back to our hotel in a taxi so that the boy could get some much-needed rest. He was already wishing that he'd gone with them.

"Darling!" Marina cried with a fake coo. "*There* is my precious boy. It's been so long!"

"Not long enough," I heard Mai whisper though he managed a lukewarm smile, managed to *appear* calm.

"Whoa! This is your mama?!" Minnie said with a gasp. "Dude! I bet she never left without her panties full of dollars."

Not even I saw the punch coming and I thought myself fairly skilled at reading Mai's body language. He strolled over to Minnie and hammered a fist to his gut without so much as a blink. He made it seem effortless, even somehow elegant. Minnie fell to his knees, the wind knocked clean out of him, and threw up in front of all of us. Embarrassing, I'm sure, but not nearly as painful as what Mai said to him after delivering the blow: Minnie was out of the band.

I always knew when Mai was truly serious and that was as serious as I'd ever seen him. He still believed it had been Minnie who poisoned dear Hazel – poison the poor shit was still suffering from – and Minnie had just made the most ill-timed, crude remark possible. His fate was sealed.

Minnie's first instinct was to laugh. I don't know if that was simply true to his nature or because of the blue pills he'd popped moments earlier, but he laughed even as Mai pulled him to his feet and pushed him out the door. Dart quickly followed him. Dart hadn't been hanging around Mai as much as he used to since Angie's death and he didn't need to be asked to go now; it was pretty clear Mai didn't want an audience just then.

I started to go, too. I hadn't exactly been Mai's choice for support lately and I knew that he knew that I'd been spending time with Minnie, but he stopped me by lightly brushing his hand against mine. He didn't want to be left alone with his mother. I think he was afraid of what he might do if he was.

"Bad timing?" Marina asked innocently. "I hope you didn't chuck him out on my account, dearest. I really didn't mind. Any attention is good attention."

"So you've always said," Mai said. "Blue, meet my mum — Marina."

Marina flashed me a showgirl smile. "Special to m'boy, are you?" she asked. "Not his usual type if I remember right."

"Why are you here?" Mai questioned, placing himself between me and his mother. "What d'you want? You need money?"

Marina pretended to be offended. She pouted, frowned and slowly shook her head. "Imagine my surprise when I turned on my telly and see none other than my baby boy there kissin' some li'l guitarist in front of screamin' fans. I didn't even know for sure you was still alive and there you were...all grown up and actin' a big rock star. Never called, never wrote. You just disappeared on me."

"How long was it before you noticed?" Mai asked. "Hmm? When you crashed? When the heroin you traded me for wore off?"

"That's a bloody lie!" Marina said sharply, shaking her head at me. "I didn't trade him for nothin'! You *wanted* to stay with Clint. You said he owned horses or somethin' and you wanted to learn how to ride 'em. I thought it'd be good for you."

"Oh, he taught me how to ride," Mai muttered, his eyes suddenly dark and cold. "I wanted to tell you *all* about it so you'd at least know what you'd done but I knew the best thing was never to see you again. I went to America. I never planned on comin' back here at all."

Now, being that I'd only just met Marina Evans, I nearly bought into it when she started to hysterically weep and threw her arms around Mai's waist in a nice show of desperation. She said repeatedly she was sorry, maybe she even meant it, and swore up and down that she was a changed woman now.

"I been clean for three months," she said.

"Slow nights at the club?" Mai asked, slipping free of her grasp.

"Actually, Popper burned down about six months ago," Marina replied. "Ain't too many hirin' girls like me now, either."

"And you've smoked your savings away," Mai said with a knowing smile, pointing at her. "There it is. There's what this is about, Blueski."

Marina adamantly shook her head. "It ain't, either! Your comin' here when you did's a godsend, darling. It's fate. I've no place to sleep tonight, I been tryin' to lay off sugar daddies. You can help me be a better person. I want you to be proud of me. I'm real proud of *you*."

The woman was good. She plugged right into Mai's guilt complex and cranked up the voltage to maximum. If he denied her, she'd have no choice but to go on selling herself to survive. If he gave in to her, he was enabling and asking for more heartache. He was screwed either way, really.

"Here," he grumbled, handing her a roll of cash. "Get yourself a hotel room and something to eat."

"I can't stay with you?" she asked, frowning.

"In our suite?" Mai laughed. "That's paid for by our record company, mum. I can hardly—"

"They won't care," Marina said. "You just got rid of what's-his-name, anyway. You've got the space and I won't be any bother at all, baby, I swear. Let me grab my things, okay? I left 'em right outside."

Marina gave Mai a peck on the cheek before scurrying out of the room. I'll never forget how helpless Mai appeared to me then, leaning against the makeup counter with wide flabbergasted eyes cast down at the floor. He slowly looked at me and blinked as if in a daze.

"Shoot me now," he whispered. "Please. Before I give her a new motor or a diamond ring."

I smiled brightly as I walked over to him and formed a gun with my hand. I put the barrel against the side of his head and made a "pow" as I pulled the trigger. Mai allowed his knees to cave and fell against me, resting his head upon my shoulder. We both uttered a quiet laugh.

"She's still out there," he murmured. "Isn't she?"

I nodded. "I imagine so."

"Damn it."

"Did you mean it that Minnie's out?"

Mai nodded without hesitation and moved away from me. "Given what he's done to Hazel — and don't think I haven't noticed he's been hurting you as well...he does more harm than good. I can't have that. There are other keyboardists. We'll get one that doesn't come with a buffet."

It may sound trivial on my part, but hearing Mai say that meant the world to me. It proved that he had still been thinking of me, worrying about me, even as Hazel clung to his arm. I could have kissed him. I probably *would* have kissed him had Marina not come bouncing back into the room yapping about some groupies outside she'd had to fight her way through to reach us.

Marina wanted to take as much credit as possible for Mai's talents, as if she had personally given him his voice and ability to compose. She taught him how to write his letters, after all, and she'd let him bang pots and pans when he was two and she never shushed him when he sang in the shower even though the neighbors told her to once or twice. The woman never shut up.

All the way back to the hotel she told me cutesy stories about Mai as a child, though most were so generic that they could have been about any child. Judging by the expression on Mai's face it seemed to me that they were. I did learn his first word was "tart" and that he was frequently mistaken for a girl as a toddler and fought with the other kids in the neighborhood quite often. I also learned that Mai was largely self-educated as he hadn't been able to attend regular school and Marina had never hired any private tutors. I was tempted more than once to whack the woman upside the head.

Minnie was still in the suite when we arrived, thoroughly occupied with Tiffany in one of the bedrooms. He'd told her about Mai banishing him and thought she'd climbed into his bed to prove she was on his side. He should have known she only wanted to score another notch on her list of musicians bagged before he went out. We left them to it.

Hazel was sound asleep, curled up on the loveseat with his stage makeup still in tact. He seemed smaller than usual, perhaps simply less of a threat in my mind. I even volunteered to cover him with a blanket before stepping into the restroom.

Dart was out hitting the local pubs, but Mai lied and said that he needed to join him at an extremely late meeting elsewhere. He gave Marina his bed and the key to the mini bar before slipping out of the room and onto the hotel roof where deck chairs and a heated pool awaited him.

Only Mai could enjoy sitting atop a roof in London, gazing out at a foggy landscape in the dead of night. It was chilly, but he didn't seem to notice. Mai never noticed the cold and loathed summer and its accompanying humidity. I found him huddled beneath his oversized black coat with the collar turned up to hide half his face from sight, smoking as he gazed upon the shrouded moon above. His knees were tucked close to his chest, causing him to practically disappear into the lounge chair.

He knew I was there before I said a word and remained silent. His pale skin appeared kissed with a bluish tint under the night sky, making his features all the more beautiful. I slid onto the lounger next to his and stretched my legs out, lying back in order to share his view of the moon.

"Is she asleep yet?" he asked in a low voice, as if we were sharing a secret.

"Drinking herself there steadily," I replied out the corner of my mouth. "Your cover is secure."

"Good work. Red base out."

"Blue base out."

Mai peeked at me out the corner of his eye and then started to giggle in his goofy way. I smiled and inhaled a bit of his smoke as I moved closer to him. Even in the cold I could feel the warmth emanating from his body.

"She blindsided me," he said, shaking his head. "I really buggered it up, too. I should've said sorry about your luck but it's *your* mess."

"Why didn't you?" I asked. "You always know just what to say to people and you've always said it before."

"Is that how I seem to you?"

I nodded.

"No shit…"

It surprised me that Mai seemed so amazed by that. Sure I'd seen him zone out now and then and, every once in a while, he'd said some unusual things but I'd always thought of Mai as nothing but reliable…secure…*together* – at least when it came to self-confidence. Everyone did. I suppose a lot of it came down to faking it.

Mai shook his head. "People are always asking me what's next for the band and for myself like I've got it all mapped out, y'know? Like, I know exactly where we'll all be a week or month from now. I don't even know for certain where I'll be tomorrow. I could fall off this damn roof for all I know. I don't know anything, Blueski. No one ever sees that, do they? No one ever realizes that I'm hangin' on by a bloody thread."

"That'd make a nice lyric."

"Bloody thread? I've already used it, you've just not seen it yet," he replied, exhaling a cloud of smoke. "Jesus, I'm quoting m'self now."

I couldn't help but laugh. "You're just down because Marina's here."

"I can't keep blaming her," he murmured, staring at the long ash dangling precariously from the end of his cigarette. "She fucked up, she knows it, but she can't change. I'm not a boy anymore, though. It's all in the past."

"The boy you were hasn't healed and he's still in you somewhere."

Mai turned and placed his head upon my shoulder, his eyes wide and curious as he gazed up at me. I put my arm around him and pulled him closer – it felt like a lifetime since I'd been able to hold him like that – and smiled.

"That was almost deep," he said. "Did you hear that on one of those telly shrink shows?"

"Something like that," I replied with a nod.

Mai patted my arm. "Gold star for you."

"Mai…Who was Clint?"

A storm rose instantly within Mai's eyes, dark and turbulent, but he didn't pull away from me. Clint was a friend of his mother's, a supplier and a customer, and that was all Mai would tell me. It was really all I needed to know. What I *wanted* to know was whether or not he'd had sex with the man. Extremely invasive, I know, but I couldn't help myself – I had to ask.

"I was just a kid," Mai replied. "He didn't really give me much choice at the time. I ran off soon after, never looked back."

"So you lied to Hazel last night."

"I can't give Hazel what he'd like. What's it matter what reason I gave?" he asked. "Hazel is too good a kid and being with me would just fuck him up. You know it would. Messing people up is what I'm good at – or haven't you been hearing those whispers about my tainted soul?"

I rolled my eyes. "That's just bullshit hype and you know it. Tiffany probably started it. Corrupting souls is sexy or something."

Mai didn't seem to have heard me. "*Why* were you eavesdropping, anyhow?"

I shrugged. "I was worried."

Mai bought that fairly easily – I figured he would – and we went on to sit in comfortable silence for a few minutes. I thought Mai had fallen asleep but then his eyes opened suddenly and turned upon me like playful daggers.

"What about you?" he asked brightly. "You've gotten all pokey about my past, so it's your turn now."

"'Pokey'?" I laughed. "What do you want to know?"

"You never talk about your folks," he replied. "Have you been keeping in touch with them at all since becoming a big star?"

I hadn't, but that had nothing to do with becoming a star. I hadn't phoned or written a single letter since I was nineteen years old – since I'd dropped out of college and ran away from my old life. I had no desire to speak with them in any shape or form because I knew what they'd do if I did.

"No," I said. "We don't get along so well."

"No?" Mai asked, sounding surprised. "I thought it was all Mr. and Mrs. Brady at your house."

"It was, growing up, but I ended up resenting the way they raised us."

"Us? You never told me you had any siblings," Mai said, suddenly excited.

"They favored me over my twin, Gray," I said. "I never thought that was right."

"Blue and Gray? Your parents *had* to be potheads," Mai said with a grin.

"Gray's dead. Gray died…in an accident. We were nineteen."

That wiped the grin from Mai's face and he stared at me with such deep compassion that it nearly broke my heart. He'd never had any siblings, but his empathy was quite genuine. I realized then that I should have told him about Gray sooner. He began stroking my hair in hopes of comforting me and I knew I could use his sympathy, his natural inclination to want to make those around him feel better, to my advantage. Finally, Gray had proven useful for *something*.

Spinning a believable tale came easily, like constructing an intricate house of cards. One half-truth stacked upon another until the foundation became solid. I told Mai that it had been a car accident that left both Gray and me unconscious. Our belongings were scattered everywhere, inside the car and on the street around the vehicle. The paramedics and doctors weren't sure who was who when we were brought into the emergency room.

I woke up; Gray didn't. My parents were visibly relieved when they arrived at the hospital and saw that I'd been the survivor. They stopped trying to pretend that they'd loved us both the same. Gray was all but forgotten.

"I kinda cracked a little over it," I said quietly. "Dropped out of school, got really depressed. My parents tried to commit me for a while, feared I was suicidal. I ran away from the institution and left town. I haven't spoken to them since."

Mai didn't know what to say so he simply kissed me sweetly and offered a sympathetic smile. He felt bad now for telling me that I didn't know what death looked like but I disagreed. I *didn't* know. I'd been given a brand new life when Gray passed away.

"I never saw the corpse, I didn't attend the funeral, but I live for both of us now," I said. "Gray's still there when I look in the mirror."

"That's fucking beautiful," Mai whispered breathlessly, moving even closer to me. "Why didn't you tell me all this before?"

I shrugged. "You didn't ask."

"Right. Next time I'll inquire about dead siblings right off the bat. Silly me," Mai chuckled. "Must be strange, lookin' in the mirror and seein' two faces like that. Do you ever miss Gray much?"

I'd have to have said no if I was to answer Mai honestly, but fortunately he let me off the hook by retracting the question as quickly as he'd asked it. It seemed fortuitous to him, even insensitive, and he apologized for asking it with a kiss to my neck. A hidden tragedy, a brush with death, a noble cause to live for – it made me irresistible.

Mai came upon me like a tiger in the wild, forceful and confident and nothing short of almost regal elegance. He was soft, tender, generous and commanding. He certainly knew what he was doing and what he wanted and I reaped every last benefit of his experience. How to time every caress, where to place his lips. His breath upon my skin, lust turning to gratification. Just the two of us intertwined on a roof, in London, on soon to be flattened lounge chairs.

We'd inadvertently roll into the pool before all was said and done – something I would snicker about for weeks to come. It was all I'd hoped for and then some. I'd taken all Mai had to give me and I wanted more. I always wanted more. I knew full well that I was not the first to be with Mai, but I believed on that night that I'd be the last. In fact, I'd have sworn to it.

That alone should have told me that I was mistaken.

Chapter 17

I BECAME PREOCCUPIED with Mai's skin disease. It wasn't that I doubted that he actually had it or anything – I believed that he did – but I wondered how it worked. How much light was too much? I asked him once what would happen if sunlight hit him – would it be instant and messy like some vampire flick, or would it be gradual with welts and sores over a period of time.

"I can't tell you, I've never tested it," he replied.

I couldn't stop wondering. In reality it was a bit of both, I suppose. If exposed he would break out, become ill, develop severe sunburn and his skin would be irreversibly damaged. Death was also a possibility, his risk of developing cancer was tremendous and his smoking certainly didn't help things any.

I only became curious because Mai and I fell asleep on the deck next to the pool, tangled up in one another and thoroughly soaked. I woke before he did by luck, really, frozen stiff and alarmed to see the sun was rising. A rare clear day for London and we were going to be directly in the sun's line of sight. Naturally my first reaction was to wake Mai immediately – and I did – though for the slightest second morbid curiosity had attempted to take over. Mai was so beautiful when he slept. Would the sun have eaten the beauty away before my eyes? Would he have been aware that it was happening? Would it be painful when the sun struck him? Would it have torn him from his sleep and caused him to scream and struggle?

As it was I shook him and he quickly opened his eyes, noticed the approaching light, and exclaimed a heartfelt "shit" before getting to his feet and running for the shelter of the roof's entrance.

I nearly pissed myself laughing as Mai huddled behind a tall potted plant and gestured wildly for me to fetch his clothes. I dressed first, near the pool's edge, and playfully waved his pants over my head. Three elderly women, fellow guests in the establishment, shuffled up behind Mai while he was cursing at me. One pinched him. Another took his picture. I'd never seen Mai blush before.

"Such a nice young man," the third said with a wink. "Be a dear and give him back his trousers before he catches cold."

The "dear" was me. How could I defy such a sweet old lady with wandering eyes? Mai attempted to glare angrily at me as I approached with his clothes in hand, but he couldn't quite manage to keep a straight face. He had his pants on when another photo was taken, this time of the two of us together near that plant. That shot would end up in the tabloids.

Everyone was asleep when we slipped back into our room. Mai curled up on the floor behind the couch and I slipped in behind him. We both slept for a few hours and then something forced me awake. Noise. Someone was rummaging through luggage.

Marina was less than thrilled when I crept out from behind the couch and caught her exploring Mai's suitcase. I don't know what she'd been hoping to find – money, cosmetics, cigarettes – but she was still empty handed when I let her know I was watching her.

It could have gone a lot of different ways. I could have made a scene, increased her embarrassment – assuming the woman *could* be embarrassed – and let everyone know that she'd been up to something. Instead I simply handed her some money and one of Minnie's suitcases full of goodies and told her to make the best of it. She left a lot easier than I thought she would. In fact, she hardly raised any objections at all. She thought she was doing what Mai wanted and even seemed a bit sad on her way out. I never regretted getting rid of her.

We left Minnie behind, alone in the hotel room, when we headed out for the airport that evening. It was to be the first real break we'd had from one another. Dart was going to visit his sister and parents back in Delsby. Hazel was off to spend time with his brother, Stephen, the only family member he cared to see. Mai and I decided to go to California to play at being tourists.

It was fun for the most part, buying manufactured t-shirts and silly trinkets that were allowed to be overpriced because they bore the name of the state, following the stars along the sidewalks and posing with figures in the wax museum (something we were nearly thrown out for until the manager realized who we were). Mai even stopped at one of those photo fantasy booths to get his picture taken "with" Angelina Jolie.

The photo fantasy thing was funny enough and then the clerk informed us that the customer before us had gotten her picture taken "with" Mai. He was one of the available cutouts and that made it hilarious. Naturally, he and I both had to pose with the Mai look alike. We signed the photo and the clerk framed it and put it on display. We each took a copy of it, too, just for laughs. It was easy to spot the real Mai – he was the one doing a screwball imitation of Elvis. That photo is hanging in that same store window to this day. I doubt it'll ever be taken down now.

It didn't occur to me at the time that Mai was simply keeping himself too busy to dwell upon his mother's abrupt departure. She hadn't said goodbye to him, from his perspective she'd simply taken his money and fled, and it troubled him more than it should have. I'd spared him from having to support her, from having the woman hooked into his back for the remainder of her life – I *knew* I had. It was hard keeping it a secret from Mai, but I'm not sorry. I can't be sorry. It wasn't like I could have foreseen what would happen. I didn't *make* her die. It was her choice, her own fault.

To keep on track – Mai and I went a bit wild on our vacation. We suddenly had a ton of money thanks to the proceeds from the albums, shirts, watches, pens, calendars, buttons, stickers (name it and Tiffany had marketed it with our name and faces). We'd not been doing much spending up to that point, however. Mai had been too paranoid, too conscientious. Two days in LA and we'd bought so many new accessories, outfits, cosmetics, future Christmas presents and shoes that we would have to buy new suitcases in order to get it all back home. That was another major expenditure – Mai had bought a nice apartment in New York, his new homeland of choice.

Mai knew that I wore contacts and colored my hair, there was no way to keep such a thing hidden after living and touring together in tight quarters for a couple of years straight. Strange that he'd never once asked me why I did it, but after I'd revealed my past with Gray I suppose he'd made sense of it on his own. Mai thought I didn't want to see the face of my dead twin when I looked into the mirror and that worked well enough for me.

I was willing to play along when he asked if he could give me a "crazy" makeover. It would be like our early days when he'd painted my face and took scissors to my hair. I'd felt the center of his world then. Everything old becomes new again.

I didn't have a clue what Mai was doing to me during this new makeover but the fact that he kept snickering childishly didn't seem a good thing. I sat patiently as he dabbed some kind of dye into my hair, waited for it to take, and then he climbed into the shower with me – fully clothed – to help rinse the excess out.

He never liked to be left alone in a room. He was a bit like a clingy pet in that respect, always pacing near the door if he was shut out or staring out the window waiting for someone to return as if starved for affection. I didn't mind, of course, because it made me feel more important. In time I'd even come to use it to my advantage. On that evening I invited him to take his clothes off and forget about the hair. He simply laughed.

Blue. Imagine that. Mai dyed my hair electric blue and then trimmed it neatly to frame my face. He wouldn't let me see it, of course, for a torturous amount of time. He sat on the counter before me, completely blocking my view of the mirror behind him, as he made a few final adjustments.

Finally he covered his mouth and uttered a convincingly horrified gasp. "Oh, dear," he said, looking afraid.

"What?"

"Promise you won't hurt me?" he asked through a sweet pout.

"What did you do?"

Mai laughed as I literally shoved him aside in order to look at myself. He'd had me worried for a few seconds, pulled a successful prank, as I looked nothing less than amazing. I didn't have any contacts in, I didn't need them to see, and the new hair color made the natural blue in my irises shine.

"Next album I think we all ought to go freak," Mai said, playfully flipping my hair. "Bitches of gloomy punk or something."

"Aren't we anyway?" I asked.

Mai shrugged. "Unusual, yes; but it's all been in a very pretty way. I'm not always pretty, you know that. You've seen me straight after getting out of bed in the evening. I'm tired of being pretty to the world all the time."

"So what did you have in mind?"

Mai smiled – his secretive smile – and jumped to his feet. "I want to go darker," he replied. "Our look, our sound. I want to bring what's in my head out in the open."

"You mean you want to let people into that dead pool you go

to when you space out," I whispered.

"You do watch me an awful lot, don't you," he remarked with a strangely startled laugh. "Yeah, I guess so. Love, creativity and death colliding. Dreams and visions, reality falling away faster than the brain can compensate. There *is* a dead pool out there, Blueski…that universal unconsciousness where all the wasted thoughts and fears and ideas go. Certain people are chosen, allowed to reach into it now and then, but I think anyone could go if they only knew to try. Imagine all the beautiful creations we'd have if they did. I want people to ponder that."

Ponder that, indeed. I nodded my head accordingly, but I was more than slightly lost – tangled in the enigmatic grace of Mai's words. A fly struggling to understand the nature of the web binding it in place. This dead pool Mai spoke of – I wondered if I'd ever been there and if it really was such a wondrous place to visit. Would most people *know* if they had gone to it or was Mai the exception? Had Mai, for that matter, really ever gone there? Was I making it all too literal? Perhaps it was mere poetic insanity but I loved Mai deeply so I suppose I was insane, too. I didn't think to doubt him.

That is the glory of *real* love. It's not about blindness, it's about illogical delusions. That's why people believe it can last an eternity and move mountains and all that. It raises unnatural determination. It makes the impossible seem possible and causes reason to lose its edge. It drives us to do things – anything – to keep the feeling alive and close to our hearts. The heart and mind work both for and against one another, especially when poisoned by the streams of love. I was far from immune.

122

Chapter 18

WE SPENT FIVE full nights and four days in California, the longest amount of time that Mai and I had ever been completely alone. He never once made any advances on me, though I gave him ample opportunity. There were only the occasional kisses that, lovely as they were, he'd have given to anyone. If ever I touched him and kept my hand upon him too long, he found ways to gently brush me aside. I was afraid that I had somehow disappointed him that night on the roof, but he seemed content to have my company and I hadn't the heart to ask.

We ran into Arieal Turner on our last night out in LA, the singer from Frothe – our touring partner back when we'd first started. It seemed a lifetime ago to me, those tour days when Basil had been with us, and Arieal had changed her physical image so much that I hardly recognized her.

The Arieal we'd known back then had been tall and boney with flattened black hair, skimpy clothes and green colored contact lenses. She was obsessed with visiting tanning beds, even though her skin was naturally a light brown and she'd believed herself to be far more important than we ever had. Coming off the stage as we were going onto it, she'd turned her nose up. If ever any of us smiled in her direction, she'd scoff in return. She'd been paired with us in hopes of garnering more males in the audience but for the most part they had preferred Mai to her as well.

Arieal's new band was called Tramp. It seemed fitting enough. Mai liked to listen to other bands whenever possible, especially those unheard of, searching for a new sound or someone new to admire. It was totally a fluke that we picked the bar Tramp was playing in that night, but Mai insisted on staying once he realized who she was.

I still can't explain Mai's interest in Arieal. She wasn't at all what I'd call attractive. She was a poster child for anorexia, had dyed her hair lavender and spiked it high enough to reach Jesus and that night she was wearing stiletto boots and baggy leather pants. Her band was playing death metal, shaking the walls, and she was poorly attempting to screech along. Perhaps Mai simply found the debauchery entertaining. For me and my ears, it was nothing more than painful.

The performance ended early after Arieal broke down in a hissy fit and threw her microphone at a heckler standing before the stage. Mai talked our way backstage and we followed her, watching as she frantically paced about her dressing room and cursed under her breath.

Arieal hadn't changed at all inside. She certainly hadn't developed a sense of humility. When she spotted us standing in her doorway she made a loud "hmph" and started packing all of her belongings into a bright yellow duffel bag. She was planning to leave the band. Death to Tramp just like all of the bands before it.

"It wasn't all bad," Mai told her. "You just aren't singing songs that suit you. It's the same problem you had before."

"What do *you* know?" Arieal asked.

"I know you and I know voices," Mai replied. "Not everyone can sing just any sort of song."

"Who the hell do you think you are to come in dropping tips like the rock pope?" she huffed, shaking her head from side to side.

"Don't you remember us?" I asked with a soft laugh.

"Hard to forget you, creepy freak," she replied, rolling her eyes at me before glaring at Mai. "Wanna get outta the doorway, Mr. Rockstar? If I want advice, I'll write to your little fan club and ask for it."

"All I'm saying is you're more suited for pop rock," Mai said. "Maybe soul or gospel, even. You don't have to get all bitchy, babe."

"Don't 'babe' me," she said. "It's always been so *easy* for you. No one cares that you sing off key half the time because you're beautiful. You can do whatever the hell you want out there and flash your little smile and shake your little ass and they'll cheer. Now *get* outta my way, you damn pop tart!"

Mai laughed over being called a "pop tart" as Arieal plowed out the door but his heart wasn't really in it. Truthfully, I believe her words had wounded him a bit, sparked his secret insecurity that Nefarious had risen to fame largely because of his pretty face. It was why he wanted the band to go darker. He needed to know he was being taken seriously.

Something beneficial did come from that chilly conversation with Arieal, however. We met Jim, the now unemployed keyboardist of Tramp, only seconds after being chewed out by the princess. Jim was a trip – tall and menacing in appearance, dressed then in a pair of standard issue prison pants and a white tank top. His arms were nearly bigger around than Mai's thighs and he was covered with so many tattoos that he barely had any white skin left on his arms and back. He had piercings in his eyebrow, nose, ears and chin. He acted as if he was on speed or being zapped with electricity at all hours of the day, but that was really due to having a mild case of Tourette syndrome. Mai slipped him Tiffany's number and let him know we had an opening in the band. He told me he had a "good feeling" about Jim as we left.

Mai spoke to Dart on his cell phone before we boarded our flight to New York. Less than a week of vacation and Dart had ended up getting married to a waitress called Nora he'd met in a Delsby bar. Mai gave him a hard time for not inviting us to the wedding and Dart replied that they'd gone "shotgun in Vegas." Mai, for some reason, couldn't stop laughing about the entire thing.

Mai was unable to reach Hazel. He'd been doing his best not to worry about the little shit throughout our vacation, I knew he had, but Hazel had always been at the back of his mind. Mai spoke to Delia, the wife of Hazel's brother Stephen. She told him that Hazel and Stephen had gone to Alaska of all places to study polar bears or some weird thing; Stephen was a zoologist.

It didn't occur to me until our plane landed and we'd climbed into a taxi that I had no home. Mai asked me where I was headed and I stared at him as if he'd lost his mind. I'd been living out of hotel rooms for years now, same as Mai. Now that Mai owned a steady address, I'd simply assumed that I'd be going home with him. I wanted it to be *our* home.

"I can't stay with you?" I asked.

"Aren't you sick of me yet, baby Blue?" he teased.

"No," I quickly replied. "Are you sick of me?"

"Definitely," Mai said with a wink. "No, you can stay with me until you find yourself a place. I've enough space. You know I don't much like being alone, anyway."

I felt a smile creep across my lips and I moved over to give

Mai a kiss. I'd intended to hit his lips but he moved suddenly and I got his cheek instead. He arched an eyebrow, flashed an odd little smile and then he laughed as he gently pushed me away.

Mai's apartment was spacious, filled with leather furniture and plush gray carpeting. He'd painted the walls a slate blue and covered them with dark paintings and the various crosses that he'd collected over the years. A sculpted angel that looked fresh out of a graveyard loomed in the corner near the terrace doors with head bowed and mouth frowning in anger.

For the most part, though, the apartment was empty and uncluttered. There were photos of us here and there but no knick-knacks, only shelves of books and the occasional painting. The kitchenette, I was sure, hadn't even been touched.

I wandered about freely as Mai checked his phone messages. A print of an angelic woman with black wings hung over Mai's narrow bed. Stacks of worn books waiting to be shelved – literary, classic books that I'd never dreamt of reading for the fun of it – sat at the foot of the bed near a mountain of CDs.

I sat down and snatched up the book opened upon Mai's pillow nonetheless and started reading it while waiting for him to come find me. It was a short story written by Oscar Wilde called "The Happy Prince" and I found myself completely engrossed in it within a few seconds. I lost track of time and shed a few tears when I'd finished it. It had been a story about love in its purest form, as well as society's shallow definition of beauty. A lesson about what true grace is all about. All of it – especially the lines about giving away the things that made the prince beautiful and his companion going off to find death – screamed Mai in my mind. Beautifully tragic in the sincerest way.

I remember those lines even now. How perfect they were – even more perfect now – like they'd been written specifically with us in mind. I have a feeling they may have been Mai's favorites as well as I could tell the book had been opened to that part many times over.

Eventually I rolled off the bed and, once I realized how much time had passed, went in search of Mai. He was sitting out on the balcony, huddled into a tight ball on a metal deck chair, holding a cigarette in one hand and a bottle of beer in the other. He was staring vacantly at the starry sky with smudged eyes, shivering.

"I thought you'd ditched me," I said.

"Sorry, Blueski," he absently replied; he sounded tired. "I've heard the most...unsettling news."

"One of the phone messages?" I asked, swallowing hard. I felt suddenly nervous.

"Hazel wants me to come see him," he said. "He says its endless dark there at this time of year, perfect for us. He sounded like his old self, but...I think he wants to leave the band."

"Why would you think that?" I laughed.

"Everyone leaves me," he replied, not even blinking. "One day you'll leave me, too."

I shook my head. "You'll never get rid of me. I swear it."

"Then you're lying."

"Only you lie when you swear," I said. "Now what's really got you upset?"

A faint smile flirted with the corner of Mai's lips as he drew in a quick puff on his cigarette, held it in, savored it, released it with a sigh. I could tell he didn't want to speak but he would. He had to speak to someone.

"Minnie's credit card ran out on him, he'd been stayin' in our room in London all this time. The manager busted in to chuck him out and found him in bed, unconscious, with a dead whore at his side. Those were his exact words," Mai said softly. "Minnie's gonna live all right. His...whore, Tiffany phoned to inform me, was my mum. Pumped herself to death with her heroin at last."

I sat down hard on the chair next to Mai, my legs having turned to rubber without warning and shook my head. All I managed to ask was, "When was this?"

"Found early this morning," Mai replied, sipping the last of his beer. "Oh, but no worries cos Tif's all over the damage control. We're saved. Fuck-a-doodle-doo."

"'Damage control?'" I asked.

Guilt. Paranoia. Near panic seething right beneath the surface – it had been years since those old adversaries had so swiftly risen and threatened to overpower me. Tiffany was working on damage control. What was the damage? Did she know I'd paid Marina off? Had Hazel or Minnie told her that I'd slipped the boy the acid stamp? The stamp. The stupid stamp. Why had I given it to Hazel and allowed Mai to blame Minnie for it? Why did Hazel want Mai to come to Alaska? Was he hoping to tell on me? So juvenile. So...

"When Minnie wakes he'll agree to state this incident is the reason he'll no longer be in Nefarious so that no one can blame his decision to overdose on being expelled by me," Mai said. "We've already prepared a statement, courtesy of Tiffany, that we wish him the best. Wish him all the best in prison, maybe, cos that's where he'll end up once they've rummaged through his buffet. As for mum...she was identified only as a random whore at the scene and publicly that's how she'll stay. It's to be our dark li'l secret, since dead whores aren't sexy and Tiffany will allow nothing less for us in the press."

"She *said* that?"

Mai offered a jagged little smile. "Why'd she go back to that room after duckin' out like she did? Clearly she stayed for Minnie's drugs, but was it for his buffet that she originally returned...or had she hoped to find me?"

I slowly shook my head, trying to formulate something intelligent to say. Mai was hurting, vulnerable, trying to reason out answers to questions that couldn't *be* answered. I didn't think it really mattered what I said then so long as I said something to reel Mai back in from the stars in the sky he was so absently focused upon. I needed to prompt him to look at me.

"This isn't your fault," I said. "You let Minnie go for good reason, what he's done now is proof of that. We all knew he hit that shit too hard, too often. And your mom...she wouldn't have joined him if she'd gone back there with you in mind. That's all there is to it."

"Is it?" Mai asked, slowly turning his glassy eyes onto mine.

"Isn't it?" I countered, nodding.

"Must be," he replied coldly. "She just never cared at all."

With that Mai tossed the empty bottle aside and rose to his feet, shuffling his way back into the apartment without saying a word. He'd not say another thing to me for the rest of the night. It made me feel uneasy.

Chapter 19

MINNIE ENDED UP getting probation, along with an obligatory stint in a rehab center when he was tried later that year – one of the perks of having a famous name. We all heard about it while heading off for the final tour, but none of us made contact in order to congratulate him. I doubt he'd have spoken to us had we tried.

Minnie was still in the hospital, of course, when Mai and I headed off to Alaska to meet Hazel. I'd pretty much invited myself on the trip – I couldn't have Mai and Hazel talking behind my back – but I'm certain Mai was grateful for my company.

I'd never seen Mai so glum for such a prolonged period of time. He hadn't returned to London for Marina's funeral but he had made certain she'd been given a decent ceremony, even if few attended it, and a lavish crypt. He hoped she'd find some peace in her new home.

He didn't speak much, not nearly as much as I was used to, and I tried not to push. It wasn't all bad, sitting in silence with Mai's head in my lap. He'd let me stroke his hair or rub his back while he gazed off into that mysterious place. It was fine so long as he eventually returned to me and he always did. I believed he always would.

Alaska cheered Mai up considerably. *Hazel* cheered Mai up, I should say. Sweet, sympathetic, love-struck Hazel. The little shit didn't mind that I'd come along, he even gave me a hug and grinned in his dopey way when I first stepped into his sight like we were the best of friends. Like he had no idea that we were rivals for Mai's affection.

The endless dark of the region was beyond surreal. All hours, day or night, it was dark. Mai was finally able to go out around noon for lunch when everyone else did without having to worry about his skin. He could watch daytime television and frequent local stores. We had to practically force him to take time out to sleep. He didn't want to waste a minute.

Unfortunately, we weren't exactly in the most exciting of places. The town consisted of a handful of homes and shops, and mounds of snow taller than our vehicle. Mai adored it. He said he wanted to give up New York and become a hermit in the Alaskan wilderness. I thought he was only joking. Time proved me wrong.

If Hazel was planning to rat me out he was doing a professional job of hiding it. He chattered endlessly about the animals he'd seen and how peaceful the land had made him feel. It had done him a tremendous amount of good to take time away from us. He didn't come right out and say so, of course, but it was obvious to me and Mai both. He'd been enjoying himself immensely, but he would have left it all behind if only Mai asked him to. The boy didn't have it in him to refuse Mai.

Hazel had made a recording with a group of local musicians simply for the fun of it. The album consisted of skillful, but, to my taste, awful country music, and the singer was a twangy older woman.

Mai got a kick out of it as he could tell everyone involved in the recording had been having a blast. He missed that, I think. Mai missed the simple *fun* of performing. Once everything becomes professional and multi-platinum business tends to take over. He wanted to escape that. So long as he was Mai Evans of Nefarious, I didn't believe he ever could.

He went without makeup while in Alaska. We all did. I found that I'd nearly forgotten what he looked like beneath the painted lips and outlined eyes. He seemed different than I recalled. Faded, somehow. He was almost paler than Hazel and, as such, seemed to have persistent dark circles under his eyes – though I'm sure his routine lack of proper sleep played a part in that. All the same, I thought he looked ill.

When I asked, naturally, Mai swore that he was feeling extraordinarily well. We met with Hazel's country band and Mai sang a horrendous, albeit hilarious, duet with their lead singer Patty. Patty made Mai look like a child, she was so tall and big boned. I couldn't imagine how badly poor Hazel fared when she stood next to *him*. Hazel recorded that duet with Mai's blessing on his video camera, following Mai as he did a strangely accurate country two-step in time to the music and danced with Patty when not singing…though I'm not sure dancing was really the word for it. The woman mostly carried him from place to place while he playfully flung his arms about in time to the music.

After their show all eight of us – Patty brought her entire band along – went out for dinner. I'd never seen so much food and booze clustered upon one table before in my life. Every single one of us, except for Hazel, got a bit smashed – especially Mai. Bad things always attempted to happen when Mai became intoxicated.

The snow, unbeknownst to us, started falling during our meal and had accumulated to a few feet before we finally staggered our way outdoors. The sensible thing would have been to simply return to our lodging as quickly as possible and sleep through the rest of the blizzard, that was what Patty and her band did, but not us. Oh, no. Mai thought it would be fun to go sledding. I agreed and Hazel, as I said before, didn't like to refuse Mai. Besides, we needed someone *sober* to head the operation.

Had Tiffany been there I imagine they'd have heard her screaming and scolding from the top of her lungs all throughout town as we climbed up the tallest hill we could find. We were not contractually permitted to do anything that could be considered a safety risk and I'm pretty sure flying down a steep hill overlooking a thicket of trees using a large piece of cardboard as a sleigh fell into that category. Perhaps that's why Mai kept chuckling in his goofy, childish way all throughout our difficult climb.

The view at the top of the hill was spectacular. Pure, untouched snow – the kind Mai had spoken to me about earlier – as far as our eyes could see. It sparkled gently, diamond dust amongst the numerous evergreens, like an endless sea of pure tranquility.

"Souls," Mai whispered. "It's all souls. Who wants to dive in first?"

Hazel didn't want to go at all. He was afraid and, I suppose, he should have been. We all should have been. There were so many standing trees waiting, hoping to break us in half, that if we weren't careful to travel down a straight path we were liable to crack our heads open.

Mai went first, lying on his stomach and facing forward because he was a fool. It was funny at the time, watching him lay down flat and vanish from our sight in an instant. We didn't know where he'd ended up, we couldn't see him at all, but when the echo of a triumphant "whoop" rose up to greet us we'd known he'd made it somewhere safely.

"Follow me, darlings, and you'll do fine!" he shouted with a giggle.

Hazel was still reluctant to go but by then it felt as though we *had* to follow suit. Mai couldn't be left alone down there. If he wandered away we'd likely never find him and the last thing either of us wanted to do was lose Mai in any sense of the word. Hazel agreed to sit down on his sheet of cardboard and allow me to push him forward. That's exactly what I did.

When I think back to that night I know I felt a strong breeze right after sending Hazel on his way. It was the breeze that made it all go wrong, the breeze that caused layers of the diamond dust to drift all around us and Hazel to veer off course. It's not easy to describe the sound a body makes as it slams mercilessly into the base of a tree, it isn't as loud as one might imagine. It's hollow and swift – startling – but it doesn't *sound* so devastating. Hazel made a wounded yelp, like a pup that's had its tail stepped on, as he clipped a tree and then he continued sliding downward. It was Mai I heard yelp next. He must have been moving forward in hopes of catching Hazel as he flew by him. Instead he became Hazel's stopping block.

I can't recall how I reached them. If I ran down the hill or slid or fell. I only remember reaching the bottom of that hill and spotting a crimson stain near one of the trees. Hazel had struck there and was clearly hurt. A few feet away I found him lying on top of Mai. Both were still.

Mai didn't appear injured as far as I could see when I leaned over his body and took a careful look. I think that's what scared me. He didn't *look* injured but he wasn't moving. His eyes were closed and surrounded by those dark circles. Inside, I thought. He must be wounded inside and that was bad. That would be the worst.

I didn't know what to do. Hazel was bleeding from his head and he wasn't moving, either. I had enough sense not to move either of them but *what* was I going to *do*? By the time I climbed that hill and found some help in my state of mind they'd likely have frozen to death. I couldn't carry them both. If I left Hazel behind, Mai would be angry with me later on and I didn't want Mai to be angry. I also didn't want him to freeze to death.

Fate was watching over all three of us that night, for we happened to be extremely close to some houses that the snow and darkness had hidden from our sight. One of the residents had phoned the local sheriff about us "jackasses" playing in the blizzard when we'd first climbed the hill; he'd started searching for us long before Hazel's accident. It *was* an accident, after all. It was the breeze to blame and nothing more. That's what I'd tell Mai and that's what I told myself. The breeze and nothing more.

It took a bit of work to get paramedics to the scene, but eventually Hazel and Mai both were transported to the nearest hospital, which wasn't all that near. I sat alone in the waiting room, pacing and drinking coffee and muttering under my breath. I didn't dare phone Tiffany, I was afraid to, but I did wish I had someone with me. Mai was hurt, that was all I could think about. What if it was serious? What would I do?

I eventually dozed off huddled up in one of the ugly plaid chairs in the corner, exhausted and medicated by alcohol the coffee had been too weak to chase away. A firm tug on my arm rocked me out of my sleep and for a moment I believed I'd died and gone to some sort of heaven because I saw Mai sitting on a chair before me.

He had pulled one of the other chairs up close to mine and sat on the edge of it, staring quite intensely at me. His eyes under that lighting appeared almost silver, his skin as fair as the snow had been, and his hair was bunched in tighter waves because it had dried naturally. The dark circles seemed more severe.

"You're really here?" I asked, sitting up with a start.

He nodded solemnly.

"Are you hurt? Thank God you don't look hurt," I said, throwing my arms around him. "You're *not* hurt, are you?"

"You are holdin' on a bit tight," he replied, attempting to tease me, but his heart wasn't in it. "I'm all right."

"You wouldn't wake up," I said, forcing myself to release him. "I was worried."

Mai nodded slowly. He wasn't really injured at all with the exception of a few bruises, he'd simply gotten all the wind knocked clean out of him when Hazel struck him and his body decided to have a rest. The doctor partly blamed it on dehydration, which came as a surprise to Mai as he really hadn't been feeling poorly.

"And how's Hazel?" I asked; I *had* to ask, didn't I?

Mai lowered his eyes and shook his head, a serious hint of devastation within his eyes. "It's terribly sad…"

Immediately I began to imagine every vile possibility there could have been. Paralyzed, in a coma, in a body cast. Dead. I felt strangely excited, perhaps even hopeful, as I hung onto the arms of my chair with ravenous anticipation.

"What?" I asked through a whisper. "What is it? He's not... dead, is he?"

"Worse," Mai replied, keeping his eyes on the floor. "The impact caused all the blood vessels in his pecker to burst and now he'll never be getting it up again. He may seriously have to consider becoming a 'she'."

Mai had gotten me good. I'd been totally drawn into his words, thoroughly convinced that some genuine horror had befallen poor annoying Hazel, and then he had to go and ruin it all with a joke that wasn't even funny. I could have slapped him for that – I nearly did. If Mai was daring to crack jokes I knew Hazel's condition couldn't be too horribly serious, after all. How cruelly he'd gotten my hopes up.

"You...bastard!" I cried, rolling my eyes and frowning angrily. "You shouldn't joke like that!"

"I'm sorry," Mai laughed. "I'm really sorry. It...just helps me not to worry so much, is all."

The clouds lifted. "There's reason to worry?" I asked.

How easily Mai mistook my genuine interest as heartfelt concern. He wasn't at all stupid, as I've said he could normally map out anyone within an hour of meeting them, but he had difficulty seeing the darkness in me. He had a good heart. He loved me. It all goes back to those illogical devotions that we so often form. He wanted to believe I had a good heart as well and, bless his soul, I believe that now I do.

"He whacked his head pretty hard, earned himself a concussion and all that, but they expect that he'll be all right," Mai replied. "It's his arm that's the problem. He's shattered it and they've had to do a bit of surgery. You know what that means."

I *did* know what it meant. Hazel had shattered his arm. He'd had surgery and a cast put on and later he'd have to deal with rehabilitation and all that sort of shit. It *meant* he couldn't possibly play with Nefarious any time soon and since Nefarious was Mai's life...

"Oh, no," I whispered, trying not to smile. "That's really bad."

Mai frowned. "Looks like it. Anyway, snow's too bad to go back to town now. I came to tell you they've set up some beds for us back here."

I nodded and followed Mai back to where the patient rooms were located, glancing in at a few of the patients we passed as I went along. They were all asleep, laying in the identical beds and gowns in darkened rooms that smelled of disinfectant. I loathed being there. I loathed hospitals. They made me think of Gray.

We slept in Hazel's room upon Mai's insistence. He hated waking up alone and wanted to make certain that Hazel wouldn't have to worry about that. Mai and I ended up sharing the same bed. He said he felt cold and with good reason; his hands were like ice. I remained awake for hours with Mai snuggled up against my back, his arms tucked in close to his chest. He never once stopped shivering.

Before Mai had drifted off to sleep he told me that he'd been lost in a terrible nightmare while unconscious, one so vivid and profound that he'd yet to shake it. We shared a bed because he was afraid but what he was afraid of – what the dream had been about – he wouldn't say. He'd simply made me promise I'd not leave him in the bed alone. It was an easy promise to keep but now I know...

He'd dreamt that death had its hand on his heart and was simply waiting to close in for the kill.

Chapter 20

HAZEL SLEPT WELL into the next afternoon, but then so did Mai and I. No one disturbed either of us, though I'm sure they'd taken turns peering in behind the curtain that encased the bed in order to spy on us. They'd learned who we were, after all. Nefarious was popular even way out in a dark tundra of a town. Who'd have thought it?

When Hazel did awaken he was in a bit of pain, slightly disoriented and extremely disheartened when he found his arm immobilized. Mai was perched at his bedside, his face was the first thing Hazel saw, and he did his best to seem cheerful.

"It's only an extended vacation," he told him. "You'll be playin' even better than before in no time at all."

Hazel didn't appear to be comforted by that. "The third album…you were ready to make it," he said, tears filling his big eyes. "Now I…"

"We'll wait," Mai said without hesitation. "We won't make it until you're back to your old self, sweetheart."

Hazel's mouth fell open as if bewildered. "You can't delay an album over me," he said, shaking his head almost violently.

"I can do whatever the fuck I want," Mai declared, sticking his nose into the air with regal superiority. "I can't be forced to sing. Tiffany doesn't know the songs are written. I can buy time."

Sweet Jesus, Mai was serious. He meant every word. He truly intended to put all of our careers on hold until that shit could use his arm again. He'd not shown that sort of stubborn loyalty to Minnie or Renna. I wondered if he'd have shown it to me were I the fool with a broken arm and I doubted it despite myself. I felt jealous. Angry. Then Hazel asked to speak to Mai in private and I saw them looking in my direction as they spoke with their heads nearly touching.

Something had to be done and I had to be the one to do it. I went to the nearest phone and called Tiffany. Mai was trying to mess up all our lives over Hazel and I knew Tiffany wouldn't allow it.

I'm sure anyone would agree that I did the logical thing at the time. The proper thing. I'd felt threatened, I was convinced that Hazel was telling Mai that I'd been the one to drug him and that I'd sent him into that tree. I was convinced that he wanted to turn Mai against me, take him away from all of us. I mean, Mai was willing to put the *music* aside for the kid and the music had always been what mattered most.

When I returned to the hall that housed Hazel's room I found Mai backed against the wall outside of Hazel's doorway by a scrawny man with a beet red face and thinning hair. I soon realized that the balding man was Stephen, Hazel's brother, and he seemed in a bit of a rage.

I guess Stephen disliked Mai just as much as Mr. Grantz had. He shoved Mai into the sitting area for a private "talk" and I stood back and witnessed every word of it. I'd planned to stand by and lend a hand in case things turned ugly, but the violence wasn't to be physical that day.

"This is exactly why I brought him here, to get him away from people like you," Stephen was saying. "You do nothing but harm. You're thoughtless, a bad influence. Are you like that around everyone or just impressionable youth?"

Mai shook his head. "I've never forced anything on Hazel, he'll tell you that," he replied.

"I know he would," Stephen was quick to say. "He worships you. I suspect he'd not say a bad word against you no matter what the hell you did. You've used him, taken advantage of him, and our family was torn apart because of it. Do you *ever* think of anyone other than yourself? Do you? Of course you don't. Your type never does. All charm and empty hearts. This mishap was a blessing for Hazel as far as I'm concerned. You can bet his arm won't be the only thing that we'll straighten out."

"You can say whatever you want about me, I don't give a shit, but don't you dare go in there and attempt to tell Hazel there is even one damn thing wrong with him," Mai said, his voice soft but cold. "Your family was a wreck before I even met your brother. He's not like the rest of you and *that's* the blessing in his life. He's the…the purest person I've ever known. The last thing I've ever wanted was to hurt him in any way."

"You sound like you mean that, Mr. Evans," Stephen said. "I believe you might. Drugs and booze, the sex and wild concerts – you think that hasn't hurt him? He doesn't need to be around that. He doesn't need to be ruined by it like the rest of you. Leave him alone, huh?"

I couldn't believe Mai didn't make any sort of response to that. He simply stood there with his head lowered and allowed Stephen Grantz to reduce him to a few inches in height. He simply stood there and absorbed every bitter word just as he'd done when Sister Mary denounced him before an entire class of his peers. He *agreed* with Stephen, I realized. He let the words pierce his heart and then he held them there to keep for the remainder of his days. The man hadn't said anything Mai hadn't already thought about himself.

"Mai?" I tried to say but my voice failed me and I only whispered it.

Mai turned his back to me and moved to gaze out the window. There was nothing but rolling white...fresh and clean... beautiful. It was no longer *his* snowy landscape as far as Mai was concerned. It had become something he shouldn't dare to touch. I was tempted to chase after Stephen Grantz and bash him once over the head, but instead I went to Mai and lightly stroked his arm.

"Mai?" I said again.

"Have I changed you, Blueski?" he asked, eyes fixated on the glass before him.

"Don't listen to that prick. He doesn't have a clue. He doesn't even know you. You bring out the good in people."

"Do I? What was good about Hazel nearly slashing his wrists because he was hallucinating?"

"You didn't drug him."

"He was around the drugs because he was around me," Mai replied firmly.

"And if he hadn't been with you, he'd be dead in some boot camp or homeless," I said. "*Don't* listen to that prick, Mai. Hazel loves you. He doesn't regret a thing, I'm sure."

"Hazel's very sweet," Mai murmured, lightly tracing the windowpane with his finger. "Now he may not play the same ever again."

"Would you really delay our album until he could?"

"Would I? Of course," Mai replied with a faint smile. "*Will* I?

You know the answer to that. You called Tiffany. I know you did."

I nodded. I found it as difficult as anyone else to lie when Mai directly confronted me about something. He didn't seem all that angry, however. He seemed almost pleased, relieved, as if I'd done exactly what he'd expected me to. Slowly he turned away from the window.

"She'll find us a bassist, then," he said. "If not, I'll fill in. I'm going to say good-bye to Hazel. Wait for me in the lobby?"

I nodded again, but I didn't go to the lobby until I'd eavesdropped on much of Mai's parting conversation with Hazel. Contrary to what I'd expected, Hazel was fully aware of what was going on. He told Mai to keep working, he even insisted on it. He also made Mai promise – not swear – to keep in touch.

"The new bassist will only be temporary," Mai told him. "If ever you're ready to come back to us, the spot is yours."

It was a brilliantly executed lie on Mai's part, I think he even believed it himself, and Hazel was grateful to have heard it. The two embraced and then I hurried on to the lobby. I didn't want to seem intrusive. I also didn't want to chance Mai seeing how giddy I'd become.

Chapter 21

I KNEW IT was not simply my imagination that Mai didn't look well when Tiffany finally tracked us down – a private plane and heavy snowplows were to thank for that – and couldn't even bring herself to yell at him. She was beyond furious that we'd been so careless, but I suppose relief that Mai was willing to return to work surpassed that. Instead of barking out orders, she simply motioned for us to gather our belongings and follow her. Back to New York we would go.

Mai was quiet on the plane, certainly nothing new, as Tiffany rattled off available bassists. She'd picked up Jim Rainey to serve as our keyboardist and, surprisingly, Renna was on the list of interested bassists. I suppose she saw no reason to continue avoiding us now that Minnie was gone. I never much liked Renna, but she was familiar and I knew Mai didn't have feelings for her. I suggested we pick her up. Mai didn't seem to care one way or the other. He was too busy writing out a poem that he was careful not to let anyone read. I was still too elated by Hazel's departure to care about his secrecy, though. I was feeling happy.

"You really let yourself run wild on this little break, didn't you," Tiffany said, attempting unsuccessfully to snatch Mai's pen away. "Your hair's limp, your face is puffy. I'm sure you've gained some weight."

"What?" I nearly choked. "He gained a pound at most. It hardly shows."

"It *will*," Tiffany was quick to say. "It starts with one pound and then the next thing you know it's twenty. 110 is far more marketable than 130 and it's my job to keep you marketable, Jeremiah. It's a shallow business, we have to roll with it as such. No more chocolate in your dressing room and it wouldn't hurt you any to actually exercise now and then. You aren't getting any younger, after all."

Mai stared briefly at Tiffany out the corner of his eye but truthfully I'm not sure he'd even heard a word of what she'd said to him. I thought she was out of her mind to even suggest that Mai had anything to worry about. He was a toothpick and a dehydrated toothpick at that. I reminded her of that.

"Water's free," she replied. "No more junk food and make sure you put sunglasses on before we get off the plane. I could fit my wardrobe in those bags under your eyes. I'm going to give you the number of my plastic surgeon. Not too soon to think about getting a little lift, you know."

"Should I take the pacifier out of my mouth now or is there something else you'd like to bitch about?" Mai asked.

"Don't be a smart ass," Tiffany said. "You know I hate that."

Mai shrugged. "Must've slipped my mind," he said. "I am dehydrated, after all. I can legally wander about a parking lot half naked and threatening to beat people with their own arms if I like. That was what's-his-face's justification last year for going ape shit after his show and terrorizing the neighborhood Target store."

I started to laugh, which made Tiffany even more frustrated, but I simply couldn't help it. Mai never once flashed a smile or giggled; I tended to crack up any time he pulled one of his deadpan routines.

"Freaky Dink is not the role model you should be looking up to," Tiffany grumbled. She never did know when not to take Mai literally.

"But I love his song about shooting da beeches," Mai said through a pout.

"Beeyotches," I corrected.

"Oh, that's right," Mai said – *finally* I saw a faint smile. "I get confused."

"Both of you, stop it!" Tiffany cried. "Honestly."

The demur smile lingered upon Mai's lips as he looked over what he'd written and made a few quick corrections. He folded it into a neat square and slipped it into his shirt pocket before slumping down in his seat to gaze out the plane window. I always thought it was funny how Mai so loathed to fly, but enjoyed spying on the miniature cities once in the air. It wasn't the height that perturbed him as much as the confined space. He never liked to walk inside of closets or shower with the shower door closed, either.

"There's an ongoing rumor that you're a real-life vampire," I mused; I was visiting our site via a laptop. "Some dork has been gathering evidence to build a case on the forum."

Mai found that rather amusing – even inspiring in an odd way. Based on the circumstantial "evidence" it seemed true: no one had ever seen Mai out in daylight hours, concerts were exclusively held in the evening, he was extremely pale, and no one had ever seen him gaze into any mirrored surfaces. On top of that, it was common knowledge that he never rode in a car that didn't have heavily tinted windows and required special lighting when filmed, photographed or interviewed. One poster added that she'd met Mai once and he had extremely cold hands.

"She was at our December show, it was below freezing," Mai laughed. "Of *course* I was cold."

"This is too funny," I said. "This person says you tried to bite them."

Mai shrugged nonchalantly. "That may be true."

It had been Tiffany's idea for Mai to keep his medical condition private. She thought he would seem far more mysterious that way. I expect that she'd been hoping for this sort of thing, gossip and reverent fans that believed whatever they heard. Some *did* believe that Mai was a member of the undead, after all. It was fortunate for Mai that they considered that a positive thing. Others thought his looks and talent were the result of some sort of deal he'd made with a demon and that was the reason mishaps and flickering lights so often occurred in Mai's presence.

"You should play this up," Tiffany said. "Bite someone during a show, draw some blood."

"We're to go that route now, are we?" Mai asked through a smirk. "Gimme your belt, Blueski. I'll beat you with it."

"I'm serious."

"So am I, Tiff," Mai said, shaking his head. "All that crap gets in the way. I'm not interested in it."

"You are always interested in making a spectacle of yourself, Mr. 'I lost my shirt again,'" Tiffany said.

"That's not a gimmick, that's just me," Mai declared innocently. "I despise gimmick rockers only looking for bucks and boobs. I won't do it."

"You know your contract with us runs out at the end of this year," Tiffany said, her voice suddenly sour. "You may want to reconsider being such a stubborn ass."

That was a threat if I'd ever heard one, Tiffany had clearly meant it to be taken as one, but Mai simply laughed at her in his slightly mocking way. He couldn't care less if the record label dropped him, he had no doubts that another would be happy to snatch him up. It wouldn't be *only* Mai that Tiffany dropped, however. Would the rest of us fare as well? Would Mai take us with him or show the same, lacking loyalty he'd had for Minnie and Renna?

"He'll think about it," I blurted. "Let's leave it at that."

I'd never spoken for Mai like that before, not when he was sitting a mere arm's length away from me. Tiffany seemed pacified, but Mai had sprung upright as if something had just bitten his back. He stared at me, sharply bewildered, but he didn't say anything. He didn't *need* to say anything. He thought I'd crossed a line. I suppose I probably had but it was too late to retract it. There was nowhere for me to go but onward, further over that line, to add one violation on top of another until it all came crashing down.

Chapter 22

THE NEXT YEAR and a half of our lives became devoted to the theme of "appearance vs. reality" in so many ways that we didn't even realize we were living it. Looking back, I can chart it out as easily as I did in papers I'd had to write for high school and college, picking out examples from our lives to prove how delusional we all were – especially me. One has to admit their mistakes in order to gain empowerment. I can admit that I did wrong.

Mai called our third album *The Dead Pool* and based it on his ideas about that place he'd tried to explain to me so many times before. It became a concept album. Every song contained similar themes and we blended the same melodies in various ways throughout the songs to create a consistent flow. We told the story of the dead pool of Mai's dreams, that strange void where ideas are born and creativity flows and souls are free of the restrictions of the flesh. The lyrics often toyed with the idea of insanity, whether or not "crazy" people aren't really the sane ones able to see and hear what the rest of us reject out of vanity or fear. He wrote of death being the ultimate freedom, a way to enter the dead pool for eternity. He wrote of love and obsession and passion and heartache. He wrote what he'd been feeling. He wrote out his soul.

The sound we produced was dark. Eerie. Mesmerizing, haunting, beautifully melancholic and uplifting, original – the words critics went on to use later seemed endless. They wrote that the album breathed, that it had a life all its own and was impossible to merely give a listen to.

"One doesn't hear *The Dead Pool*, one *feels* it," my favorite review read. "One feels a part of it. Every thundering roar of the drum, the wail of guitar, throb of the bass and the voice of Mai Evans sounding like an angel singing soulfully from Satan's choir – all creep beneath the skin and fester like an addiction that can only be fed by listening to the album again. There is something spooky going on here, folks. There's also an achievement to be applauded that will surely enter rock history in years to come for its originality, vision and sheer enjoyability. Buy the CD, get lost in the morbid beauty, take a trip into that dead pool in your mind."

We all knew that we'd created something big during those studio sessions. It also felt that we were inviting something – I don't know the right word. Wicked? Unnatural? We were inviting something unnatural into the room with us, opening the door wider with every song we finished, blurring the line between reality and that place Mai so often drifted off to even further all the while.

I can't explain it in any way that makes logical sense, I can only note all of the odd things that went on. Flickering lights, doors opening or shutting without reason, the window that refused to remain shut, and the voice. That damn voice droning on in the background of our recordings.

Things became – and would continue to be – particularly odd during our recording of the song "Tainted." I swear that song rose from some grave and worked its way to freedom through Mai. I know that sounds melodramatic, maybe even hilarious, but it *is* true. I said before that Death seemed to be in love with Mai and that song was an open invitation to let its affection be known.

An unexplained power outage forced us to end the session when first we attempted to record it. Dart checked the fuse box and found everything in order. More than that, he found our particular studio was the only portion of the building to have fallen dark.

The second attempt to record nearly left us all deaf. The song began with a piano solo from Jim, which was followed by my guitar and then Dart and Renna. Jim played his piano fine, but when I struck my guitar we were bombarded by horrific, shrill feedback that scraped out the speakers like a dying feline. My ears rang from it for days.

I told Mai to drop the song. I *hated* that damn song and I'd not even heard it played all the way through yet. Don't get me wrong. It wasn't a bad song, it was probably the most melodic and meaningful track on the album, but I loathed the way it made me feel. My part of it was low and growling, my guitar rigged to sound as though its voice was melting or dying somehow. Renna's bass was low in pitch and carried the throbbing pulse of the song.

The piano was high and furious, accompanied by a recording of a sighing sort of hum/chant that Mai had found somewhere – I didn't ask where. The voice was androgynous and dry and warped, it went high and dragged low as a song on a cassette tape quickly becoming tangled in the gears of a stereo might. I hated the voice. I hated the goose bumps it called to the surface of my skin, the sense of displacement it evoked within. I hated the way Mai could sit and stare, totally focused upon it when he played it by itself, no longer mentally in the room with us at all. It was the sound he'd often heard in his troubled dreams.

That voice – the entire song – took Mai away from us all, away from himself. When he sang it his voice was in perfect form, low and rolling silk, and he claimed to have no recollection of starting or finishing it. The song *frightened* me, though it's only now that I understand why. It made us all nervous, but Mai refused to cut it and so we'd gone for lucky number three.

The third time was a charm, so to speak. The lights flickered when Jim began to play. The window flew open and this amazing breath of wind charged in and enveloped the entire room. The sheet music scattered, Mai's microphone nearly fell over, but he motioned for us to keep going and go we did.

Those sounds made it onto the final recording, the rattle of electricity and the banging windowpane, the restless wind and scattering pages. Mai liked them there. All of us played without making a single mistake. Mai sang the entire song facing that opened window with glaring eyes as if he was taunting something we couldn't see. The end result was amazing. The song was perfect. I hoped to never hear it again.

Naturally, I hid my seemingly irrational fear of the song from Mai – it did *sound* ridiculous to be afraid of a song – but he admitted to me quite freely that he didn't much like listening to it, either. He'd written it after waking from that nightmare in Alaska he'd yet to describe to me. He said he woke suddenly with the melody roaring inside of his head and the lyrics on the tip of his tongue.

"I had to record it," he told me. "I had to let it out, stand up to it. We'll never play it live, though. That would be a bit of a betrayal, wouldn't it?"

I'd followed that with another of my obligatory and clueless nods, a relieved smile on my face. I didn't care what reason Mai babbled out so long as it meant I wouldn't have to play the song again.

Mai wanted to look "dead" for the photo shoot. Not dead in some zombie sort of way, just faded and a bit harsher than usual. The photographer shot him in black and white and that, combined with the lighting and shimmering shadow smudged about Mai's eyes, turned him gaunt and stern. He was still elegant, still pretty, but now it appeared refined. Mature. Stunning.

The rest of us were made to look like agents of death, dressed in identical suits with spiked wings mounted on our backs and black and white paint upon our faces. It was a riot, really, wearing costumes and posing with the most intimidating faces we could manage. Mai sat on the floor before us and each of us placed our hand somewhere upon his back or shoulders. He stared at the camera grimly with a smoldering cigarette between his fingers. That became the image printed upon the actual CD.

For the cover, Mai stood before a mirror in black and white, glum and depraved. The mirror's reflection was bright, the background colorful; Mai's image was removed from the glass – a wink to all of those undead rumors that pleased Tiffany beyond words.

Jim "dead people come to me at night" was a nice addition to our new image. He looked a bit like a demon from hell and he enjoyed trying to convince people that he was as bad as he looked, even though we learned early on, when he cried over a Hallmark commercial on TV, that he wasn't.

We were all feeling pretty good when it came time to release the album. Despite Tiffany's angry protests, Mai had refused to release a single to the public before the album's launch. It was fairly unprecedented, to promote an album that people had heard nothing from, to trust them to keep faith they'd not be disappointed, but Mai was stubborn. He was also proven right. *The Dead Pool* sold even faster than *Aberration* on the day of its debut.

The last tour had gone so smoothly – in terms of an inviting public, anyway – that we'd all sort of forgotten what it was like to be in the center of flames. Controversy rose overnight and flew worldwide in a matter of months. The denouncements, bannings, angry letters and hurtful accusations began anew and sort of blindsided us all. Especially Mai.

The old haters returned to the public eye feeling venerated. They claimed our latest album was the cliff all of the lemmings were being lured to right from day one, that Mai had finally showed himself for what he really was: dangerous and manipulative.

The album, as I said, described reality in all of its harsh detail – a world where all beautiful things are destined to die upon creation and his dead pool, where all was immortal and inspired. There were some, quite a few by the end of it all, who claimed that Mai's message was clear. They claimed that the entire album was simply a campaign to encourage suicide – and that could spell disaster for all those morose and excitable teens out there.

Mai was horrified, even remorseful, that anyone would hear such a message in his work. He hadn't meant any of it to be taken literally – *we* all knew that – and he certainly didn't want anyone to harm themselves over it. He wanted to speak out the instant the noise started, but Tiffany forbade it. So far, all of the fuss was only helping the sales and that was what really mattered. In all of our years together, Tiffany *still* hadn't learned that she couldn't successfully forbid Mai from doing anything – and when Mai sought to strike back, he did it with finesse.

He remained silent, appeared subdued, for a week or so. He remained quiet while sales increased and Tiffany charted out our future tour and booked us on the Gary Trevors late night show. It would be the first time since that ancient kiss incident that we were allowed on live television in the US and Gary's show was seen worldwide. It was the perfect time to strike.

They wanted us to perform "Tainted." It had become the most popular song, as well as the one that took the most heat during the debates; but we, as a group, refused. I felt a bit badly for old Gary at the time. He hadn't a clue what he was in for that night. We'd warned him that we had a point to make and he assumed that it would have to do with the controversy. Controversy fueled ratings so he was all for it. He became Mai's unwitting accomplice.

The plan was for Mai to step onto the stage, we'd play the song we'd performed in rehearsals and then Mai would go over to Gary's desk for a chat. Mai even reviewed the questions and listened as a staff member informed him of what would or wouldn't be allowed by the censors. He was being extremely well behaved, he even smiled once or twice at Tiffany as she paced about the green room. No one knew what Mai was going to do, no one besides me and the band. We were Mai's accomplices.

We were already standing on the stage when Gary delivered

our introduction. Our instruments were plugged in, we'd had our sound check and appeared ready to play at any second. Mai was out of sight, waiting behind the burgundy curtains and listening for Gary's introduction to come to an end. We had a lot of fans seated in the audience wildly cheering for Mai to step out.

Jim forgot that we weren't supposed to play unless Mai signaled us. When we later watched the show, we heard the tiny "ding" of a piano key being poked as the curtains moved aside to reveal Mai. As far as I know, Jim laughs about that to this day.

Mai approached the microphone with his head lowered and hands folded behind his back, walking quickly and confidently. The fans whooped, but Mai held his hand up and silenced them. It had been announced on our website that Mai had something important to say and they were all eager to hear it. They had no idea, of course, that Mai wasn't going to *say* anything at all.

The lights focused upon Mai's face as he lifted his head, allowing everyone to see that he'd had black stitches painted over his lips with such startling detail that they appeared quite authentic. He stood motionless for a few seconds, simply staring at the camera, before he pulled a handmade sign out from behind his back and held it in front of his chest for all to see. It read:

"Don't kill yourselves. I would explain why, but my management says I'm only a singing whore."

Mai held the sign there for quite a while, until a couple of the fans giggled, and then he tossed the sign aside and flashed his trademark grin – the devilish grin reserved for pulling pranks or showing off before a crowd. Then he waved at me and we played the music while he simply stood there and silently protested before a collective audience of millions. We played well but the near deafening applause that broke out when we finished was solely for Mai's defiance. We all knew that.

The applause went on for so long that they had to cut to a commercial and Gary came over to shake our hands. When the show returned, we were all huddled next to Gary's desk; but Mai wouldn't speak to the man. He simply smiled or shrugged or frowned. Once he held up another little sign that listed Tiffany's cell phone number and asked people to call if "dissatisfied with our service."

I answered the questions about our tour and things of that nature and that was it. We were out of time. When the cameras were shut down, Gary shook his head at Mai and called him a jackass. Mai laughed.

"You're either incredibly stupid, kid, or an arrogant genius with a lot of balls," he told Mai. "Either way, come do the show again some time when you actually plan to sing."

Incredibly surreal, that's what it was. Gary Trevors was a legend in his own right. During his four decades on television he had seen the best and worst in entertainment come and go, he was considered an expert in judging who was worth the hype and who was a passing fad. In his characteristic way, he'd given Mai one of the highest compliments imaginable and Mai appreciated it.

"Thank you, sir," he replied with a nod. "I will."

And we did. We'd appear on Gary's show once more as Nefarious toward the end of our tour, but Mai would visit it twice on his own – not counting his stints as a guest host and sitting for a primetime interview conducted by Mr. Trevors only weeks after our first appearance.

Having the support of someone like Gary thrust us even further to the top, off somewhere into the atmosphere. At the time I'd thought us invincible but it never works like that. When one finds they've reached such a high peak there's nowhere to go but down – and the source of decay always comes from within.

Chapter 23

TIFFANY REFUSED TO speak to Mai directly after that show, but then her cell phone started ringing off the hook and she became giddy with greed all over again. People wanted to interview Mai. People wanted to interview her *about* Mai. Everyone wanted to hear the story behind Mai's stunt.

The rest of us were pushed into the background. I suppose that's why I didn't initially notice the collapse looming over our heads once we started the tour. Mai was constantly busy doing other projects in between shows. Photo shoots for magazines and a future calendar, interviews, other talk show appearances. He went back to Gary Trevors' studio to tape the primetime interview and acted as a guest host while Gary was on vacation (he was nothing short of excellent behind that desk). We caught a rerun of the primetime show halfway through the tour. We were in Dallas.

Mai explained on the special that the dead pool was simply a metaphor and that people only needed to close their eyes to get there. It was ideas and dreams, creativity and talent. It was something everyone could strive to touch while alive.

"Can't do much if you're dead, now, can you?" he'd snickered.

Gary asked Mai about the other songs and his writing in general as well, whether all of his focus on love came straight from actual relationships or perhaps just one major relationship that he'd not yet healed from. Mai said it was neither. He wrote about ideas, about muses that he picked from all sorts of places.

"I fall in love with people everyday," Mai said. "Someone I see on the street, in a film, on the telly – whatever. I'll find something so beautiful about them that I become obsessed, inspired and I create. It's a compulsion. It's being in love with the *idea* of them and what they represent to me in my mind. The idea of love. I never write of anyone who I've actually been intimate with because intimacy shatters the magic.

"It makes it really difficult, really hard, cos I want nothing more than to have this person, touch this person and I can't. It creates a burning sort of vulnerability. It's keeping that painful desire bottled up inside that makes it all fall in place. I can't have what I want and somehow that makes me function properly. Most people think I'm insane," he laughed. "Maybe I am. I think you have to be a li'l off kilter to create art."

"Have you ever had a love that wasn't only an ideal?" Gary asked.

"Oh, sure," Mai said with a sly laugh. "Plenty. The ideal is always better."

I took offense to that. Jim and Dart had laughed over it as we watched together in our hotel room, but I'd nearly burst into tears. *I* was one of those loves Mai was dismissing as a failed ideal – unless, of course, I wasn't considered a love at all. I wasn't sure which was worse, but Mai wasn't around to confront. He was never around anymore.

If he wasn't working, he was always off in a gym or visiting a nearby arcade to burn off energy on one of those dancing machines. I don't think he had bothered to sleep for more than minutes at a time in a month or more. He'd been bouncing off the walls, collapsing into sleep when exhaustion took over, and living off of his cigs and sodas and chocolate chip rice cakes or "chocolate-coated Styrofoam" to use his words. None of this was for health reasons, of course. There was nothing healthy about the way Mai ate or celebrated or behaved. Little sleep, poor nutrition and yet enough energy to stomp on a dance pad for hours on end – I should have realized that something was seriously amiss.

I found Mai upstairs in the hotel's exclusive fitness area, walking as fast as he could on one of the treadmills. He looked slightly ridiculous to me, dressed in a tattered black tank top and sagging jeans plagued by holes in the knees that were threatening to slide off his slender hips at any second. The lit cigarette hanging from his lips completed the look.

"Check it out," he panted, smiling at me. "At this rate, I'll be in Memphis in half an hour. If I was really walking, that is."

"I saw your primetime thing with Gary," I said, crossing my arms.

"Oh, shit! That was on again?" he asked. "I've missed it twice…"

"You really never write about anyone you've been with?"

"Not after I've been with 'em," Mai replied curtly.

"You just move to one and then another? Use them and toss them away?" I asked, shaking my head. "Inspired one day and disinterested the next?"

Mai forgot he was supposed to be walking and was nearly thrown off the treadmill as a result. He stepped off the machine with a grunt and stared at me as if I'd grown two heads, panting and coughing in an attempt to catch his breath. His face was flushed, his eyelids heavy. He looked as though he'd not understood a word I'd said.

"Why are you yelling at me?" he asked.

"How can you even *ask* why? I'm one of those people you dumped. Here I wondered why you'd not touched me again. Now I know I must not be ideal enough. People *aren't* ideals, Mai. That's a daydream!"

"Wh-what the hell are you…You're shittin' me, right? This is a prank?" he asked hopefully. "Cos you know—"

Mai's voice abandoned him and his eyes turned upward, threatening to roll back in his head. He told me he was feeling dizzy, his voice a mere whisper as he stumbled his way back onto one of the chairs behind the treadmill, still struggling to return his breathing to normal. I thought he was being a ham, playing it up to deter us from having a serious conversation. He told me his chest was hurting and I shook my head. Then he fell limp in the chair and the cigarette slipped from his lips and burnt his neck. I knew then that he wasn't playing around.

I tossed the cigarette aside and started shaking him. I didn't really know what else *to* do. I grabbed a bottle of water and poured a bit of it over his head and into his mouth. It was a near minute before he opened his eyes and coughed and gazed hazily in my direction.

"What h-happened, Blueski?" he asked, taking hold of my hand; he seemed afraid.

"You passed out."

"What?" he laughed. "No I didn't! I, uh, guess I'm ready for some sleep is all. H-Help me up?"

Mai was visibly shaken, frightened, and I felt my anger fading away. He acted as though he didn't recall what we'd just said to one another before his tumble and I didn't have it in me then to pursue it. He *did* ask if I was angry with him, he had a nagging worry that I was. I said I wasn't.

"You should see a doctor," I said, watching as he chugged down the remaining water in the bottle. "You're shaking."

"I'm fine. I promise," he replied with a smile. "I only need some sleep. I've a photo thing…somewhere…for something. Tomorrow, isn't it? Downtown, I think?"

I nodded. He was to become a cover boy once again, posing for one of countless magazine covers. He was going to be busy all night long, sitting first for the shoot and then conducting a meeting to discuss our next video. I wondered if it might be too much for him but I couldn't confront him. He'd become all smiles and witticism, a sure sign that he was planning to avoid the issue.

So it was that I helped Mai back down to our room in silent worry, still fuming over the Gary Trevors show and unable to express it. Mai collapsed on top of the closest bed, which wasn't even his, and passed out within seconds. No one said anything, but Renna was staring hard at Mai. Either she was worried too, or she'd also been angered by what Mai had said on the show.

We had plans to play tourist the next day, Dart was excited over the possibility of scoring a genuine cowboy hat, while Tiffany planned to take Mai to the cover shoot and listen in on the phone meeting about the video in the evening. We were to regroup at the tour bus near dusk so that we could head off to the next stop on our tour during the daylight hours.

Things didn't exactly go according to plan, of course. Tiffany found she couldn't get Mai out of bed and it wasn't even due to spite on Mai's part – he simply couldn't will himself to rise. She phoned me, frantic, convinced that Mai was only trying to anger her.

"You talk to him and *make* him cut it out!" she shouted at me. "I'm putting the phone to his ear now."

There wasn't anything I could say to Mai to change the situation. Every response I got from him was slurred and inaudible as if he had a mouth full of Novocaine. Tiffany was in the process of stripping him down, changing his clothes while he babbled to me about some dream he was still half in. Tiffany managed to get him dressed, but she needed me to drag his ass out of the bed and into the waiting car outside.

It was fortunate for Tiffany that I hadn't been far from the hotel when she'd rang, because it would have taken forever to get a taxi at that hour. Tiffany was pulling on Mai's wrists and forcing him to sit up by the time I'd entered the room. He looked like a child with his face scrunched up in a pout and hair sticking out in every direction, but at least his eyes were open. He turned to face me when he heard my footsteps.

"Save me," he said. "Make her go away."

"Blue's here to help me drag you down to the car!" Tiffany said with a grunt, yanking on Mai once again.

"I only just went to sleep for Christ's sake! It's early," Mai insisted, freeing himself from Tiffany's grasp yet again.

"It's nearly seven," Tiffany replied coldly.

Mai began patting his shirt pocket in search of his cigarettes only to find them missing. He huffed under his breath and checked the pockets of his pants as well. Still no luck. It was rather comical to watch him as he first became frustrated and then completely bewildered when he realized that he was wearing a dark purple shirt made of nylon and clean blue jeans instead of the ratty exercise garb he'd fallen asleep in. He looked at me with wide eyes, his mouth hanging open – a face that clearly asked "what the hell?" without a single word being spoken.

"You stripped me whilst I slept?" he asked Tiffany, sounding horrified. "You took my clothes off?! I feel so…so…violated!"

"Oh, shut up," Tiffany replied, trying, I think, not to laugh. "I'd been trying for half an hour to get you to do it yourself and all you did was grumble."

"I doubt she saw anything she hadn't already seen before," I said; it came out more caustic than I'd intended.

"Still fuckin' rude," Mai muttered, swinging his legs off the side of the bed in order to search for his old clothes. "Where'd you put 'em?"

"Just take these, we don't have time," Tiffany said, throwing a fresh pack of cigarettes at Mai. "Get your shoes on and take these, too. I'll get you some water."

Tiffany handed Mai a couple of pills. Small and innocent looking white pills that I'd never seen before, but then I'd never had much to do with that particular form of drugs. Mai didn't seem at all surprised by them, however. He popped them into his mouth and downed them without hesitation when Tiffany gave him the water. I asked what he'd taken and he told me that they were aspirin. Actually, he *swore* to me they were aspirin and then it all fell into place.

I still didn't know the name of the pills, but I did know that they had to be uppers of some sort. As I walked Mai down the lobby stairs and out into the parking lot I realized I'd seen him popping pills on a number of occasions over the past few months. I'd not thought much about it at the time. Aside from the hyperactivity, Mai had always behaved normally and he'd taken the pills in such a casual manner that it had never *seemed* suspicious.

I blamed Tiffany for it. She was the one scheduling the phone interviews during the afternoons and photo shoots that spanned the free evenings. She was the one who arranged all of the extra projects Mai had been doing away from the rest of us. We were playing shows at night, every night, and traveling during the day. The rest of us caught our sleep on the bus or on the planes, but Mai had been writing or doing those interviews or working on Gary's show. Tiffany had been drugging him to make it possible and that day, before the precious photo shoot, Mai had experienced his first crash.

"I don't have any lipstick," Mai complained once we'd all piled into the back of the car.

"Use mine," Tiffany said, rolling her eyes.

"If I wanted lips that bright I'd kiss a fire hydrant," Mai said. "Have you got any, Blues?"

I shook my head. "I don't carry that shit with me."

"Well, I don't, either," Mai replied, shaking his head. "We'll have to stop somewhere. There's no time to get made up at the shoot and they always fuck it up, anyway."

"We're nearly thirty minutes late as it is!" Tiffany nearly hissed. "We are *not* stopping so you can buy some damn lipstick!"

"You're the one that bitched I shouldn't be seen without my mask on," Mai declared, staring at Tiffany with devilish glee. "If I stay like this someone hiding in a bush might pop out and snap a photo of the real me and then surely the world will end. Or even worse, the magazine crew will pick some color that–"

"Fine! We'll stop at a drugstore or something – just shut *up!*"

Mai smiled, looking quite satisfied with himself, and settled back in the seat next to me. He cuddled up against my arm but I moved away trying to make my expression as stern as possible. Mai blinked, rubbed at his eyes tiredly and arched his eyebrows.

"What?" he asked innocently. "I know I stink, but you can

always turn your head the other way. It's Tif's fault for not showering me while she had my clothes off."

"You *know* what," I replied. "Those weren't aspirins you took. Now I know why you passed out yesterday."

"Passed out?" Tiffany asked, perking up immediately.

Mai quickly pulled away from me and shook his head as if I'd annoyed him. He kept his eyes focused upon the window as I told Tiffany about Mai's collapse after stomping on the treadmill at the hotel. He denied passing out and Tiffany wanted nothing more than to believe him. It was better for business.

"They're only energy supplements," Tiffany told me. "Perfectly harmless if taken properly. You *did* use them properly, didn't you? Jeremiah?"

Mai shrugged. "Maybe I forgot how many I'd already taken a time or two," he replied nonchalantly. "Maybe I took a whole handful. Maybe today I'll take *two* handfuls."

"Don't be a smart ass," Tiffany said. "How many are left in that bottle I gave you? Answer me."

Mai wouldn't answer her. He wouldn't even look at her. He refused to look at me, as well, and that spoke far more than any words could have. He'd bought his own bottle of the pills, possibly more than one. He'd had to in order to keep up with everything going on around him.

"This is your fault," I said, glaring at Tiffany. "You're the one picking at him over what he eats and does and says. You schedule too much shit back to back and your solution was to feed him *pills*? Even after all the crap with Minnie?"

"I asked for 'em," Mai said softly, staring now at his trembling hands. "Okay? I asked for 'em. Now it's done. They're gone. Okay? So let's drop it."

I never believed Mai, not on that day and not now as I think back. It *hadn't* been his idea to turn toward the drugs and yet he'd gone along with it and, for reasons I couldn't understand, he'd chosen to protect Tiffany after I'd yelled at her. Tiffany remained silent, quite eager to allow Mai to take the fall.

I suppose that was why I'd dropped it after that, Mai simply seemed too vulnerable to badger. I hadn't really realized how easily Mai could be manipulated if the proper buttons were pressed, though I don't know *why* I hadn't. As defiant as he was, as stubborn as he could be, Mai wasn't really that hard to control when his nature was used against him. Tiffany knew that. I knew that. It wasn't long before we ended up taking advantage of it together.

Chapter 24

WE HAD SUCH a good time that day that I forgot why I'd been mad at Mai to begin with. On the way to the photo shoot we stopped at a convenience store so he could purchase mauve lipstick and dark eye shadow, and the clerk's puzzled expression was priceless. Then, as Mai stood outside using the window as a mirror to put on the cosmetics, an old woman wandered by and gasped when she caught the reflection of his face in the glass. Mai simply offered his smart grin and then smacked his lips together to even out the color as he wished her a "good evening." I couldn't stop laughing.

Mai kissed me as the woman quickly passed us by – shaking her head and grumbling under her breath as she went – to blot his lips. Mine became the same shade as his. He admired his handiwork and smiled at me, but he didn't look into my eyes. I assumed he was simply embarrassed over the pill business. I'm glad I didn't know the truth.

The photographer at the magazine shoot turned out to be Basil Hallford's brother Ryan, but neither Mai nor I knew of the relation at the time. He was short and stocky with rather silly curly hair all teased up into a brown bush atop his head – he certainly didn't *look* like Basil – and he had a habit of snapping his teeth together every time he finished a sentence.

"Look like death," he told Mai. "Stare hard at me, no feeling on your face at all."

It wasn't hard for Mai to follow the instruction, he'd made that face on a number of occasions and he was still fairly tired. Ryan took a few playful shots as well. Mai ate a couple of doughnuts and had a few sodas and then he'd started feeling pretty good. He laughed and cracked jokes and flashed his funny faces. He seemed quite happy.

When the shoot ended Mai fell asleep almost as soon as he'd climbed into the car, leaving Tiffany to handle the phone meeting on her own. I allowed Mai to use my lap as his pillow and stroked his dirty hair with my fingertips. He grumbled uneasily and frowned and twitched. When I put my hand upon his chest I could feel his heart racing madly, hammering within as if trying to break free of his body.

We ended up getting a head start to our next location – everyone else was already on board the bus and ready to go when Mai and I arrived. Tiffany was extremely animated when she hung up the telephone and insisted on a group meeting. I could tell Mai didn't want to speak to her, he only wanted to sleep, but there was no getting out of it. She had wonderful news, she said. "Wonderful," coming from Tiffany's lips, was rarely good at all.

"Zaurus wants to meet you," she said with a toothy smile and excited eyes. "Can you believe it?"

Silence. We all greeted Tiffany's enthusiasm with sheer, ignorant silence. I was relieved to find that I was not the only one unaware of who or what Zaurus was supposed to be. We all started looking at one another with blank expressions on our faces.

"Smashing," Mai finally said, his voice dripping with sarcasm. "I'm off to bed, then."

"I can't believe you're all so clueless," Tiffany said. "*None* of you knows who Zaurus is?"

"I do," Renna reluctantly admitted, rolling her eyes slightly. "Why should we get excited? By 'us' you mean 'him,' anyway, right? Zaurus wants to meet *him*."

Renna pointed at Mai as she spoke, though she didn't bother to even look in his direction. Mai seemed a bit wounded by the bitterness in her tone. Had he been doing projects without the rest of us? Yes. Had he done any musical projects? No, and he didn't plan to. He was loyal to Nefarious and found it hurtful that Renna was suggesting otherwise.

"Zaurus wants to meet all of you and do some sort of collaboration," Tiffany said. "He is only *the* biggest thing in Europe right now. You'd have the world on a string if you teamed up with him. Imagine the possibilities. Write a song together or something. Sing at his shows, invite him to yours."

"See?" Renna grunted.

Mai shook his head. "I don't like the sound of it," he said. "The tour's killin' me as it is and besides…I don't want someone else taking credit for getting us noticed. Our songs have already made it to Europe, we'll expand our shows there on our own eventually. Plus I don't know anything about this person."

"I knew you'd say that," Tiffany said, shoving a DVD into Mai's hand. "I knew you'd need some convincing so I bought this while you were doing the shoot. He wants to fund your next video and I suggest we take him up on it. It'll be spectacular."

Tiffany had referred to Zaurus as a "he" but I was less than convinced as to what Zaurus's true gender was. I wasn't the only one. We all watched the DVD that Tiffany gave us together, cramped inside the main "room" of the bus with our eyes glued to the television screen.

The first music video we watched had Jim snickering within seconds. Zaurus was tall with narrow shoulders, tiny breasts, long dark blue hair and a manly face. That's not to say the face was wholly unattractive as makeup can work wonders for anyone but it was *shaped* like a man's face. The chin was strong and nose slightly large. The eyebrows were painted on and the sapphire eyes were actually quite lovely.

"Drag queen!" Jim cried. "It's gotta be!"

"Boobs are too small to be fake," Renna said.

"Hey, hey, now," Dart jokingly scolded. "Lotsa people don't know what Mai is at first, either."

"They do as soon as he opens his mouth," Jim said. "This one sounds like either."

"Maybe both," Renna remarked.

"Quiet!" Mai said, though he was smiling. "I can't hear."

I won't lie. Zaurus was incredibly talented, even though I found him/her a bit creepy. The guitarist was far more advanced than I was, the drummer was more energetic than Dart had ever been and the woman serving as the bassist could probably have outplayed Renna any day – though none of us had the courage to say that out loud.

"Isn't that…it is!" I cried.

Minnie. Minnie was in the video playing a piano. See, when we played London I mentioned two people of importance in our audience. Marina Evans had been one of them. Mr./Ms. Zaurus had been the other.

Zaurus had come to check us out, to size up the competition and had apparently been impressed. When word spread that Minnie was out of Nefarious, Zaurus snatched him up without hesitation. It had taken some time, but eventually Zaurus left a message at our studio about wanting to do a project together and now the message had finally caught up with us.

Musically, technically, Zaurus was far beyond Nefarious. There had been a number of times when we'd been unable to play what Mai had in mind while he was composing certain songs because we'd simply lacked the ability. Tiffany had even offered to bring in session workers that could possibly pull it off, but Mai had refused. It was the only way Mai had ever compromised his music, tweaking it so that we wouldn't have to be replaced in order to create it. I'd not realized what a tremendous compromise it had been until then. I couldn't even *imagine* where Mai might take his art if he had access to Zaurus' people.

I'm sure I wasn't the only one to notice how much better their music was compared to ours, but vocally Mai was by far the better of the two. Zaurus could carry a tune, but he/she tended to screech and the thin voice often cracked. Even with the aid of machinery the transition from note to note was rarely smooth. It was probably intentional, meant to add to the mystery, but it wasn't as nice to listen to.

We watched a brief interview that was included on the DVD as well. Zaurus sat rather stiff in the chair and never once looked directly at the camera as she/he answered questions with automatic yet seemingly spontaneous responses.

"I never give anything away and I've never loved a soul," Zaurus said. "I'm not the one having anything taken away when I'm on the stage. I'm not the one falling in love, they are. They enjoy it. Music is much like prostitution in that respect. If they want to pay me to steal their hearts, I'm all for it. It's their choice to spend and give admiration but I never love anyone and sex is overrated. It takes too much from you and then its over. Instant gratification is for fools that can't find other means of pleasure. Unless you're hoping to breed, what's really the point of it?"

"What a load of bullshit," Jim stated, shaking his head.

"Probably can't *get* anyone to sleep with it," Renna said.

Dart laughed in agreement but Mai remained fairly stoic. He'd given so much of himself away that I believe he'd found Zaurus' words quite meaningful, maybe even inspiring. He found beauty in Zaurus at any rate for I could see admiration in his eyes. He made us stop at a music shop and picked up all of Zaurus' albums. He listened to them one after another throughout the afternoon. I didn't feel threatened over it, though, because Mai and Zaurus didn't plan on meeting one another in person any time soon. Meeting would have ruined the magic.

Chapter 25

IT WAS RAINING outside on the day we were to film the video. We'd driven throughout the day, slept, performed to a packed auditorium that night and tried to sleep again before the morning wake-up call was scheduled to barge into our hotel rooms. It turned out that Tiffany had already agreed to allow Zaurus to fund our video – she'd done so long before making the announcement to us that Zaurus even had interest in us – which meant that he/she was producing us from afar.

The only condition was that we make the video for "Tainted," as that was the song fans most wanted to see – and since we never played it live at our shows, Mai felt a certain obligation to please them. He exchanged emails with Zaurus, sharing ideas and concepts, and within mere days we'd had a plan to follow.

The format was much the same as it had been years ago when we filmed "Clarity." We would begin inside the hotel in another rented conference room and again had permission to take the lobby stairs over for an hour or two. Once finished at the hotel, we'd go on to an abandoned asylum that Mai had read an article about for the remaining shots.

Zaurus sent a man named Tommy over to act as our director, a short and chubby guy with curly brown hair and a dark brown beard. He made all of the sets himself, free of charge, simply because he loved to paint and adored our music so much. Much to our surprise, and Renna's outrage, Tommy brought a surprising guest along with him – Minnie.

I was actually a bit pleased to see Minnie and he'd do me a great favor before departing for London the next day. He didn't seem to hold any hard feelings about what had happened between us. He and Mai didn't speak much but I shared a hit or two with him before moving down to explore Tommy's sets, which were nothing less than fantastic.

Statues and paintings had been brought into the lobby, along with fine rugs and lavish pieces of furniture. It was a posh place anyway, but by Tommy's hand it suddenly became a magnificent mansion when captured upon the lens.

The conference room became a foreign landscape – it's extraordinary what paint, canvas and talent can create. On the floor lay a painted lake that looked so incredibly realistic that everyone who saw it felt compelled to touch it to make certain it was indeed canvas. It was an overhead view of the water, making it appear as though one could easily fall right in and drown. Another fantastic mural hung on the wall, one of a rolling field of grass and flowers of red and gold basking beneath a blazing sun. The green seemed to go on forever with *such* depth. Tommy told me he'd simply followed sketches that Mai had mailed to him and had considered it easy to do. *Easy*.

I suppose I should explain "Tainted" before I get into the video we made for it. The song tells the story of a person living their life inside their personal daydreams and delusions because it's the only way they can find security. When forced to face reality, where cruelties are considered a mere factor of life, they choose the freedom of death to escape it.

The video would be a perfect analogy, a visual telling of the story. Mai was playing a patient in an asylum, believing himself free to roam lavish palaces or float peacefully on the surface of a pond, while in reality he's confined to a cell. Committed for life in an institution. Mai hoped to raise the question of what was worse, to have someone completely out of touch but content in their own world, or forcing them to join ours.

For the daydream sequences, those being filmed first, Mai was absolutely stunning. After two hours in the makeup chair he emerged with his hair combed back, dressed in fitted trousers and an ornate red jacket. His face was covered by more powders and paints than usual. His skin was slicked over with a shimmering lotion, his eyelids and lips were rose-kissed, his eyebrows darkened and lashes coated by mascara. Jim snickered that he looked like a girl and he did – in the face, anyway. He also seemed majestic, almost ethereal. Beneath the lights he appeared to shine.

Tommy filmed Mai strolling along walkways and descending the stairwell, inspecting the paintings and touching the statues. Close-ups were taken of Mai singing and then we were filmed playing our instruments while Mai went into the conference room to give the shots needed there.

Mai went back to makeup to change his clothes and face for the reality scenes, while the crew packed up our equipment and Minnie and I shared another treat. Mai filmed more scenes in the conference room in his new attire and then met up with us in the lobby. He resembled the living dead: dressed in baggy gray patient garb and face painted pale and ashen – or so I thought. He joked that he'd simply taken all the paint off his face to achieve the desired effect. I *hoped* he was joking, anyway.

The asylum was a horrific old building made of gray brick. Many of the windows were boarded over with "no trespassing" signs posted everywhere. The barbed-wire fence that had once posed a deadly threat to those confined to the asylum yard was now dull and thoroughly rusted. Everything was overgrown and neglected. I loathed the place enough as it was and then Mai informed me that patients had been tortured to death inside of it.

"The great science of the age," he said.

I hated it when Mai cheerfully dropped morbid facts upon my lap.

Jim and Minnie were both dressed in sea-foam colored scrubs to play the asylum's staff. Dart and Renna had remained back at the hotel, chatting with people they'd met in the bar. I'd simply tagged along to keep an eye on Mai.

The four of us toured the place while Tommy oversaw the lighting, strolling down the vacant halls side by side. We saw labs, tubs and wires once used for shock therapy. We peered cautiously into the various rooms and cells. Narrow rooms with no windows, cement floors and heavy locks upon the doors – there was no word for the former patients' living quarters other than cells. All were technically empty now – all except for the room we'd be using, but they hardly felt unoccupied. The walls were sighing. I heard it and I know that Mai did, too. They sighed exactly like those in Mai's old building. We weren't alone.

Everything ran smoothly in the beginning. Tommy filmed Mai lying on a bed in one of the cells. He filmed the door unlocking seemingly on its own and then Mai wandering cautiously out into the hall. He roamed a few corridors, sang a few lines of the song and then it was time for Minnie and Jim to take him down as staff would have done going after an escapee during the asylum's heyday.

Both enjoyed it a bit too much in my opinion: the chance to plow Mai over and carry him off to a padded room where a bed fitted with restraints awaited. They pretended to give Mai a shot, Mai fell limp and then they began to fasten the restraints about his wrists and ankles.

There was a lot of giggling during the restraint sequence from Jim, Minnie and Mai, as well. Minnie made a crack about bondage and Jim added that Mai seemed suspiciously well rehearsed. Tommy had to shut the camera off; he was laughing, too.

Tommy left a camera mounted at Mai's bedside and was about to leave the room when the light overhead flickered. The rest of us were out in the hall, admiring the shots Tommy's assistant Neil was reviewing on a monitor, when the door to the padded room suddenly slammed shut and trapped Tommy and Mai inside. The bang echoed all around us.

"Funny!" we heard Mai shout. "Open the damn door!"

Minnie and Jim pressed their faces against the small window in the door, snickering and mocking Mai…and then they tried to lift the handle. They couldn't. Neil inserted the master key Tommy had left in his charge into the lock. It slid in with ease but refused to turn. Now Tommy was irritated. He banged on the glass and yelled for us to stop our playing, but we hadn't done anything to cause the door to close, let alone jam, in the first place.

It's safe to say that Mai lost his shit at that point. Tommy had also given Neil the restraint keys: if Neil couldn't get in, Mai couldn't be set free. Minnie and Jim had fallen silent, concerned, as Mai started yelling and tugging violently at the restraints. We could all hear it lurking beneath Mai's screams, a low crackling within the walls and over our heads. Disjointed. Electric. Alive.

We could only watch as the light inside the room flickered madly before power throughout the entire building died and a truly horrific howl erupted from inside the room. We were all left in darkness and I could smell smoke. I could smell burnt flesh. Mai had become suddenly silent and through the small square window the slightest flicker of light, dim and brief like a flame drowning in melted wax, could be seen.

The door to the padded room was standing wide open when Neil finally got the generators up and running and restored the lights in the hallway. Smoke, thin and white as fog, hovered in the doorway.

A live wire lay on the floor, twitching and hissing. The light that had been hanging overhead was shattered upon the floor near the bed. Tommy sat lifeless in the corner.

I was first to enter the room, foolish in retrospect given the jittery wire. Mai was lying completely still with his eyes open and fixated upon the wall opposite to Tommy. He was facing the camera, eyes dark and glassy and lips slightly parted. The camera was on – I can't explain *why* or how – and it was filming. It had been filming the entire time despite the power failure.

I hastily turned the camera off and took Mai by the shoulders, shaking him a bit rougher than I should have. His skin felt like wax, cold and stiff, and his eyes…Honestly, I thought he was dead for a few terrifying seconds until I saw his eyelashes flutter.

"I saw it. I saw *you*," he said, his voice less than a whisper.

I shook my head. "What the hell happened?!"

Mai blinked and seemed to become more oriented. It was almost like he'd forgotten who I was for a minute but I could see recognition in his eyes now. "Blueski? Let me go. Please? Let me up. *Please*," he whispered, a tear rolling down from his left eye. "I want out. I need to get out before it gets me…"

It didn't occur to me then that Mai wasn't solely referring to being released from the restraints about his wrists and ankles. I shouted for Neil to give me the keys. He did so without hesitation and then left to dial an ambulance – though looking at Tommy it was pretty obvious that he was beyond help. I'd never seen a fresh corpse before. It was strangely invigorating. Life affirming, somehow.

Mai went into shock over it all. He'd bruised himself during his struggle with the restraints and couldn't, or wouldn't, speak to anyone about what had happened. Faulty wiring was later blamed for Tommy's death, but it didn't cover the incident with the door jamming and opening or the fresh scratches I found near Mai's throat and chest as I helped him off the bed. He shuffled out of that asylum resembling someone else, someone frail and afraid. He'd always been haunted. Now it seemed his demons had decided to perform before us all. I couldn't help but think of the old saying about reaching into the abyss – or, in this case, Mai's dead pool – and something following you when you withdrew. Mai had been reaching into it his entire life – and now something had most definitely answered his call.

It was fortunate that Minnie was with us that night. He gave me something to calm Mai's nerves and Mai took it without saying anything. Mai remained close, clinging haplessly to my arm, afraid to be left on his own for the rest of the night. When he and I were finally alone, right as Mai was beginning to fall asleep, he told me that he wanted to end it all. He wanted out of Nefarious. He wanted out of the spotlight.

"I don't want to do this anymore," he murmured, resting his head against my shoulder. "I'm...so tired."

"That's just the drugs," I said with a smile.

"No. No, it's not, Blues," he said. "I wanna go away. I wanna leave. It's all gone so wrong...out of my hands. Everything seems to be wrong and now Tommy...Tommy...We should never have...I shouldn't have...Can't I just leave? Can't I go?"

"No," I replied quickly, harshly. "You can't leave, Mai. You can't just ditch the rest of us. What would we do if you did? Our contract is up in a few weeks and Tiffany won't want to renew us without you."

"You...you guys can play for anybody," Mai said, his voice becoming sluggish. "You'll do fine."

"No, Mai. We're in the middle of a tour, we've got tons of commitments and *you* want to take off just because there was a freak accident? Don't be so selfish!"

Mai fell silent and stared out from lowered eyelids, totally lost in thought. He'd wanted me to support him, to tell him that it was all right if he wanted to quit, but I couldn't do that. How could I? If Mai left Nefarious, he'd be leaving me even more than he already had. Worst of all, I wondered who he'd be leaving us for. Zaurus? Someone we'd not heard of? Did he simply want to go solo?

"The tour," he finally said. "Right. We'll finish the tour. I have to finish it."

I nodded and then Mai succumbed to sleep, and I was able to freely make a phone call to Minnie. I told him I'd be in need of his services again before he departed the next morning.

Chapter 26

IT SOUNDS AWFUL, I know, to abuse trust and slip someone drugs without their knowledge, but I did it for the benefit of all of us. Besides, Mai had willingly taken pills to keep himself awake and full of energy earlier, so I didn't see how my giving him pills to make him indifferent to his environment was really such a crime. If Mai no longer gave a shit about where he was or what he was doing, I reasoned, he'd lose those thoughts of wanting to leave the band.

On stage Mai became rather listless because of it. He still sang beautifully so long as he didn't have to move around. He lacked the energy to belt out the notes and walk about at the same time. The fans didn't notice. They came out to stare at him and scream and throw things. Mai probably could have gotten by without singing at all, he could have just stood there at the microphone and they'd have been happy – but singing was too important to him.

I may have started it, but, in the end, it became everyone's sin. We all knew. Renna, Jim, Tiffany and even Dart all looked the other way as Mai went from being ignorant about the drugs to indulging in some he'd scored on his own. He varied between manic bursts of energy to total, nearly incoherent lethargy and depression. I added a more than ample dose of booze into the equation on the night Tiffany approached Mai about renewing our contracts and Mai signed his name to it without much hesitation.

The plan was to wean Mai away from the drugs' influence as soon as the contract renewal became official – it was our means of self-preservation – but I'd opened a dangerous door that I wasn't certain I wanted to close. Mai became completely dependent on me during that last half of the tour. He had to be watched, needed constant guidance and I was more than happy to volunteer. I loved it.

It really was funny at first, after all, the crazy things Mai started to do. It was funny to see that no one seemed to care what the hell Mai did while on the stage because he was a rock star in their eyes and nothing more. He'd stop in the middle of a song and start rambling out bizarre poetry that he'd written. He often took off his shirt and cut at his flesh with a razor – a practice he'd been carrying out most his life, only he'd had the sense to keep the cutting out of anyone's immediate sight before. A few times he flashed his bare ass for the entire crowd to see.

Some shows he performed sitting on the floor. Other times he'd lay on his back. Sometimes he didn't sing at all, but simply let the fans take over and used the opportunity to drink from the flask he kept in his jacket pocket. He'd laugh or cry for no reason. He'd reinvent lyrics. He'd go into fits and extend notes or repeat phrases until he exhausted himself and had to stop. In Chicago he screamed one word until he became so winded he literally fell over in a stupor. I had to pick him up and pull him offstage.

No one ever said anything to Mai's face or to any of us except for the time he tried to go out on the stage without any clothes and security wouldn't let him pass until he agreed to put some pants on. Almost every time he made a spectacle of himself it ended up in a magazine and tabloids were simply eating it up. Whenever Mai read something he'd supposedly done he would show the article to me and say: "I didn't do that. Did I?" The opportunities to mess with his head became endless.

I would be criticized later for allowing it to go as far as it did, but I felt that Mai owed it to me. I was in love with him, I always had been and what did he ever do in return? He'd reach out and push me away over and over again, needy and then thoughtless. Wonderful and cruel.

Besides, people need to understand how difficult it is to really see the changes in someone so close to you. Seeing Mai every day, I never noticed his weight getting less, the bags under his eyes darker and puffier…I never noticed how much he had aged in a year. No. It wasn't a matter of not noticing the decay – I didn't *want* to see it.

"Tainted" won us two awards, one for best song and the other for best video. At the awards show, seen around the world, Mai's only comments at the podium were, "We're all dead" and "Thanks." He'd then nearly fallen over and proceeded to drop the award on the floor as he bumped into the bleached blonde who was supposed to guide us all back off the stage.

Even though Mai declared it "ghoulish," all of Tommy's footage, including that taken inside the padded room, had been sent to Zaurus and edited together to create the finished product. Words really can't express how beautiful the video turned out and how appropriate it was to be the last ever released by Nefarious.

Mai stepped out of his cell, dark and dreary, looking like walking death, and entered the hall of the lavish palace resembling a silver and rose angel. Zaurus blended images and made several comparisons between the dream and reality as Mai walked and sang. When Mai was taken down and injected with a sedative he was shown lying upon that painted pond. Digital effects were added to make it appear as though Mai sank beneath the pond's surface when the restraints were put on – surprisingly painful to watch.

The flickering light in the padded room was left intact, as was Mai's terrified thrashing about on the bed. The video ended with Mai pressing his hands against the painted field of green and then backing up as if about to run into it. Zaurus digitally placed Mai inside the painting, making him appear free to roam in the sunny field, while the fading shot was of Mai's glassy-eyed stare beneath the fickle light.

The video's massive success resurrected a few old debates. Once again, Mai was accused of promoting suicide; people took the images too literally, and Tiffany opted to revive the whole "Nefarious is cursed" craze herself. I agreed to help her. People were already questioning whether something paranormal had been to blame for Tommy's death – Mai certainly seemed to think it was – and if the other mishaps and deaths before it could also be attributed to the same. Another appearance by the so-called spooks said to follow Mai around would give people something to talk about other than Mai's odd behavior. No one would have to know the spooks were completely fabricated by us.

It all unraveled at our annual campus performance. It was hard to believe five years had passed us by. Most of our original fans had already graduated from the college and moved on, but they always came back to see us whenever we rolled into town. By then, we'd started holding the shows at the local sports arena to accommodate everyone, performing on a small stage in the center of the football field.

With all of the attention being placed on "Tainted" winning the awards, the fans were demanding that we play the damn song at least once and Mai no longer cared to refuse. I told Mai I wouldn't play the song, but he didn't care. He said none of us had to play it. He said he'd do it himself and give the crowd an acoustic rendition instead if he had to and I knew he'd at least *try* to make good on that threat. I quickly changed my mind. I wasn't about to help weed myself out of the group, but I also had no intention of playing that song. I came up with a plan, some harmless sabotage to get people fired up and spare us all the pain of having to perform that particular piece, and ran it by Tiffany. She was in on it just as much as I was, I must mention that, though she'd go on to publicly deny it and become absolved of responsibility.

It was only meant to be a small thing. We'd rigged the equipment beforehand to short out when we readjusted and switched gears to play "Tainted." There would be some sparks, some smoke, some scary crackling – that sort of thing. Mai would remember the incident at the asylum, a thing which haunted his dreams nearly every night, and freak out. His genuine reaction would play into the whole scam perfectly and cause people to believe it hadn't been planned. End of story. End of my having to hear the damned voice Jim would have programmed into his machine to growl out at us all.

The problem was that it started to rain, light drops that turned into heavy fists upon our backs, and the wind was vicious. Mai was knocked off of his feet more than once and eventually decided to sit on the stage floor to keep from being blown away. He changed his mind and decided he didn't want to play "Tainted," he thought it was unsafe to play *anything* in the swelling storm, but Tiffany would have had my ass if we ended the show then and there. I was the one that insisted we press on and press on we did.

How could Tiffany or I have known that the man we'd hired hadn't been as qualified of an electrician as he'd led us to believe? How does a person test such a thing? It wasn't only his lack of skill that caused the tragedy, of course. *It* was there, too – whatever Mai had seen at the asylum and believed to have been on the stairwell with us long ago. Knowing all that I do now I realize he was right about that. He'd always been right about that.

It was over in a matter of seconds. The rain grew heavier, thunder growled, the sky flashed with lightning. Mai remained seated, watching as the wooden planks of the stage beneath him became overly saturated and waiting for Jim's piano to start the song.

It began with a low buzz, deep and unnerving. Renna fiddled

with her amp and a near deafening "pop" fired out. She fell back as if she'd been shocked, unleashing a shrill shriek as she did so, and ended up tumbling right over the edge of the stage. She fell a good three feet to the soggy ground below with a splat. Dart left the drums to peer over the edge of the stage to check on her. I took my guitar off, moving purely on instinct, and tossed it aside just as sparks began shooting out of my own amp.

Seconds later a fire started, the blaze unrelenting despite the deluge from above. A bolt of lightning sent a spotlight crashing down on Jim's head. He fell flat upon the stage floor without so much as a gasp. Mai – stupid, stoned Mai – was still sitting in place and staring with a look of awe about his face. The fans were screaming in horror. The ground beneath our stage was glowing. *Alive.* The entire football field had become one huge, live wire, carpeted by electricity.

"Don't move," Mai suddenly said into his microphone. "Don't get out of your seats, the stands are safe."

The damn microphone! He might as well have been holding a lightning rod, for God's sake. I snatched it out of Mai's hand and threw it as far from him as I could. I'll never forget how he stared at me once I'd done that, perplexed as if I'd somehow betrayed him. It haunts me to this day.

"It's passing me by again," he whispered, lowering his head.

Had Mai been more coherent I imagine he'd have been a handful, nearly impossible to keep still; but that day he simply sat in a heap and allowed me to hold him. Not that my holding him protected either of us in any way, luck – or perhaps cruel fate – did that. Either way, we remained unscathed until the main power was shut down and it became safe to exit the stage.

Jim survived his injuries. Multiple crashes on his motorcycle and jackass stunts had given him quite a resistance to physical blows. He received a concussion and nothing more. Renna hadn't been so fortunate.

No one could tell whether or not she'd survived the initial shock and fall, since her body continued to be electrocuted while lying in the wet mud. Regardless, they told us she hadn't suffered much and we chose to believe that. We met her family for the first time at the hospital. Strange, too, because I'd never once imagined that Renna had parents and a sister that loved her. Not once in all of the years I'd known her. One never really seems to know people until they've passed on.

We were scheduled to perform on Gary Trevors' show the same day Renna's funeral was to be held. We'd been committed to do the show for weeks and Tiffany was adamant that we show up as planned.

"Renna's death was tragic," she told the staff at Gary's show. "But she wouldn't want us to stop doing what she loved. She'll be there in spirit."

It sounded poetic, of course, and it wasn't as though the staff members were going to try to talk us *into* ditching their show. So we went.

Mai didn't even try to protest. He hadn't said or done much of anything since the day Renna died other than drink and smoke and use whatever I had handy to give him. We simply toted him along with us like a walking suitcase. I even took to leading him about by the hand when necessary. He was always quite content so long as a cigarette – lit or unlit – was in his mouth. He'd blink and cough and follow. He'd taken to coughing a lot since the concert; the chilly rain had settled into his bones.

I did Mai's makeup before the show. He wouldn't bother to do it on his own, he simply sat before the mirror staring blankly at his reflection, and he became agitated whenever one of Gary's people attempted to touch him. He let me work on him, though. He'd let me do just about anything in those days. When I gazed into his eyes I saw only myself – truly a hollowing feeling looking back on it now, but it filled me with pride at the time. I'd never felt so important.

Mai remained colorless no matter what I did as I still hadn't the skill to work foundation as well as he could. I decided to take the extreme approach and enhanced how pale he was, making his lips and eyes darker. He seemed to glow beneath the lights, ghostly and ill. He looked beautiful to me. I kissed him sweetly upon his lips when I'd finished. He tasted of stale bourbon and nicotine.

"Are you ready?" I asked.

"Sure," Mai replied with a flat smile. "Where…is it we are? What am I doing?"

"Gary's show," I said. "We're performing 'Redundancy.' Remember?"

"But what am I doing?" he questioned, sounding rather lost, staring hard at his reflection as if he didn't quite understand what he was looking at.

"You're going to sing," I stated, swinging Mai's chair around and pulling him to his feet. "You're going to sing like you always do and you'll be fine. There will be only a quick interview with Gary before we play. You'll tell him we're all sad but determined to carry on and all that. You get along good with Gary. It'll be easy."

"Easy," Mai repeated, staring at the mirror yet again. He sniffed sharply. "I-I need a minute, Blueski. Watch the door?"

I knew damn well what Mai needed to take a minute for. A fix. A quick sniff or stick of his latest poison of choice. I could have stopped him but I didn't. I was the one that had turned him on to the stuff, after all. He'd have left me if he went clean. He'd have left all of us. Surely people can understand that, the fear that was motivating all I did. There's nothing worse than being in love with someone who is no longer around. Mai might have been rather absent in such a state but he was *there*, I could still reach out and touch him and kiss him and take care of him. He still came to my bed when afraid to be alone. He needed someone, and Dart and Jim were hardly ever around anymore.

Gary came into our dressing room just as Mai was stepping out of the bathroom. He smiled at me, genuinely cheerful, and then his eyes fell upon Mai and all color drained from his face. It had been a good six months since Gary had last seen Mai and he'd been hearing all of the rumors. Now he saw the truth for himself.

Gary was horrified, to say the least, but Mai didn't seem to notice. He was preoccupied with brushing imaginary lint off the shoulders of his jacket and actually appeared quite startled when Gary put his hand on his arm. He gasped, coughed, sniffed sharply, then giggled as he stumbled haplessly against the wall behind him.

"What's goin' on?" he asked Gary in an overly excited manner.

"I could ask you the same," Gary replied glumly, turning to look at me. "How long has this been going on?"

"What?" I asked. "He's fine. We're all just a bit down because of Ren and Mai's a little under the weather today but it's fine."

"He's under *something*," Gary muttered, shaking his head.

"I am fine," Mai said. "I'm fine and...I'm...fine. They're putting my bassist in a hole in the ground as we speak, probably next to Tommy, and here we all are. Remember Tommy? The man died right before my eyes and we won an award. It's great, isn't it? Fine. It's what we're all about cos it never stops. You can't stop. It won't stop."

Mai quickly shook his head as he rambled, smiling like a maniac, his eyes having grown wide and tearful. I simply lowered my eyes and refused to look at him. Gary took him by his narrow shoulders and shook him hard enough to cause a few bones to pop.

"You're too damn good to end up some rock cliché, kid," he said. "It won't happen on *my* show. I won't allow it."

"But I…I…I wanna sing," Mai said tearfully. "Please? It's all I can do."

Gary shook his head. "I'll let you sing, but there will be no interview," he said. "I won't help you make a fool of yourself. Sometimes walking away is the best thing you can do, you hear me? Stopping is the only way to go on. I've seen it time and time again, son. Time and again. It's not too late for you. Now. Showtime is in fifteen minutes. Try to pull yourself together."

Mai stood in a stupor long after Gary had left the room, staring straight ahead with eyes unblinking and mouth hanging open dumbly. I wondered if anything Gary had said managed to cut through the tangled fog in Mai's brain. I think it confused him more than anything else, made him feel as if he'd disappointed the man. He hated to disappoint anyone, even self-righteous talk show hosts.

"Who the hell does he think *he* is," I said.

"He's afraid I'll fuck up his show?" Mai asked, his voice barely a whisper. "I can't sing anymore?"

I shook my head. "He's afraid you're fucking yourself up," I replied; I couldn't lie about that.

"Oh," Mai said with a blink. "Well, that's nothing new, is it?"

I shook my head and we both started to laugh. Mai laughed until he wept. I had to touch up his eyes before they called us out onto the stage.

Chapter 27

THE AUDIENCE CHEERED madly from their seats as we made our way onto the stage. The performance was meant to mark the grand debut of our new bassist, a lanky guy with greasy-looking hair who Tiffany had picked out herself called Rom. He was supposed to come out mid-way through "Redundancy" and replace the bassist from Gary's house band who would be starting the song with us.

Tiffany thought that a more dramatic approach, but the only dramatics the audience was to see that day would come from Mai and backstage – backstage, out of the public's sight, they would come from Hazel. That's right. Stupid, healed, concerned Hazel who had placed himself in the audience that night. His presence made for the beginning of a nightmare.

Mai didn't even *make* it half way through the song. He shuffled over to the microphone with an unlit cigarette dangling from his lips like a wandering sheep in a field might mosey over to its feed box. He coughed before signaling us to start and then didn't say a word when his time to sing came. He didn't even open his mouth. Dart and I stared at one another and extended the introduction; thankfully, our guest bassist was able to think quickly enough to do the same.

The second time around Mai began singing, but his tempo was too slow and he kept changing the words. He broke down right in the middle of the chorus. He fell silent, slightly catatonic, with his eyes focused directly upon the red light of the camera before us. His eyelids fluttered. He opened his mouth as if to speak but only coughed violently. Then his knees gave out from under him.

I was a bit frightened by it all, I didn't know then that Mai was mostly faking his collapse. He went down hard, taking the microphone stand along with him. A horrid screech erupted from the mic upon impact with the floor. We all stood frozen for a few seconds, simply staring down at Mai as he lay motionless. He'd landed face first upon the shiny blue floor with his arms tucked in close to his chest and his hair hanging over his eyes. He seemed so small as we stared down at him. So fragile.

Gary shouted for a doctor before shoving the camera away. Its focus fell off to the side, the picture projected now one of darkness – though the viewers at home were still able to hear all that was going on.

"Give him room!"

"Turn him over!"

"Give him some air!"

I don't recall uttering so much as a gulp myself. I only remember the panic audible within the audience and the sound of my own heart thundering in my chest as crew members began to swarm all around Mai's body like locusts. Some were fearing him dead, but I knew that he wasn't. I could hear him wheezing as he breathed in and out.

The show cut to a commercial and Mai was carefully carried backstage where they laid him down upon a long, green couch. A woman covered him with a blanket, a young intern fetched a glass of water, while another woman started running a cool cloth over his face and neck. Mai was alert again by then, frustrated that no one would light his cigarette and slapping at anyone who dared to touch him.

As luck had it, a doctor had been in the audience and he made everyone clear the room when he arrived backstage – everyone except for me, because Mai refused to be totally alone with the man. Mai didn't trust doctors.

Mai had a fever, his pulse was elevated and his lungs sounded as though they were filled with fluid. Dehydration, a bit of malnourishment, pneumonia and the drugs – the doctor was astounded Mai *hadn't* dropped dead yet.

"You should be admitted to a hospital," he said. "Tonight."

Mai moaned woefully, his eyes widening. "No, no, I don't need to do that," he insisted. "Tell him, Blueski. Tell him, please? I won't go."

"We can't force him," I said.

"That's right!" he cried, struggling to sit up. "I only fell down cos I couldn't remember the words, the words were all mixed up and I didn't know what to do. I had to do *somethin'*, so I fell. That's all. I can't go to the hospital. I've got a, uh, a, uh...what am I doing tomorrow, Blues?"

"Another calendar layout," I replied.

Mai nodded emphatically and then collapsed, falling off of the couch and onto his knees with a grunt of pain. He really couldn't get to his feet, he didn't have the stability, so he simply backed himself into the nearest corner and hugged his knees close to his chest. He was shivering wildly. Tears were streaming down his cheeks in a silent but steady flow. He turned his face away from us.

I wasn't sure what to do with him. It had always been Mai's department, knowing how to talk people back down to the ground so they could feel safe again. All I could think to do was to grab his arm and drag him to his feet but I didn't see how doing so would help him any.

That was when I heard Hazel harping at someone just outside the door, trying to weasel his way into the room. The doctor opened the door to speak to him, but he didn't know who the hell Hazel was and would most likely have not allowed the little shit to enter. Then something odd happened. Something came over me and I stuck my head outside the door and gave Hazel permission to come inside. *Why* I did that, I'll never know. I suppose somewhere deep inside I knew that Hazel could reach Mai in a way I couldn't and I truly didn't want to see Mai die – not huddled up in the corner of some backstage green room, anyway.

The time away from us had done Hazel some good. He'd added a bit of color to his hair, streaks of gold to dance with the natural white, and his face was as youthful as ever. He appeared to have completely recovered from all of his injuries. He seemed even stronger, actually, more confident. He gave me a somewhat disdainful glare as he stepped into the room and the doctor stepped out to give us some privacy.

Hazel was angry with me. He blamed me for the pathetic state Mai was in – he blamed all of us – and the glare he gave me let me know it. Hazel wasn't the type to waste time yelling or scolding right off the bat, however. He was worried about Mai and that was his top priority. He'd have preferred for me to leave the room, I'm sure, but I didn't. I remained near the door and watched as he slowly approached Mai, bouncing with each step as he always did, like a little doll on the march.

I didn't catch what Hazel said when he first sat down next to

Mai, but it prompted Mai to turn his head and look at him. He stared with mascara streaked eyes, a black trail of tears running down his cheeks, looking as though he didn't believe Hazel was actually there before him. Hazel put a hand on top of Mai's and Mai shivered almost fearfully.

"Y-You look good," Mai whispered.

Hazel nodded. "You don't," he said.

Mai laughed. "I...no. No, I'm not good," he slowly confessed. "I'm...sorry I haven't called you but I wrote...for a while. I-I wrote...but then I stopped cos I thought maybe you hated me and it got so hard...to hold the pen..."

Hazel shook his head. "I got all of your letters, Mai. I loved 'em," he said with a smile. "I couldn't ever mail you back because you were always moving around, but I did answer them. You can read the letters later if you want."

I'd never seen Mai become so totally elated and horribly morose all in the same instant. He'd written faithfully to Hazel at least once a week ever since we'd left the brat behind without my knowledge – at least until his mind had become too hazy. What had Mai written to the little shit? He hadn't spoken much to the rest of us, not *that* much. I was fuming. Envious. I managed to maintain my silence, however...somehow. Mai was thrilled Hazel had been pleased with the letters. It also terrified him.

"Wh-Why are you here?" he asked.

"Your letters stopped and I saw on TV what happened to Renna. Horrible. I, um, also started hearing some things and then I saw a new picture of you in this magazine and I got scared," Hazel replied. "How did this happen, Mai?"

Mai hugged his knees even tighter and started rocking slightly, muttering under his breath as tears flowed from his eyes. He shook his head as his bottom lip began to tremble and lowered his eyes. He didn't know. He had no answer to give Hazel, but he didn't really need to say anything. Hazel knew.

"I hope you're happy!" we heard Tiffany shout; she nearly knocked me over as she came charging through the door. "We're no longer on the list of guests that will be scheduled on this show. You planned this, didn't you? You did this on purpose. *Why* do you hate me so much?"

"This isn't about you," Hazel stated; I was surprised by how stern he sounded.

"I did ruin it," Mai whispered. "I ruined it. I messed it all up and…and…everyone saw. Everyone saw. They're always watching and whispering. Always."

"We want people to stare and whisper, that's how the game is played!" Tiffany continued to yell.

"That's what *you* want," Mai nearly shouted. "I *never* wanted it! I never…I only wanted it to be about the music."

Tiffany made an almost convincing smile of sympathy as she walked over to Mai. She patted his cheek in a patronizing manner and laughed. "Oh, sweetie," she said with a sigh. "It never has been. Now do I need to ask security to carry you out of this room and force you into that ambulance that's waiting outside? You're being a selfish little brat – you know that?"

"Back off!" Hazel cried. "I'll get him to the ambulance, just let me talk to him alone."

Tiffany shrugged and promptly took her leave. I didn't. I remained near the door, able to eavesdrop with relative ease as Hazel softly commanded Mai's attention back to him.

"I don't wanna go," Mai said with a whimper. "I like it here. It's dark here."

"You need help," Hazel said.

Mai nodded. "It's all gone wrong. I can't…can't think anymore and the noise…the pool…it's too much. It doesn't make any sense, does it, Hazel? I don't wanna do this anymore. Is that terribly wrong of me? I…I'm so tired…I want to run away."

"I'll run with you," Hazel stated, wrapping his arms around Mai's fragile frame; he cringed when he felt the bones of Mai's spine through his shirt. "We'll leave it all behind together. You don't have to do anything you don't want to do anymore."

"He can't just leave," I said. "We need him – the band needs him."

"What is *wrong* with you?" Hazel hissed. "Can't you see the problem? Are you *blind?*"

"Mai's only a bit overworked. He'll get over it."

Hazel's aggressiveness mounted. He removed his wallet from his pocket and took out a photo he had of the three of us. It was from better days, when Hazel had first begun to play with us. It was only then, with a side by side comparison, that I could finally register how gaunt Mai had become. I felt ill.

Then Hazel pulled another trick on me. The dim-witted

sunbeam actually proved himself clever by telling me the first and probably only lie he'd ever told anyone in his life. He pulled me off to the side, out of Mai's hearing range, and whispered into my ear that he was only saying whatever was needed to get Mai out to the ambulance.

"Wait for us outside," he told me. "I'll get him out there."

I believed him. How could the little flowery face possibly deceive me? How could precious Hazel ever even *think* to concoct a lie? What a fool I was. Hazel helped Mai sneak out a back exit and put him in the passenger seat of his rental car after I left the room. While I stood outside waiting near the ambulance like a total moron, Hazel was driving Mai to the nearest hospital he could find outside of the city. Finally – *finally* – my paranoia was realized: Hazel had stolen Mai from me.

All hell was about to break loose.

Chapter 28

INTERESTING BIT OF trivia – to me, at least: there is a close resemblance between the symbol for "love" in sign language and the sign of the devil so many fans enjoy flashing at concerts. I don't believe it is a coincidence. Yin and yang, positive and negative, shadows and light, love and hate – without one half there can be no other and it's all interchangeable. Love can create hate. Hate is so often driven by love. It sets our souls on fire and poisons our blood. No one is immune – not if the love that's tainted their system is genuine. It's true that absence makes the heart grow fonder. It also causes the poison to thicken.

Mai was considered missing for five whole months. The mystery of his disappearance dominated newspapers, magazines and television programs alike. One of the most famous faces in all of the US had seemingly vanished without a trace. Fans feared him to be dead. I feared it something much worse.

What actually happened was this: Immediately after escaping the studio, Hazel took Mai to a hospital out of town where he was treated for pneumonia and dehydration. Once Mai was well enough, Hazel snuck him into some obscure drug rehabilitation center, where he completed a program and cleaned out his system. He even gave up smoking, except for maybe two or three cigs a day – a pretty huge cutback for someone of Mai's habit.

When all of that was said and done, Mai went back to live with Hazel in some shed of a house in Alaska. Buried deep in snow and trees, far from towns or neighbors or any form of actual civilization, Mai finally got his wish to become a domesticated hermit.

Hazel had been keeping himself busy working on all sorts of projects during his time away from us. It turned out he was a pretty fine singer and he'd been doing the vocals for a new band called "Rei" whose members — strangely enough — had never even met one another in person. They each recorded their contributions and then sent them to one another via email. Bizarre and yet strangely efficient. They managed to come together with incredible harmony and Hazel found he actually preferred singing to playing for the time being, as his hand still felt a bit tight while working the strings.

On top of that, Hazel offered guitar lessons once a week when he ventured into town, and designed websites for people and companies the rest of the time — all things he'd been able to do while his arm had been on the mend — to earn some decent money.

Mai remained in Hazel's home for weeks on end, learning how to cook, playing in the snow and writing loads of poems while Hazel continued working on his various projects. Mai ate frequently, devoured tons of movies and even became proficient enough to survive the war while playing Hazel's Playstation. Mai was, in a sense, doing absolutely nothing with his life — and he'd never been happier. Puttering about a snow-covered house, singing to himself and learning to bake bread — it just didn't seem right, not for someone like Mai. I had to make him realize that.

I only found out where Mai was and what he'd been up to when, after months of worrying myself sick, I happened to hear a message that he'd left on Tiffany's answering machine. Tiffany's and not mine. He sounded so damned content, so giddy, that it made my stomach churn. He said he planned on never returning to Nefarious. He said he wanted to get a shack of his own near Hazel's and remain some domestic sloth forever.

Tiffany was livid, naturally, but she wasn't going to do anything about it. For all of her past bullying she knew she couldn't go to Alaska and have Mai dragged out by the ear if he didn't want to go, especially not after Dart and Jim had admitted they were actually pleased Nefarious was finished; they'd been far more bothered by Renna's death and the weird shit around them than they should have been.

I knew then that it was up to me. *I* had to be the one to get him back and make the others remember how good things could be. I mean, that was the *real* reason Mai had left that message. He knew I'd hear it and he knew I'd come after him. He was counting on it. He needed me to get Hazel out of the way because he couldn't do it on his own.

I honestly didn't have any plan in mind when I made the journey to Alaska, no specific purpose for the gun that I'd brought along. I was only acting on instinct and my gut told me to come prepared for anything. It would take me a few days to track them down, as Mai hadn't given Tiffany his exact address. I found the building that Hazel gave his lessons in first.

I ran into Hazel – quite literally – as he was leaving his last guitar class for the day. We made small talk, I started things pleasantly enough, but Hazel wasn't in the mood to listen to anything I had to say. He almost seemed afraid to be alone with me.

"Mai's better now," he told me. "You'll make him take up old habits again."

"Mai made his own decisions," I stated, already irritated with the boy. "No one forced him to do the things he did."

"You didn't discourage it, either. You knew how all that stupid gossip and how Ren and Tommy's deaths got to him – and you did nothing to try to help him," Hazel said. "You know all it took? Asking. I *asked* him to stop and he did. You never asked, you did the opposite. Don't think I don't know. I know all about you," he said, putting his face uncomfortably close to mine, "*all* about you."

I don't know which of us began the pushing after that – probably me. Hazel then started running toward his truck and I knocked him down flat. He kicked back at me, which surprised me, and even managed to strike me fairly hard once or twice. He wanted to get back to Mai before I had a chance to find him, to warn him that I'd come. I couldn't have that.

"What do you think you know?" I asked breathlessly.

"I know you drugged me and that day…on the hill…you pushed me," he panted, darting out of my grasp. "I hit the tree because of you."

"That's ridiculous!" I laughed.

"Mai believes me," he was quick to say. "I know other things, too – like about your twin. It's *amazing* what you can research online."

My voice came back like a crackling old-time radio, "What have you told him?!" I croaked, horrified. "You little shit! You act so sweet and perfect…*that's* how you get people! No one can *ever* do good enough next to you. Sweet, stupid little Hazel – he'd *never* tell a lie! But you're going to tell Mai you lied to him about me!"

Hazel quickly shook his head. He wouldn't have, either. Not even if I'd put the gun to his head. Hazel would never compromise his precious morals for anyone. I had to stop him. I had to make sure I had time alone with Mai. I only needed a chance to speak to him and it'd all be fine again. It had to be.

I hit Hazel with the butt of the gun as he attempted to open the truck's driver's side door. He fell forward and whacked his head against the window. Cracks branched out like frost around his skull just before the glass shattered completely. He bounced back and fell onto the ground, his snowy locks of hair quickly turning crimson. He didn't get up. His eyes were closed. I checked his wallet, found his address and then I turned and ran back to my own car. I left him there in fear someone might happen by at any minute. I couldn't risk being spotted at the scene with Hazel's blood on my hands.

It took some work finding the house, as it truly was isolated behind a fence of blanketed evergreens and rolling mounds of white. It was a beautifully bright day, sunny and crisp. I knew Mai was awake, since all the blinds inside the house were tightly closed. The timing was definitely in my favor, as Mai would be unable to flee; running out of the house would have potentially been his death. I found the front door unlocked and quickly, silently, let myself inside.

The smell of badly burnt brownies and the sound of Mai cursing softly greeted me as I closed the front door behind me. I couldn't believe Mai lived in the place, it was such a drab little cottage. Plain wooden walls and floors and simple pieces of burgundy colored furniture. There were a few photographs and paintings on the wall, some I recognized as the same ones I'd seen in Mai's apartment. He'd been sneaky indeed to smuggle them out unnoticed.

The house was easy to map out. Down a short hall were the bathroom, laundry room and bedrooms. Directly before me was the kitchen where I could hear Mai snatching a pan out of the oven. Quietly, I followed the sound, entered the kitchen, and began watching him.

He looked incredibly well. He was wearing an old pair of blue jeans that hung low on his hips and a dark blue shirt. He had his ass back, some meat on his bones, and no longer stood with the defeated slouch I'd gotten used to. His hair had been cut fairly short and settled in wild waves about his earlobes. He was poking at a pan of nearly petrified brownies with the tip of a knife.

"They're not supposed to be this hard, are they?" he murmured, thinking I was Hazel.

"Probably not," I replied.

I thought Mai might cut himself, he jumped so sharply upon hearing the sound of my voice. His expression was mixed as he turned around to face me, not entirely cold but certainly not as warm as I'd hoped. I suppose that was because he'd not given anyone his exact address and he'd certainly not been expecting me.

"Blues," he nearly gulped. "Wh – How'd you get here?"

"Ran into Hazel," I said. "He told me he had some errands, but to come over without him and stay for dinner."

"He did?" Mai asked. "Really? What sort of errands?"

I shrugged. "I didn't pry," I replied with a laugh. "Why the interrogation? Aren't you happy to see me?"

Mai smiled, briefly, and made a quick nod before setting his knife aside and moving forward to give me an embrace. I tilted my head to kiss him and he quickly turned away. A cold chill shot down my spine and I suddenly became aware of the weight of the gun in my pocket.

"H-How have you been, Blueski?" Mai asked. "You look good."

"I've been worried to death over you," I replied. "You look fantastic, though. I guess a hermit's life agrees with you."

Mai smiled, a more genuine smile, and nodded. "It's great out here," he said brightly. "I don't miss the city at all."

"Great for you," I said with an unintentional sneer. "You're content playing 'snow bunny' while the rest of us are left high and dry. You can't live your life hiding here, Mai."

"I'll die if I go back," Mai said. "It can't go back to how it was, Blues. If you care about me at all you have to know that."

"If *I* care about *you*? All I've done for you, all I gave to you and you just up and abandon me. I thought I meant more to you than all your other 'throw aways.' You saw me. You've been the only person to really *see* me and now I see you were just fucking with me all along. 'Screw 'em and toss 'em aside.' Have sex and move along. Take and take all you can until you make people crazy. Well, you have to give something back now. You *owe* me!"

Mai seemed more than a bit startled. Mostly his fear rose because I'd begun to yell at him, but he'd also caught sight of the blood smeared about the side pocket of my coat. He may have even seen the handle of the gun. He made very careful eye contact with me – very careful. He'd never completely forgotten the day I'd started shouting at him after seeing his interview with Gary, the day he'd gone on to pass out on me. He recalled how angry I'd been then. As angry as I'd just become in Hazel's kitchen.

"I don't understand," he said softly, shaking his head. "What is it you think I owe you? I added you to my band. I've never treated you as anything less than a dear friend. I–"

"You can't call someone you've made love to *only* a friend! You can't play with people like that! I won't let you get away with it."

"Wha...Who are you here yelling for?" Mai asked, truly struggling to put his words together. "I've not really been with anyone since I let Jeanie go on her way and if someone's told you dif–"

"You've been with *me*! Do I not count? We've had something real all these years and then you just decided to run off with Hazel without so much as a 'see ya later?' You didn't even call me – you called *Tiffany*. You can't just leave me!"

I don't know how the gun found its way into my hand, but there it was: poised and aimed directly at Mai as I screamed at him rather hysterically. My vision was blurred by the tears that had flooded my eyes, but I could see the absolute horror that had taken hold of Mai's face. He fell back against the oven behind him as if I'd shoved him, his pale eyes wide and focused upon the gun. He was afraid.

"Baby, I...baby, we've never..." he whispered. "You and I have never been together like that. I had my zombie days, but that's not something I'd forget. Unless, of course, you jumped me *during* my zombie days – in which case that'd hardly–"

"Don't try to charm your way out of this! We were together in London, on the rooftop by the pool. Our picture ended up in a tabloid afterward. Should I find that tabloid? Should I *prove* it to you or will you just admit it now?!"

Mai was shivering, still tracking the gun, but he seemed to be processing his thoughts far more quickly now. He remembered the two of us sitting together on that rooftop right after his mother had butted back into his life. He also remembered that tabloid I'd mentioned. He had quite a different take on both.

"We talked for hours by the pool," he said slowly. "You told me about Gray and why you'd left home–"

"And then you made love to me," I interrupted.

"No. No, I didn't," he said, shaking his head. "Then this couple came out and started splashin' about in the pool and I joked that *they'd* start goin' at it soon," Mai replied. "You ended up dozing off for a bit and I went back inside cos I was pretty wiped out myself and the sun was about to come up. I went back to our room, but there was no place to lay so I tucked myself away behind the couch. You were beside me when I woke up and mum was gone."

"Why are you lying?" I cried, shaking the gun at him. "*We* were the ones in the pool. *We* woke up late and you had to run to beat the sun. *I* had to bring your clothes to you. That's when someone snapped our picture by that plant you'd hid behind."

"That picture was a fake," Mai was quick to say; he sounded almost angry with me now. "Remember? It came out and we all had a good laugh cos it was so obvious that they'd pasted our heads onto the bodies of some porno scene. *Remember?* You were a foot too tall and there was no tattoo on my arm and they had us both standing in the sunshine. They still joke about it on our website, you can see it for yourself."

I found myself gritting my teeth, struggling to remain calm. "But you loved me."

"I *don't* love you!" Mai shouted.

Mai regretted what he'd said almost before he'd even finished saying it. His eyes widened further, he briefly covered his mouth with his hand, and then he quickly shook his head at me. "Oh, that came out wrong," he said a bit too quickly. "That – I didn't mean that like it sounded. I thought I'd just misheard you that day, after you saw the interview, but…you really thought…All this time you really believed we…All the extra petting and kissing, how possessive you got – I get it now. Jesus. Here I thought *I* was the crazier of the two of us."

"How dare you!" I growled, shaking the gun again. "Now you're *mocking* me?"

Mai shook his head. "No! That was a dick thing to say and I'm sorry," he said – he sounded sincere. "It's just…Fuck. M-maybe you dreamed it? Maybe you dreamed it happened and you got confused. Like when you dream the phone's ringing and once you're up you can't recall if you missed a real call or not."

I couldn't believe that Mai had just compared the two of us experiencing one of the most passionate moments in my life to a phone ringing. He must have read the outrage in my eyes, because he started checking the clock and eyeing the door. Was it too early in the day to run – that was what he wanted to know. Unfortunately for him, it was only three in the afternoon. The sun was still burning brightly.

"H-Hazel shouldn't be much longer," he said. "He'll help us sort this all out. It'll be okay."

"Hazel said his class was running pretty long. I don't expect we'll see him for a while."

"His class?" Mai asked, slowly placing his hands behind his back. "I thought he'd errands to attend."

I *had* said errands earlier; Mai had caught me in a lie. It struck me as inexplicably funny for whatever reason that I'd been busted by the same man who only months earlier couldn't even manage to zip up his own pants. I laughed out loud whole-heartedly, a sound that spooked Mai even further. I'd seen Hazel: Mai believed that I'd been honest about that; but now he was afraid of what I might have done to him. Hazel wasn't going to be showing up any time soon – if ever again – and he knew it.

"I didn't really mean for it to happen," I said. "Do you believe me?"

"Didn't mean for what to happen?" Mai asked.

I didn't answer.

"What did you do?" he questioned, his voice suddenly forceful. "What did you *do*?!"

"Don't worry, he's not dead or anything," I replied. "I'm sure of that."

"'Don't worry?' Don't worry! Is he outside? Is he out there?" he said, making a motion for the door.

"The sun's out, dumbass," I said, unconsciously wagging the gun at him to shoo him back into place. "You can't go look for him!"

Mai glared at me – I mean *glared* – and started trembling. I imagine he was picturing a number of horrific scenarios. Hazel shot and bleeding to death in the snow or stranded and freezing to death as we spoke. For a few seconds, I thought he might attack me and then he simply unleashed a weary sigh. He seemed extremely melancholy. Strangely sympathetic.

"Why are you doing this?" he asked. "Tell me why."

"I love you," I replied without hesitation. "Everything I've done was for you."

"So you *did* drug Hazel," he said solemnly. "And you pushed him into that tree?"

"That was an accident," I replied. "The wind knocked him off course."

"'The wind,'" Mai repeated. "And, um, now? What'd you bring that gun for? To kill Hazel? To kill me? What?"

"I don't want to kill anyone," I laughed. "I only came to take you back with me. You can't abandon all we had. Can't abandon your music and your fans."

"I'm not drugged anymore, Blueski," Mai said, lowering his eyes. "I won't go back with you. You can't *make* me go back with you."

"You can't hide here living a life that isn't yours!" I cried. "You can't become someone you aren't and run off to some new life. At first it feels like you can, but you can't. It always comes back to haunt you."

"Like you and Gray," Mai flatly stated.

Now it was my turn to falter. Mai spoke as if he knew something about me. He *did* know. I think now he'd always somehow known something was amiss and not once had he said a word about it. Maybe he'd been able to see right through me all along, after all.

"It's all right, I understand why you did it," he said softly, sweetly. "I imagine it was horrible for you to wake up in the hospital, your twin beside you in a coma and no one's sure which is which. Blue was the one your parents favored and you could see the hope in their eyes when the doctor asked you for your name. So you lied. Right? Blue was the one in that coma, Blue was the one who died, but you lied. It didn't take 'em long to see through it, though. Did it."

I wasn't in Mai's snowy Shangri-la. I was back in an antiseptic-smelling hospital. Staring at a figure in a bed. My free hand found its way to my hair and I raked at it to drag myself back. "I didn't do anything wrong!" I protested. "It was an *accident* and they'd have blamed *me* if I told them the truth. I wanted *Gray* to die. *I* wanted to be the one they wanted. I wanted…"

…to be loved. How clichéd it all sounds now. I hadn't killed my twin on purpose – that's the honest truth – but once people started suspecting that I wasn't actually Blue, they all whispered that I'd intentionally crashed the car. My parents sent me away to be evaluated, but they couldn't prove anything. *No one* could prove anything. I ran. I broke out of the facility and I ran. I changed my appearance, kept Blue as my name. I ran until I'd found Mai; but, in the end, I couldn't become the person he'd wanted me to be, either.

"You can't shape yourself to match anyone's expectations, sweetheart," Mai said. "I'd hoped you'd learn that on your own. You can't expect anyone else to change to fit yours, either."

"How did you know about me?"

Mai shook his head. "Only a guess, really," he replied. "That and Hazel did some checking. He came across a report that Blue Hensington was believed dead, that a staff worker at an institution was gravely injured when a patient escaped. Hazel thought that patient was you but I…"

But I was willing to give you the benefit of a doubt until you showed yourself to be a psychopath – that's what I believed Mai to be thinking. I was still holding the gun on him, but Mai seemed to be feeling less intimidated by it. He didn't believe that I'd really do him any harm. I didn't believe that I would, either. I'd spent years trying to be someone else, someone others would desire to embrace, and now I was exposed and bleeding out before Mai. Before my love. My obsession. I might have dropped the gun, then. I could easily have burst into tears and pleaded for some sort of absolution that only Mai could give. We might have gone to get Hazel and I'd have begged for forgiveness for letting things go so far.

Then Mai stupidly made a mad run toward the back door behind me and the lucidity fell apart. I took his desire to flee to mean that all of the sincerity he'd displayed was false. Fake. I couldn't let him leave me alone in my shame – not when he was a sinner, too.

Chapter 29

MAI STRUCK MY hand with the kitchen knife with which he'd been chipping away at his ruined brownies. He'd had his hand on the handle of the back door and was about to fling the thing wide open when I grabbed him and he'd reacted on instinct.

The knife bit deeper into my soul than my flesh – but my first thought was for Mai. It was insanity for him to run outdoors. The sun wouldn't have killed him instantly, of course, but it would have severely burnt and marred his skin. There would be swelling, he'd become seriously ill and would not, in all likelihood, have even made it back to town. Not to mention that the fool was barefoot and the snow outside was several feet deep. He'd rather run out and risk his life than remain indoors with me – had it really come to that?

"You could die out there," I said firmly.

"I don't wanna fight you," he said, shoving me away. "Just keep away, all right?"

"I can't. I love you and I know you love me, too. We were meant for each other. We've *always* been meant for each other. Everything else got in our way, but now it's different. Forget the band, forget Hazel. You and me, we can go somewhere together. Okay? Just the two of us like when we went to California."

"I can't do anything until I know Hazel's all right," Mai stated, shaking his head.

"You're *not* leaving this house to look for him!" I shouted, slamming my fist against the door. "That little shit doesn't matter anymore."

Mai shook his head again and took off running. It was such a small house that the chase was hardly any effort at all. He went toward the front door, but I fired the gun at it and forced him to turn away. I placed myself between both exits, gun ready to fire again and started to smile.

He ran down the hall, the only place left for him to go, and I was quick to follow. There was a third exit, a sliding glass door in the bedroom hidden behind heavy curtains. The room was pitch black until Mai started tearing at the curtains, threatening to flood the area with light. I quickly yanked Mai down to the floor and readjusted them.

"Why are you trying to run from me?" I asked. "You want to get yourself killed?"

Mai simply glared and clawed his way to his feet with a pant. He slammed the door behind him as he ran out of the room. I followed and watched as he paced restlessly, entering and exiting rooms, opening and closing doors. He did it to throw me off guard. He did it so I'd be taken back when he suddenly turned and made a second attempt to run through those sliding doors in the bedroom. Typical stubborn Mai – he really wasn't going to stop. He would have kept running in circles until he finally managed to slip out a door or crash through a window and then he'd have been lost to the sun.

God forgive me but I hit him. I ran straight at him as hard as I could and smashed him against the wall. I held him there as I snatched down the curtains guarding the glass and proceeded to tightly wrap him inside of them. There wasn't much Mai could do after that, all tucked inside the heavy material. He couldn't free himself, couldn't run, couldn't strike out at me. He could hardly even breathe. I dragged him out of the bedroom, leaving the door wide open behind me. I left him rolled up in the hallway and marched throughout the house, opening every door and raising all the blinds I could find. I flooded the entire hall with light. I created a deathtrap.

I pulled Mai into the laundry room at the very end of the hall where there was only a round window the size of my head shuttered shut from the outside. I dumped him in the corner between the wall and washing machine before shutting the door behind us, and then I shook him out of the curtains and out into the open.

Even while gasping for air, Mai punched at me. He cursed and kicked and continued to punch, but he'd wasted too much energy to pose much of a threat to me. I managed to lay him flat on his stomach and sat on his back before I pinned his arms down at his sides with my knees. I could feel his slender bones cracking beneath his flesh. I could feel him struggling in vain to get out from under me. I had him.

"You're hurting me," he whimpered. "Get off…"

"Not until I believe you'll keep still," I said, pressing down on Mai's shoulder blades with my hands. "I've opened every blind and door. One step out of this room and you'll drop before you reach an exit."

"Tell me where he is," Mai said, his voice scarcely a whisper. "Is he all right? Please…just tell me he's all right and I'm yours. Okay? I'll do anything you want, baby, I will. Don't hurt him cos of me…"

I didn't say anything.

"Blueski? *Please.* I-I didn't realize…but now I do. Now I know and it'll be…different…I didn't know how much you loved me. I didn't know. Phone Hazel some help if he needs it. You…you don't have to tell me anything. Okay? I…I can't…catch my breath. Please. Anything. I'll do…any…thing…"

It was fascinating, watching as the life faded from Mai's body. He couldn't breathe properly with me on top of him, my weight was too much for his thin chest, and his words faded from whispers to mere rasps of moving lips. His eyes became unfocused beneath heavy lashes. Slowly he ceased to move and the lips fell into a relaxed pout. The eyelids lowered. He looked extremely peaceful. Almost like an angel.

I didn't let death take him, then, of course. I was quick to roll off of him once he'd slipped into unconsciousness and then propped him up into a sitting position in the corner. I reasoned he'd have no idea how much time had been lost to sleep when he came to. If I told him it was still light outside, he'd have no choice but to take my word for it. I'd have him completely dependent on me once again.

Mai was a clever bastard, though. What I didn't know was that he'd faked exactly how short of breath he'd become and really hadn't passed out at all. He pretended until I left the room and quietly snatched Hazel's wrist watch from atop the dryer. He checked it and then hid it in his pocket. He wasn't daring enough to flee the room – he'd gained enough sense not to run out into the sun – but his thoughts of abandoning me were far from dormant.

He really did doze off for a bit while I was gone because the sound of the door closing behind me caused him to jump with genuine fright. I'd left my coat in the living room, but the gun was still on me, out of immediate sight. I'd brought Mai a drink and something to eat, as well as a first-aid kit. I'd made him bleed and I felt genuinely remorseful about that.

"Are you hurting?" I asked.

Mai slowly shook his head. "It's not too bad," he replied. "Did you—"

"He'll be fine," I said sharply. "Let's not talk about it anymore, all right?"

I don't know if Mai believed me or not, but he said nothing more about Hazel for the rest of the afternoon. He remained still as I washed his face and tended to his scratched cheek and temple and busted lip. I felt his eyes burning into me the entire time I worked on the wounds.

"I didn't mean for any of this," I said. "I really...I just couldn't seem to stop myself."

"I know," Mai said, lightly caressing my hand with the back of his. "I only wish you'd spoken to me sooner. Before..."

"Beating you up and locking you in a room isn't a normal way to open a discussion?" I asked with a crooked smile.

"Most would have started with torching my car or something," he replied. "Maybe cut holes in my clothes?"

We both started to laugh. Mai laughed until pain seized his side and then he groaned and shook his head. I stroked his hair, pushed it away from his face and smiled. He looked a bit tired – but how beautiful he was! He didn't hate me for how I'd behaved, he felt responsible for it. That's simply how Mai was. He wanted to take care of it, make it all better somehow.

"I am sorry, Mai," I said. "Not just for this but...before...I never wanted you to be sick, you know?"

Mai nodded. "Forget about it. So...where is it we're to run off to?"

I shrugged. I really hadn't thought that far ahead.

"I think I'd like to see Scotland," he said. "Someplace like that, green and open."

"Scotland is green and open?" I laughed.

"Isn't it?" Mai asked with a smile. "Bloody hell I'm feeling tired. Really wore myself out, I think."

I leaned forward and kissed Mai's lips. He returned the kiss almost on reflex and flashed a fatigued smile before slumping down low in the corner and closing his eyes. I sat beside him and allowed him to use my shoulder as his pillow. His sleep was genuine, he had exhausted himself trying to run away from me, and I eventually joined him.

Mai was gone when I came to. I felt betrayed all over again.

Chapter 30

I FOUND MAI sitting in the kitchen on a wooden chair, resting his elbows on his knees. He was staring down at the floor, a cigarette in one hand and the cordless telephone in the other. The cigarette was half spent and topped with a neglected excess of ash.

He had my gun. I knew he'd taken it, but I wasn't at all worried. Mai wouldn't have fired it on me even to save his life – I was confident about that – but I entered the kitchen as quietly as possible all the same. He knew I was there, but he didn't turn his eyes upon me. He looked guilty.

"Did I wake you?" he eventually asked, clearing his throat.

I shook my head. "Maybe," I replied. "Maybe I knew you'd left and that's what woke me."

"I'm right here," Mai said, smiling faintly. Finally he looked in my direction. "I've gone nowhere."

"Give me back my gun, Mai. I know you have it."

"Why?" he asked. "You don't need it, do you?"

"It's mine," I replied. "Give it back."

Mai shook his head. "I tossed it out the window."

I knew Mai was lying. His voice caught in his throat and he swallowed hard upon finishing his sentence. He didn't want me to get my hands on it because he knew what was about to happen. He was fearful of what I might do.

"Where did you really put it?" I asked.

"I tossed it out," Mai quickly replied. "I swear."

"You only swear when you're *lying*!"

I'd just forced Mai to his feet when I heard the sirens. A police car was fast approaching. Mai lowered his eyes and told me that he was sorry, not even bothering to pull away from me. Sorry. He'd called the police on me as if I was a common criminal and he was *sorry*.

"Do you want them to lock me away?!" I cried, shaking him angrily. "That's what they'll do. I've proved myself crazy for them – my mom will be thrilled. Where's my gun?"

"It's not like that," Mai said, frowning sharply as I started searching him for the weapon.

"Why did you call them? I told you I didn't want to hurt anyone. You have to know I never wanted to hurt *you*!"

"You're hurting yourself," Mai said, finally breaking away from me. "You need help, help I can't give you. I'm not good for you to be around. I only make it worse and I'm sorry. I never meant…"

"That seems a running trend with you."

A tear rolled down Mai's cheek and he quickly shook his head. He'd been thinking about what I'd just said. He believed that was his curse – his *real* curse – just as much now as he had before. Maybe even more so than before. Anyone he allowed to become close to him ended up poisoned by that force, that place he believed he'd reached into too deeply. The police were closing in, coming after me, and now his guilt was nearly overwhelming.

"I have your gun," he said. "I'll, uh, help you run if you want. We'll get you some help somewhere private. No one will have to know about it. No one has to be hurt. It's either that or you allow the police to escort you. You choose. I'll be behind you either way."

What Mai was thinking, I'll never know. He allowed me to reclaim my gun and I held it to his back as we slipped out the back door of the house. We made it appear as though Mai was my hostage in case one of the officers happened to spot us. We managed to escape into the woods unseen, however, protected by the towering trees and starless night sky.

Mai knew it would only be a forty-five minute walk at most to reach the main highway. It was three-thirty when we began the hike – it seemed we'd have plenty of time. We walked side by side, marching over the endless carpet of untouched snow. I sensed that Mai wasn't planning on running from me anymore and put the gun away. He intended to keep his promise to walk to the road with me. I believed he'd also remain close if I agreed to get some treatment. He'd feel obligated to.

"You think I'm crazy?" I asked softly.

Mai shook his head. "No," he replied. "I think…Well, I've no room to call anyone crazy. Have I?"

I laughed. "You've had your moments."

"I think you need a break is all," Mai said. "Get away, collect your thoughts. Get yourself rid of me."

I frowned. "I'll never be rid of you, Mai," I whispered. "Part of me will always be wherever you are."

Mai fell silent and I wondered what he was thinking. Mai *did* have love for me, maybe even more than I'd realized. All of these years together he'd actually been the one taking care of me until he started burning out and I'd repaid him by popping at the seams. I felt a little ashamed over it all.

It snowed fine and soft flakes that melted instantly upon our skin as we walked. No one had been in the woods since the last major snow, which was firmly packed beneath our feet. Everything was still and untouched, beautiful and dangerous. Neither of us had even an inkling that we'd strayed off the main path until the ground fell right out from under us. We'd inadvertently stepped over the edge of a sharp decline that had been concealed by the drifting mounds of white.

Down we went, crashing into one another along the way. Mai was practically swallowed up as I landed on top of him, hammering his body down into the awaiting bed of snow in the process. I rolled off to the side and quickly thrashed about in the white powder to find him. He was laughing when he resurfaced – not an amused laugh but strangely heartfelt nonetheless. He was laughing because he knew that we were screwed.

I don't know how it was that I'd managed to fracture my leg on the way down when I'd had Mai to cushion me, but my knee was hurting like hell. I didn't know exactly where we were – at the bottom of some natural pit, a sinkhole, a ditch that seemed to drop miles down from the road we'd been walking on. It was like being trapped in a box of ice, surrounded by high walls of white. Mai attempted to climb back up, but it was impossible. He wasn't tall enough to reach the surface and the snow and ice continuously gave out beneath him when he attempted to climb.

"Well, this isn't good," he said in a surprisingly light tone of voice. "I believe we may be slightly fucked."

"There has to be a path somewhere," I said. "One that goes back up to the main road. Right?"

"Possibly," Mai replied. "We'll never spot it now, though."

Mai was right. Just as we'd been unable to see that we'd gone off course, we couldn't see much beyond the immediate white around the area in which we'd landed. Any of the standing mounds could have been hiding a road or a trail or a hill we could climb to get back on higher ground. Or they could simply have been mere mounds of snow waiting to collapse under our weight.

Standing snow has much in common with the rolling sands of a desert or the endless waves of an ocean in that it seems to go on for an eternity and causes all it touches to look identical, obscured – especially beneath the moonlight. There was a risk that if Mai went exploring he might lose all sense of direction. Not only would we be separated, but he wouldn't be able to find the main road or make his way back to me even if he did. The only thing we both knew for certain was I couldn't possibly march through the snow on my wounded leg. He could have left me alone and taken his chances, he probably *should* have, but he didn't. Why?

"You should take the weight off that leg," he said.

"It's too cold to sit," I grumbled, though I did do as Mai said and collapsed upon the ground.

"Want to cover up with my coat?" Mai asked, moving as if about to remove his jacket.

I shook my head. "You need it."

Mai shrugged and then sat down beside me. He put his arms around me. He *hugged* me. After all we'd gone through, all we'd done to one another, Mai hugged me. "I never was much of a boy scout," he said apologetically. "I guess I missed the chapter on avoiding cliffs."

I nodded. "Seems like it," I said, not quite able to match the smile in his eyes. "This is my fault, not yours."

"Nah. We had to run from cops I called."

"You only called them because I went psycho," I stated.

Mai frowned thoughtfully and then jokingly agreed. "You've a point there. All right. We'll blame this one on you, baby Blue."

"You still call me Blue?"

"Only name I know to call you by," Mai replied with a shrug. "I wish you'd have told me about all of that sooner. You make a lot more sense now that I know."

I'd never imagined that Mai had seen me as some sort of puzzle, especially since he'd once referred to me as "simple." He'd believed that I'd been raised in a Brady environment, with parents who adored me in a nice, secure home. He never really understood, then, why I'd behaved as a wallflower and so easily identified with those underdogs he sang about. Now he knew. The mystery was over.

"I guess you'll get to see what happens when the sun hits me," he said suddenly, staring up at the sky. "Don't worry, I'll move over some in case I do happen to burst into flames. I won't take you down with me."

"That's not funny," I was quick to say. "Not funny at all."

"Not at all?" Mai asked, looking disappointed. "I thought it was."

"I'd *want* to go with you. I won't be able to live with myself if you die because I got us stuck out here."

"Don't be an idiot."

"I'm dead serious," I said, grabbing his hand. "I'd follow you to heaven."

"That's sweet, darling; but I don't believe either of us would be allowed in heaven," he remarked, quickly kissing my hand. "Seriously, though. Whatever happens to me, you promise you'll not hurt yourself. Even from hell, I'd be wracked with guilt if you did."

I made the promise, but it was one that I'd not be able to keep. Time passed like the wind, racing past us unrestrained, and we watched as the sky grew increasingly lighter. Mai seemed painfully beautiful to me, watching the sky with a graceful sort of anticipation. He was nervous, I think, but the uncertainty also excited him.

To die at the hands of the sun... it was too surreal for me to visualize. Strange how fascinated and curious I'd been over such a thing through the years only to feel horrified when it was about to actually happen. It was nearly five in the morning. There was, at best, an hour remaining before Mai would be in danger. He could cover his face with his coat if he had to, but then he'd not be as protected from the cold winds and falling snow. The odds of both of us surviving an entire day, stationary as the snow slowly buried us alive, were slim. It seemed wrong for Mai to simply sit and wait to be taken.

Fate seemed to be in agreement with me. Once the sky lightened I was able to see a large rock not far from us protruding slightly above the accumulating snow. If I stood upon it and Mai climbed upon my shoulders, he'd have a fair shot at pulling himself onto the main path we'd fallen from. He still had a chance of making it to the highway so long as he moved quickly. He at least had to try.

"You can get indoors before it's too late," I said, having told him my plan.

"If I make it back up there, I'll not be able to reach you without falling in again," he said, shaking his head. "I won't leave you here alone."

"Send someone back for me. I'll wait. Now help me get to my feet. You've got to hurry."

Mai was nearly frozen, as was I, and getting to his own feet proved quite a challenge. His muscles were stiff, his skin bleached and lips blue. I suppose I must have looked the same. He did manage to somehow get us both on our feet and I carefully climbed onto the rock.

"I may fall," I warned him. "Be quick."

"I don't like this," he nearly whined. "This isn't–"

"Do it or I'll shoot myself right now, right before your eyes."

"*That* isn't funny," he said, crossing his arms.

"I wasn't joking."

I really *wasn't* joking and Mai must have known it because he grumbled at me and came closer. I put my hand upon his cheek and kissed him before he climbed onto my shoulders; it was a kiss he readily returned. His ascent back onto the main path was hit and miss as his hands were numb and his arms were shaking uncontrollably. I started pushing him once he'd left my shoulders.

The last time I saw Mai alive was after he'd just reached the surface. He was lying on his stomach and peering down at me, making certain he really couldn't reach me, with a great deal of uncertainty swirling about his smoky eyes. He didn't want to leave me alone. He didn't want to wind up by himself when the sun rose. He was afraid for both of us.

"You'll never be alone while I'm around," I told him. "And you're going to reach the road. I'll be waiting here."

Mai nodded. "All right. I'm going to run. I'll either make it or my insides will explode from smoker's lung," he said.

I shook my head, compelled to smile. "I love you, Mai. I always did, always will."

Mai smiled at me – *the* smile – and I felt as if I'd been forgiven. As if I'd been blessed. "Me too, Blueski."

Then he was gone, on his way. Racing time. Racing the light. I don't know if he ran as he'd told me he would. I don't know if he was afraid or determined right up to the end. All I know is that I sat on that rock and watched the sun slowly rise in silence. The night was once again put to death, all shadows were chased away, and Mai was dead.

I knew he hadn't had time to reach the highway, secure a ride and place himself indoors. He couldn't have. I imagined his face burning and swelling up. I imagined him falling ill and being unable to continue on. I imagined him collapsing in the snow and dying alone. I'd killed him as sure as if I'd shot him point blank. I'd *killed* him. I regretted helping him climb up to the main road. If he had to be taken that day, I'd at least have wanted to hold his hand in the end.

I felt a cool breeze caress my cheek, I heard the surrounding trees sigh and became convinced that Mai had left the earth and wanted me to do the same. It seemed only fair considering that I had once sworn that I'd never leave him alone, a promise that meant much more to me than the one I'd made to him earlier that morning. Thirty minutes after the sun had been blazing brightly in the sky above I pulled out my gun, put it to my head and squeezed the trigger. I never once doubted it was the only way he and I could still be together.

Chapter 31

THE ADVANTAGE OF being dead is that time becomes an abstract concept. From China to Texas in the blink of an eye – it's fantastic. The downside was that a lot transpired during my fumble from flesh to spirit and there was no way to ask people on the street for a nice summary of all I'd missed.

A newspaper on display informed me that I'd been dead for nearly eleven months. It also informed me that Mai was still alive and for some reason – I'd missed the steps from there to here – had begun a flourishing solo career. Back in the public eye once again and his album had been produced by Mr. and/or Ms. Zaurus.

The paper had written a lengthy article about Mai and his career to honor the debut of his first solo album, and to publicize the "one-time only" joint show he was giving with Zaurus at The Razor soon. It offered few tidbits of information that I didn't already know, though I was surprised to read that Mai was only twenty-seven. I had never found out his exact date of birth during our time together, but I'd certainly never considered that he was younger than me.

I read most of the article over the shoulder of some giggly teenager and discovered I was able to knock it right out of her hands when she attempted to turn the page too soon. I carried the entire paper out of her reach and laid it flat on the ground around the corner. I believe I gave her quite a start considering it was not at all windy that day.

Mai's current single was called "You" and he'd played the piano featured in it himself. He and Zaurus had also co-written a song together entitled "Crossing Lines." Both were selling extremely well.

I can't lie and proclaim to have been happy about this turn of events. I'd died for Mai, I'd believed that he had died as well. Not only was he alive, but he seemed to have betrayed himself by stepping before the cameras once again. He'd been so miserable earlier, so content to hide away. It didn't make sense. Was he happy now? Did he know I was dead? Surely he *knew* that I was dead.

I'd gained a strange sense of clarity about myself since death removed me from my body. The mind can become so cluttered, the limbs heavy and burdensome. I could see all of the mistakes I'd made and I could make sense of them. Only by dying did I learn exactly who I was, what my purpose had been from the beginning and who I was now free to become. It was liberating. I wanted to share the feeling with Mai. The only question was how to find him.

It wasn't nearly as hard as I'd expected it to be. Now free of the physical limitations that had governed all that I could or couldn't do during my twenty-nine years on the planet, I only had to learn to think outside of them. I wanted to be near Mai. All it took was picturing him in my mind, desiring to be close to him, and close to him I became.

I found myself in a spacious studio, surrounded by cameras, hanging backdrops and blazing lights. There were three stools in place, two side by side, and one near the camera. An interview was about to take place. I could feel that Mai was in the building. I wondered if he was able to feel me, as well, as I set off in search of him.

Passing through doors was an interesting experience. I found my instinct was to reach for the doorknob as I always had, even though I only needed to place my head through the wood to get a glimpse of the room beyond. I found Zaurus' dressing room first and caught the star in the middle of a wardrobe change.

That's another perk of dying: one can find out all sorts of things kept tightly guarded by the living. Supposedly no one knew Zaurus' true gender – that was part of the gimmick, part of the mystique. I can safely say that most gimmicks are lies, illusions of grandeur that make the truth seem comparatively dull and insignificant – and this was certainly true in the case of Zaurus.

A woman playing at being a male that cross dresses – that's what Zaurus was. She wasn't pretty in the eyes of the public, not when compared to most of the other females in her profession, but when she changed herself enough to raise questions she'd become instantly attractive.

I saw the proof of this while peeking into her room, as she

hadn't yet put a shirt on. That was the real reason she didn't let anyone close to her, for fear that they might kiss and tell. Naturally, I was curious as to whether or not Mai had learned what I now knew or if he'd chosen to maintain the mystery. I suppose it didn't really matter one way or the other.

The sound of Tiffany's nagging voice lured me further down the hall to Mai's dressing room after I'd left Zaurus to dress in peace. Tiffany had her arms crossed, she was in the middle of one of her tantrums, and her eyes were focused upon the bathroom door. Mai had locked himself in.

"Necessity is *not* the point," Tiffany was saying, her tone short and agitated. "People are dying to see chemistry. You created it for the video – keep it up until the concert."

"Kissing on live television has been done a billion times," I heard Mai say with a grunt.

"But, baby, no one kisses like you can," Tiffany retorted; I think she was being sincere. "And everyone loves to watch you do it."

"Why don't I just unzip my pants and go at her, then," Mai said. "Why not the entire crew? You want a bit of it, too?"

Tiffany rolled her eyes dramatically and threw her hands into the air. "I'm not talking to you. I *can't* talk to you when you're like this."

That's why I get like this, Mai thought.

I *heard* Mai's thought. I heard it as surely as if he'd said the sentiment directly in my ear and I laughed. The light over the mirror beside me flickered as I took a few steps toward Tiffany. She shivered and shook her head, grumbling before turning to storm out of the room. Tiffany was the one behind Mai's solo career, still holding onto him as tightly as possible. I'd figured as much. I couldn't believe that Mai hadn't rid himself of the woman yet.

"Is she gone?" Mai asked timidly.

I said that she was, I answered out of habit, and slowly – cautiously – the bathroom door crept open a few inches. A lovely gray eye surrounded by gray and charcoal shadow peeked out at me and then the door opened wider.

It was almost like seeing Mai for the first time all over again. Perhaps I truly *was* seeing Mai for the first time. I saw him in shades of black and gray, oddly enough, just as I do whenever I think back to memories of our past. His hair was down to his shoulders, wild as ever, and he was dressed in dark jeans and a concert T-shirt; the band upon his shirt was the one for which Hazel had been singing months ago. He slipped into a tailored jacket – a dark blue one, I believe – and then seemed to look right at me.

"Took you long enough," he said with a smirk.

I opened my mouth, but no words came to me. It had felt as though he'd seen me, as if he'd spoken to me, but then I sensed someone behind me – walking *through* me. Zaurus.

"Takes awhile to get it all in place," Zaurus replied lightly.

"Has Tif harassed you yet?" Mai asked.

"It was my idea, actually. I sent her to harass *you*," Zaurus said.

"Really," Mai nearly purred. "So you do want me after all, ay?"

Zaurus pretended to be annoyed and Mai laughed. He crept up beside her and moved forward to kiss her neck. She sharply pushed him away and started for the door. "The kisses are only for the cameras," she said. "And get a serious breath mint in you before the interview starts. You reek like an ashtray."

It seemed more than a bit rude to me, but Mai was smiling brightly enough when Zaurus slammed the door behind her. I remembered that Zaurus claimed she had never loved anyone. I suppose the fact she seemed to have no sexual interest whatsoever was what Mai found appealing about her.

I stood off to the side and watched as Mai fidgeted for a few seconds with something in his pocket before taking a seat in front of the lit mirror. He took two small pills, downed them with bottled water, and then stared hard at his reflection as if he was searching for something.

I leaned in close and peered over his shoulder, staring at his face through the glass. I had no reflection, there was no visible trace of me at all until I reached out to touch the mirror's surface. The glass began to fog up around my fingertips.

It began as a few small streaks and grew into a fairly large patch of white outlining my hand. Mai saw it. He jumped out of his chair, rubbed his eyes, and then nervously peered over his shoulder. He felt me near him, could see my handprint on the glass before him, and didn't seem to know what to think of it.

Slowly, reluctantly, Mai lifted a trembling hand and reached for the print. His hand was nearly on top of mine when a member of the television crew suddenly burst into the room and startled us both. I pulled my hand away to get a look at the portly young man and Mai did the same.

"Five minutes, Mr. Evans," the man announced.

Mai nodded and quickly straightened his jacket. My handprint had already faded away by the time he looked back at the glass. I think he convinced himself that he'd only imagined it as he made his way out of the room.

I hung back for a bit to study my empty reflection in the mirror. I put my hand to the glass again – and again produced a foggy impression. I kept it there for what felt like a few seconds and the foggy web grew, branching out farther and farther until it devoured the entire surface. Only a space the size and shape of my hand remained clear.

I ran my hand through one of the light bulbs next and noticed my touch caused it to flicker tumultuously. I had no reflection, my body couldn't be readily seen by the human eye, but there were ways to make my presence known. Mai was going to notice me – I was quite determined about that. I only had to find a way to let him know that it was indeed me that he was sensing.

The interview was already underway when I wandered back into the studio area. Mai was seated next to Zaurus with his legs crossed, a cigarette smoldering between two fingers and a pleasantly demur smile on his lips.

"Let's talk about you for a moment, Mai," the plastic blonde reporter was saying. "You've had a crazy year, a lot of tragedies, but now you've left Nefarious behind."

"It was pretty much already gone," Mai said. "I didn't so much leave it as, uh, let it die, I guess."

"Any truth to the rumor Nefarious disbanded because of a curse?" the reporter asked with a wink. "That the others were afraid they might be the next to die if they remained close to you?"

"You're close to me. Are you fearing for your life?" Mai countered coyly.

"Be serious."

Mai shrugged. "You'd have to ask Dart and Jim if they believe in that bullshit. I can't speak for them."

"That's seriously the best you can give me? Come on, now. Everyone knows you vanished for something like five months and remained hidden for nearly a year after you were found. You really expect us to believe there was nothing suspicious behind that decision? What was it really? Illness? Drugs? Did someone hold you hostage?"

"Hold me hostage?" Mai laughed.

"Everyone knows no one's allowed to touch him but me," Zaurus said brightly.

Mai shook his head and lowered his eyes. "My leave was for personal reasons," he said. "I needed to sort some things out."

"So what caused you and Blue to end up in those woods?" the reporter hounded. "Blue dead and Hazel Grantz in the hospital – you nearly frozen to death. Hardly sounds like sorting things out. You've kept mum about the whole thing long enough. Surely you can give us *something*."

There had been a lot of speculation as to what had transpired that day and the bubbly reporter was eager to dredge it all up yet again. I didn't much like him at all, he was superficial and bronzed and empty. He reminded me of Jeanie.

Apparently, Mai hadn't made it to the highway. He'd left me and ran as far as he could with his coat wrapped about his head. He came to realize that he wasn't going to make it in time and considered giving up. Then he noticed a billowing trail of smoke rising into the air and spotted a house nestled within the trees.

Mai made it as far as the front yard of a simple little cabin before collapsing from exhaustion and developing hypothermia. He managed to crawl beneath the bushes that lined the front of the home before passing out. The bushes protected him from the sun and falling snow until the homeowner happened to discover him and brought him indoors – by then he was only barely breathing.

Mai told the police that there was a third person in the woods with us. He said that he and I were running from an attacker and became separated. My apparent suicide and dozens of other details placed numerous holes in Mai's story, but he'd refused to change it. I was curious to know what Hazel had told them. I was curious as to where the dimwitted sunbeam was now.

"Blue's death isn't something I'll talk about," Mai stated, clearing his throat. "I've said that countless times."

"Fair enough, fair enough," the reporter chuckled. "What about the other members of Nefarious? Do you still speak to them?"

"Sure, we keep in touch," Mai replied; I could tell he was lying. "Dart's on his second honeymoon right now and, um, Jim's playing with another band."

"And Hazel? How's he been?"

Mai was becoming restless, more uncomfortable beneath the

increasingly heavy lights directly over his head. He felt trapped. He didn't want to discuss Hazel anymore than he'd wanted to talk about my demise. He hadn't seen Hazel or so much as telephoned him since a few days after I'd tracked them down in Alaska. The despair visible within his eyes was priceless.

"I'm sure he's fine," Mai replied. "I'm, uh, advertising his band today."

"Can we talk about current issues?" Zaurus asked shortly. "I'm not sitting here for nothing."

The rest was all boring banter and business, promoting the songs and the show at The Razor. Mai spoke briefly about working with Minnie again. I got the feeling that Minnie had been less than hospitable.

The reporter tried one last time to get Mai to speak about his relationship with me and how he planned to cope with the anniversary of my death right at the interview's end. I moved in closer, between the camera and Mai, for once as eager as the reporter to hear Mai's reply. Did he miss me? Was he saddened by my absence? Did he know I was standing an arm's length away?

Mai shivered involuntarily as I reached out and ran my hand along the side of his neck. I couldn't touch him but I was able to feel his warmth – and his anxiety. He stared right through me and then quickly turned his eyes upward as the lights overhead flickered. It conjured up bad memories of the day Tommy died, I'm sure – a day Mai still occasionally relived in his nightmares.

"I heard the shot," he whispered. "I heard the shot right when I was getting under the bushes and I knew…What do you want me to say? What should I say? We'd been mates for years…"

Mai's voice faded away and he lowered his head, shutting down completely. Zaurus seemed almost genuinely concerned. She placed her hand upon his leg and leaned over to kiss his cheek. Mai returned the kiss, locking onto her lips, inadvertently giving Tiffany exactly what she'd wanted all along. Finally the reporter seemed satisfied that he'd managed to squeeze something out of Mai no one else had gotten before.

Zaurus pulled away from Mai and leapt out of her chair as soon as the cameras stopped rolling. The reporter gave a fake farewell and went to speak to his assistant. Mai sat alone and smoked, not looking up at anyone until I caused the lights to flicker once again. That prompted him to practically flee the studio.

I followed Mai back to his dressing room. He looked over his shoulder more than once as he walked, feeling as though someone was watching him. He quickened his pace until he was practically running toward the door and threw himself into a corner once he was inside the room. He ran his hands over his face and moaned under his breath as he sank down to the floor. He was breathing hard.

I really couldn't control the lights very well. They flickered when I was near them regardless of whether or not I wanted it to happen – I made a mental note to stay away from them. Later, I'd discover that televisions, radios, telephones – all things electrical – were also incredibly sensitive to my presence.

Mai was still huddled in the corner when Tiffany entered the room – she found him hugging his knees and staring down at the floor. She had a surprisingly warm smile upon her face; and when she called his name, she did so in a gentle and patient way. He didn't look up at her.

"I apologize," she said. "The station is going to apologize, too. I specifically told them not to ask—"

"They'll always ask," Mai stated, his voice rather flat.

"Not always," Tiffany laughed. "They'll forget as soon as you do something else to get them chattering. Now, come on. You need your rest. You're recording tomorrow."

Mai nodded with an unexpected complacency and rose to his feet. He walked alongside Tiffany in silence, lost in his thoughts. He didn't think she was right about the media forgetting such a huge story, he couldn't imagine being able to top it, but he would. In a matter of months he would do something that would live on forever.

Chapter 32

MAI HAD TRADED his New York apartment for a smaller one in Chicago. The place had come furnished, so Mai hadn't done any of the decorating himself. He also hadn't bothered to unpack a single thing. Nearly every belonging he had remained tightly sealed inside large cardboard boxes all stacked in the center of the living room. Only a television, a radio and Mai's clothes had been set out.

I found all of cupboards and the refrigerator bare. A mountain of mail, all forwarded from his former address, sat unopened and forgotten near the front door. Many of the envelopes, I could see, were fan letters. Some were bills. Most were from Hazel.

Now I knew the separation was not Hazel's doing and yet I guessed that Mai was unhappy about it. He'd pushed Hazel away. It seemed as though he'd pushed everyone away and it was because of me. I'd done it. I'd prompted him to isolate himself, but everyone knew Mai couldn't stand to be alone.

That was why he'd returned to the spotlight. That was why he was partnering with Zaurus and about to collaborate with — imagine this — Arieal Turner in the studio the following night. He was keeping busy so that he wouldn't have time to think or feel. A fine plan until a dick reporter refuses to let a matter drop.

Mai took a hot shower, popped a number of Tylenol PMs to put himself to sleep and then collapsed upon his bed wearing only a pair of pants. It was a dead sleep, heavy and unshakable. He didn't so much as twitch. I watched him the entire time, as the sky lightened and darkened outside his covered windows. His body trembled every time I dared to lay a hand upon his skin. I whispered into his ear and hoped that somewhere in his dreams he was able to hear me.

It was Tiffany who made Mai get out of bed. She banged on his door and let herself in with the extra key she'd had made for herself for those (frequent) times when he didn't answer her knocks. Mai did little more than grumble at her for nearly a minute as she shook his arm and swatted at his hair. Finally he opened his eyes and sat up as if startled, eyeing the room suspiciously.

"You're alone?" he asked.

"Who would I allow to see you like this?" Tiffany countered, rolling her eyes. "Bed head and chapped lips."

"I'm all dried out," Mai said, peering cautiously over Tiffany's shoulder; peering in my direction. "Why's it so cold?"

"You fell asleep wet and half naked," she replied. "What's with you, anyway? What are you looking for?"

Mai shook his head, rubbed at his eyes, and pushed Tiffany away. He seemed tired, groggy from the pills, and flustered. Tiffany had interrupted his dream. He'd been dreaming about me.

"I saw Blue standing over me. Over my bed," he said as he lit a cigarette. "Watching me."

"Don't start," she warned. "Blue's dead and you can't freak out every time someone brings up the damn fruitcake. The whole mess is history now."

"That *mess*," Mai snapped, "nearly killed me. You've no idea. No idea…"

"I don't," Tiffany agreed. "You won't talk about it. You're the one who didn't want the world to know Blue went psycho."

"Because it was my fault," Mai was quick to say. "I told you that. Why are you here so damn early, anyway?"

"It's not early, it's six freakin' o'clock," Tiffany replied. "Go get dressed. Make yourself presentable. I'll make you some coffee… assuming you *have* any in this dump."

Mai remained still and silent until Tiffany started to walk away and then he swiftly flipped her off and disappeared into the bathroom. It was fun watching him dress, seeing how he behaved when he thought no one was watching. The low humming under his breath, the swaying in time to music rattling inside his head. He didn't really even look in the mirror as he got ready. He dressed promptly. He didn't so much as run his fingers through his hair.

I rode with Mai in the car, hovering about the seat beside him and across from Tiffany. I put my hand on the window and caused it to fog up. Twice Mai wiped the fog away so he could peer outside once again and then he gave up. Tiffany raised an eyebrow and Mai shrugged innocently.

"I guess I'm hot," he joked but his eyes remained solemn. "The mirror did that, too. Yesterday."

Tiffany shook her head and reached for her cell phone. She'd already let the matter go.

Arieal Turner had finally found her niche singing songs for animated movies. She was currently working on a sequel to the first film she'd done and Mai was to be her guest star. Their duet would play during the end credits.

Show tunes weren't to Mai's taste, but he *did* have the voice for them when he chose to and there weren't many projects he bothered to reject anymore. He arrived at the studio fifteen minutes late. No one seemed surprised. Arieal had already recorded some of her solo verses and was working on another when Mai appeared in the sound booth to review what he would need to sing. Arieal greeted him with a glare.

Not much had changed between the two of them, though it was Mai's unwanted advice that had gotten Arieal where she was now. She had no love for Mai and he enjoyed provoking her. Some things simply remain the same regardless of how many months pass us by.

I was around while Mai recorded his verses and then joined Arieal for the chorus. I honestly didn't aim to interfere, though I did wonder out loud what Mai was doing lending his voice to such a hokey song obviously geared for mass market pop rock stations. Mai kept shivering whenever he wasn't singing. Once I came too close and his microphone screeched.

Mai promptly fled the room when the producer played back what he and Arieal had recorded. Their voices were fine, perfectly on pitch and harmonious, but they were drowned out by an unnatural static. The producer isolated the noise, trying to determine what had caused it. It was heavy sighing. It was the same as the voice Mai had recorded and used in "Tainted." Low, distorted, unintelligible, except *I* could understand it. It was me. The voice was mine. Mai had recognized that as well before his hurried retreat.

Time loses meaning to the dead, I'd already experienced enough to know that. People don't realize how abstract a thing time really is. It has no clear beginning or end and everything, past and present – as well as things to come – are all swirling about in an orderly, infinite chaos.

Everything suddenly made perfect sense – where that voice Mai had accidentally recorded while alone in his bedroom for

"Tainted" had come from, what he'd felt hovering just out of reach when he'd nearly fallen over the stair rail and became trapped in that coffin and padded room. There really *had* been something there. A force. A presence from that dead pool he'd reached into so deeply.

I'd become one of those things Mai had always sensed reaching back at him – except I wasn't in the pool, I'd never fallen into the abyss. I wondered if there were others floating freely, if they had been the whispers Mai had so often listened to in those moments when he'd zone out and leave the rest of us behind...or if it had somehow always been me.

Subconsciously, I must have been aware of my destiny right from the beginning. That was why I hated that voice when I'd first heard it; I'd hated the truth it represented. Our fates are all somewhat predetermined. Our journey may differ slightly depending on the paths we choose but, whether we like it or not, all paths lead to the end fate has chosen for us regardless of how fiercely we try to fight against it. Everything old becomes new again. Every beginning is formed by the end and on and on it goes.

In dreams we sometimes catch glimpses of scenes that we find ourselves unwittingly acting out later on. I'd done the things I had because I was meant to. I'd felt it was my duty to kill Mai right from the beginning and the beginning is always the start of the end. Mai knew this as well. That's why he'd fled the room. That's why he'd locked himself in the bathroom and refused to speak to anyone. No one could reach him. No one could enter the room but me.

Mai had a lit cigarette in his mouth and had another clutched between two trembling fingers. He was huddled on the floor, staring sharply at the full-length mirror that hung upon the wall across from him. He wasn't staring at his own reflection, however. He was looking for signs that I was near him. I put my hand on the glass and gave him what he wanted.

Mai was strangely subdued as he watched a thin web of frost coat the mirror's surface. He rose to his feet and approached the glass without hesitation. He put his hand on top of the imprint I'd left and inhaled sharply over how cold the surface was.

"Is it finally my turn?" he asked softly.

I took my own hand off of the glass and slinked around behind Mai, brushing up against him as I did so. Mai caught a blur of movement in the glass, a dark shadow over his shoulder, and quickly spun around to face me. I backed away, waited to find out if he could see me. He couldn't. Playfully, I strolled over to the sink and turned the faucet on. Then I prompted the automated towel paper dispenser to fire out a few clean sheets. Mai watched with a face set in stone, scarcely blinking, swallowing hard. I think he was actually quite terrified.

Mai's solution, once he was able to command his body to do so, was to childishly cover his eyes as if hoping he was only imagining things. He took in a deep breath, exhaled, puffed away on both of his cigarettes, and then courageously stepped forward in order to shut off the faucet. The room became silent. Still. Mai seemed to relax a bit. To spite him, I turned the water on yet again and he quickly backed away.

"What is this?" he asked, his eyes darting all about the room. "Just get it over with and *take* me already if that's what you want!"

I shut the water off. Mai backed up against the mirror and startled himself. I know he caught a glimpse of my face imposing over his own reflection when he turned around. I know he did because he dropped one of his cigarettes and shook his head and laughed until his laughter turned to tears. He knew. Finally, he *knew*.

"You *have* come to take me," he said, sounding rather pathetic. "Take me, then! Bloody hell, you've waited long enough."

The fog lingered upon the surface, but my image must have faded away because Mai howled angrily and proceeded to ruthlessly attack the mirror with the small metal trash can near his feet. He shattered the glass, screaming and practically sobbing all the while.

Security busted in on him at that point. It took three men to subdue him. He continued his incoherent rambling even after he'd grown physically still. One man appeared afraid, another amused. The third simply wanted to shut Mai up. Mai did, eventually, quiet down once they removed him from the restroom. He felt safe out in the open hallway, away from mirrors and the automated towel machine. He felt safer to simply be near other people.

Needless to say, that marked the end of the session. Tiffany took Mai by the arm and rather forcibly led him back to the car where he sunk into the backseat and attempted to disappear. She didn't blame him for the static on the song, but she did blame him for the money she cost her by leaving early and having to replace the mirror.

"I ought to make *you* pay," she said. "I just might. You don't pull stunts unless *I've* arranged and approved them – got it?"

"I think I've lost my mind," Mai whispered, almost miming the words.

"What else is new," Tiffany laughed. "Are you using again?"

"Huh?" Mai asked.

"Are. You. Using," Tiffany retorted. "Tell me the truth so I know what to do with your sorry ass."

Mai innocently shook his head. "Nothing but the occasional booze and those pills to make me sleep. Sometimes those pills you got prescribed to me for anxiety, but never all at once as you've repeatedly forbidden me to do," he replied. "If I was using, I wouldn't think I was losin' my mind – now, would I?"

"Don't get short with me. You know damn well I've yet to figure out how your twisted mind works."

"I saw Blue in the mirror," Mai whispered. "I know I did."

Tiffany simply rolled her eyes. She had no interest in listening to anything else Mai might have to say. She didn't believe in ghosts and she wasn't, I'm sure, at all convinced that Mai really wasn't on some sort of drugs. Mai remained silent and stared down at his hands. His body never once stopped trembling throughout the entire ride home.

Chapter 33

THEY SAY THAT curiosity killed the cat, but I really didn't see the harm since I was already dead. I couldn't stop thinking about Mai's mound of unopened mail, specifically all of those letters from Hazel lying neglected upon the floor. What was it that Hazel had to say that Mai was apparently afraid to read?

Thinking about Hazel drew me to him within the span of an eye blink. He was someplace sunny – California, I'd later learn – singing for his new band. Apparently, they had finally seen the wisdom of playing in the same room now and again. He wasn't at all like Mai while performing, he bopped around and grinned and thoroughly enjoyed himself without paying any attention to his surroundings whatsoever. He was exactly as I'd remembered him, goofy and annoyingly energetic.

I could also see inside of him now – one of death's many blessings. I believe I finally saw the boy in the way that Mai had, finally understood what it was that Mai needed from the little shit and what the little shit could do for me. Everyone has a part to play; some simply need a nudge or two to get them on their way.

The interview I'd watched Mai conduct with Zaurus and Malibu Ken was playing on a muted television backstage after Hazel had finished his set. He probably wouldn't have paid any attention to it, since he was too busy making faces at himself in the mirror, had I not bumped the television panel and caused the volume to increase. His eyes became glued to the screen the instant he heard Mai's voice.

I was rather mesmerized by the program myself as I noticed a pale, white glow could be seen next to Mai whenever the lights flickered over his head – a white haze exactly my height and build in shape. There weren't really any distinguishable features, but it *was* my silhouette captured briefly on film. Mai's near anguish as he squirmed before the camera was more than apparent. There were times he almost looked downright afraid.

Hazel hadn't told the police that I'd been the one to attack him because Mai had visited him in the hospital before the officers arrived and begged him not to. It had never set well with Hazel, of course, to attempt to lie to authorities. He wasn't a very good liar when he was doing it for reasons he found less than noble and he hadn't wanted to protect me. He'd gone along with it for Mai's sake, of course, and then Mai had left him with only one of his enigmatic poems as an explanation.

I know these things because I followed Hazel home that afternoon and spotted the poem unfolded upon Hazel's nightstand. It was dated five days after my death, two days after my body had been discovered, and apparently Hazel had never bothered to put the thing away. I could only stomach to read it once, though the last lines meant as much to me as they evidently meant to Hazel.

"The more I suffer, the better off you are," the lines read. "The only way to prove my love was to turn and walk away."

I claimed those lines as my own – I don't care what anyone might say to the contrary. Those were meant for me.

One thing that was always true about Hazel was how insistent he became once his mind was made up about something. He had Mai's current address, he'd gotten it from Mai's previous landlord, but he'd never gone to Chicago to see him face to face. He'd chosen to simply write letters to which he'd never received replies and allowed Mai to have some space. Suddenly, he got it into his head that he needed to go to Mai – but what he planned to do seemed a mystery to me at the time. Mai was more bullheaded than anyone I'd ever known – if he didn't want Hazel to see him, Hazel wouldn't get near him.

Tiffany became an unexpected ally in that respect. Despite all of the negative things I've said about the woman, Tiffany did hold a place in her cold, little heart for Mai. She'd given him a piss test and it proved that he was clean, yet his strange behavior continued. He kept expecting to see me. He couldn't be still, couldn't shake the raging anxiety that I was breathing down his neck. Watching him. Waiting for him. Everyone around him thought he was coming unglued.

Tiffany gave Hazel a key to Mai's apartment, but that wasn't where Mai had gone after losing his partnership with Arieal. Hazel found Mai in that old building back in Delsby, up those narrow white stairs, in the room down the hall where the light filtered in like gentle rays of the sun through the cross on the window. He found Mai huddled in the far corner, sitting upon that nappy, brown carpet, wearing the same clothes I'd seen him in at the studio and clutching a nearly spent white candle. The flame was burning tall.

Mai looked as though he hadn't moved for hours, perhaps even days, as I wasn't quite sure how much time had passed since I'd last visited him. His clothes were wrinkled, his hair dirty and wayward, and his hands were streaked by melted wax that had dropped from the candle and hardened on his skin. Hazel made a soft gasp when at last Mai came into his sight, cringing a bit at the sight of the gathered feathers and fallen birds weighing down the plastic all around him. Sunny Hazel wasn't accustomed to a place where decay thrived so freely.

Mai looked up at Hazel with wide eyes, surprised at first and then horrified. He'd gone to the building where he and I had shared our first genuine kiss, a building no one besides us knew about. He couldn't understand how Hazel had been able to find him there. He didn't know that I'd guided Hazel without the little shit even being aware that I was doing so.

"Mai? What are you doing in here?" Hazel asked softly.

"I'm waiting for Blue," Mai said.

"You're *what?*"

"You can't be here," Mai said suddenly, his voice shaky but stern. "You have to go away! Get away from me."

"Mai, you're scaring me a little," Hazel said. "I've been to your apartment, I saw that you haven't even opened my letters. You won't take my calls. Tiffany says that you haven't been taking anyone's."

"Go away!" Mai shouted. "I'm not safe to be around. Haven't you learned that yet? It's true what they say about me. Not in the way they think, but it *is* true. I am cursed and if—"

"There *is* no curse," Hazel said rolling his eyes – and then focusing hard on Mai. "There's never been a curse. You know I don't blame you for anything that happened and you shouldn't blame yourself for what Blue did. It was out of your control."

"It still is," Mai whispered. "Blue's here, you know. Here, I think, to kill me."

"That's ridiculous," Hazel laughed, shaking his head in that annoying little way of his. "You know how silly that sounds?"

"No one believes me, but I've *seen* Blue. I wasn't sure at first; I thought it might've been…but then I saw Blue's face in the mirror. Just as close to me as you are now, Hazel."

"Sure it wasn't a dream?"

A dream. Blaming it all on a dream. Now Mai knew how *I'd* felt when he'd said nearly the same thing to me. It's not a pleasant state to be in. Losing trust in one's own perception of the world is quite possibly the most terrifying thing there is. If one can't believe what one sees or hears, how can he or she believe in anything?

"All that we see or seem is but a dream within a dream," Mai whispered.

"New lyrics?" Hazel asked.

"Edgar Allen Poe," Mai replied with a faint smile. "You'll die if you stay around me, Hazel. You've come too close too often as it is. Go back home. Please? Just forget me."

"You oughta know I can't do that," Hazel said. "I wouldn't *want* to do that. You're only letting your guilt get to you, that's all. You told Blue to wait, you said you'd be back. Blue didn't wait. That's not your fault and in no way should you feel like you did wrong by *not* dying, too. You do know that, don't you? You *can* see that?"

Mai lowered his head and Hazel quickly knelt down before him and forced him to make eye contact. Hazel wasn't completely off the mark, I suppose. Mai *had* asked me not to do anything, to wait for him, but I'd been tricked. I'd believed Mai was dead. I felt I'd owed him my life. In some way, Mai had to be feeling the same or he'd have been able to meet Hazel's gaze.

"You don't understand," Mai said. "It won't stop. It won't stop until I'm dead, too. It can't cos that's always how it was meant to be. Mum always told me so. I was supposed to die when I was a boy, but something got in the way and I came back. Don't you see? That's how I knew about the dead pool in the first place. I went there and messed everything up. All that crazy shit – all those people who've been hurt or killed – it's cos of me."

Hazel shook his head, trying and failing to follow Mai's logic. "I don't understand any of that. I don't – What are you talking about?"

Mai lowered his eyes, already regretting that he'd said anything at all. It was something he'd never told anyone, after all. Something Marina Evans had forbidden him to ever speak about, though he saw little point in honoring her wishes now.

"I was about seven or so when mum nearly got us both killed," he said. "She was wasted and she'd had another row with her latest twat. She shouldn't have gotten behind the wheel, but…you know how that goes. She was going too fast and some animal ran in front of us. She swerved right off the road and down into a pond. It wasn't even all that deep, but we'd flipped and landed upside down…"

Hazel and I listened together as Mai described what it was like to be locked inside of a car quickly sinking into a large body of water. How the water slowly started trickling in. How Marina had been too dazed to tell him what to do. The selfish cow eventually managed to get herself out to safety, but Mai had been left to drown. She claimed she couldn't get to him, but I think we all wondered if the woman had even really tried. At any rate, it had been up to a total stranger who had just happened by to dive down and fish Mai out of the water.

"I was dead and he brought me back," Mai said. "I was off in that place, in between, and he pulled me out of it. I've been able to feel it reaching to pull me back ever since, like part of me never really left it. Mum told me time and again I should have died that night, that I should've *stayed* dead, and maybe she was right. I think maybe I should have. All these things happen around me, to *people* around me, like it's trying to make up for letting me go."

Hazel frowned, blinked, and then gently grabbed Mai by the shoulders yet again so he had no choice but to look him in the eye. "No offense, Mai, but your mom was a total bitch," he said.

Mai stared at Hazel for several long seconds, his face set in stone, and then he laughed. It was a genuine, goofy sort of laugh that made Hazel smile, even if it was short lived. "Maybe," he said with a nod. "Doesn't mean she had it wrong."

"You can't mean that."

"I should've went with Blue. I should've gone back after… when I heard the shot. I should've gone back."

"Stop that!" Hazel shouted, giving Mai a sudden shake. "Don't even think like that, all right?"

"It's what Blue thinks."

"Blue isn't here anymore. You only think you saw—"

"I *did* see!" Mai insisted, shaking himself free of Hazel. "That's what I've been trying to tell you. I've always seen and heard things. The dead pool's a real place, ever since that night I've been able to feel when it's near – and now Blue's become a part of it. If I don't go–"

"If you really wanted to go, you'd have done it already," Hazel said, his voice surprisingly stern. "You'd have killed yourself years ago if you really wanted to die, but you didn't because you don't. I know you don't. You *told* me so yourself when I took you from the studio, remember?"

Mai looked ashamed of himself. "Yeah, I remember, but–"

"But, *nothing!*"

"I knew you wouldn't believe me," Mai whispered. "I don't know why I even told you. No one believes me."

"I believe that *you* believe everything you've said," Hazel replied; a bit patronizing, if you ask me. "That's why I'm going to stay with you for a while. Nothing bad will happen and you'll see that everything can be okay now. Blue's gone. The past is the past, yeah? That's all over."

Now Mai had a serious dilemma. He wanted someone to keep him company – he wanted that desperately – but he still believed that Hazel was in danger so long as they were near one another. He wanted to send Hazel away, but then the shit went and hugged him. Hazel won everything with one of his teddy bear embraces.

"Don't even try to tell me to go," Hazel said. "I won't leave you."

"But your band…"

Hazel shrugged. "They can wait. Besides, we've always got email," he replied. "I'm gonna make sure you stop hurting yourself. Or else."

"Or else what?" Mai asked with a defeated laugh.

"I'll have to beat you or something," Hazel replied with another shrug.

"Jesus. I'm really fucked," Mai whispered, lowering his eyes once again. "I feel like I did when I was drowning. I don't…I don't even know how I got here. How did I get here?"

"You mean right back where you got sick of being before? Tiffany got you there," Hazel said. "And that Zaurus person, of course."

"No, I mean *here*. I don't remember…How did *you* get here? I never told you about this place," Mai said, his eyes darkening slightly.

Hazel shook his head, shook his head because he genuinely

didn't know; but he wouldn't admit it out loud, and got to his feet. "Can we leave now?" he asked. "Head back to your place? It stinks in here."

A tired smile crossed Mai's lips and then he reluctantly nodded and allowed Hazel to help him to his feet. They left together, walking side by side. It was nearly morning by the time Hazel opened the door to Mai's apartment and Mai laid down upon his bed for a much needed rest. Hazel snooped all over the place, searching for food and drugs, and found that Mai had little of either. He poured all of the alcohol he could find down the kitchen sink, but left Mai's Tylenol PM and anti-anxiety pills alone. He even made a quick list of items he planned to purchase at the grocery store later on, like a tiny domestic diva on a mission to forge a new home.

I watched him as he did all of this, silent and irritated, hoping he'd somehow feel my glaring eyes upon him. He didn't behave as though he felt like he was being watched; however, before going to bed, he turned and seemed to look straight at me.

"You can't have him," he said, voice soft but firm. "Understand? Leave him the hell alone."

Did I imagine that Hazel had spoken directly to me? I can't say for certain. It certainly sounded as if he had. It had sounded like a challenge but why had the boy told Mai that he was imagining my presence if he believed I was around? What exactly was the little shit up to?

It turned out that a lot of people had noticed my silhouette during Mai's interview. The message boards remained in an uproar over the next few days. Some were outraged, believing it was a publicity scam, while others were excited that a "spook" had made a live appearance.

Mai was oblivious to all of the chatter – Hazel made certain of that. Hazel kept Mai busy; they spent their time grocery shopping, brushing off Tiffany and recording acoustic songs on a tiny tape recorder in Mai's bedroom. They were recordings that Mai refused to listen to for fear that the voice – my voice – would make an unwelcomed appearance.

I chose to keep my distance during all of this. I simply hung back, watched and waited. Mai was beginning to lose his uneasiness. He didn't remember to feel afraid so long as Hazel was nearby to lean on. That was the way I wanted it.

Jealousy, surprisingly, was no longer such a strong issue for me by then. Envy, perhaps, and dismay, most certainly, but I didn't feel jealous of Hazel. Mai would have clung to anyone, it just so happened to be Hazel who was closest to him – and Hazel just happened to be good for Mai. I could see that. Hazel never asked for anything from Mai other than friendship – and that Mai keep clean and refrain from harming himself. Mai had no problems complying with such terms, so long as he wasn't left on his own.

Hazel didn't understand Mai as well as I did, however. He didn't understand Mai's fascination with the constant decay of life or his strange desire to seek out punishment. Mai would never stop his downward spiral, he would never be able to shake his belief that he truly belonged inside the dead pool. His career, his relationships, his entire lifestyle – he had to be removed from all of it in order to truly be well again. He needed to surrender to the call of the pool, to allow himself to give in to it at last. Hazel couldn't make that happen, he didn't know how to, but I could. Mai had to be removed from his life as I had been from mine. That was to be my gift to him.

Chapter 34

THE SHOW IN which Mai was to perform alongside Zaurus was ridiculously overcrowded. It reminded me of the concert that cost those people their lives with fans all packed like sardines against the metal railings, screaming and bumping into one another in a solid mass of blurred faces.

Basil was there. He'd been hired by a music magazine to photograph the event – or so he told security – but I could see deceit in his eyes. I couldn't understand how I'd ever been fooled by the man when now it was so clear how corrupt he was. Those accidents that had occurred during our music video – the faulty safety net and stubborn coffin – hadn't been accidents at all. Interesting how sins write themselves upon the faces of the living and how easily dead eyes can see them. I simply *knew* that Basil had tried to hurt Mai in the past and he was planning to do so again now.

I followed Basil to the side of the stage as the show began. Zaurus had dressed in a suit and slicked back her hair to make herself look more like a man. Mai looked as he always did, masculine but undoubtedly pretty. A large sheet of glass had been placed across the center of the stage, keeping Mai and Zaurus separated, but nearly able to touch. The glass had been Zaurus' idea, to tease both the audience – who couldn't really *see* the glass was there – and Mai. They were singing their own songs, taking turns singing the other's lyrics. The final song would be the original they'd written together.

The show was half over when Basil stopped photographing and started wandering around backstage. He kept eyeing the rafters, the lighting, the hooks and ropes that operated the curtains. I knew my suspicions were correct when he started poking at one of the knotted ropes. He was after Mai.

It all happened so quickly that I don't even have all the details to give. What I *meant* to do was to work one of the hanging bags of sand loose so it would fall and render Basil unconscious. What happened was a chain reaction of falling weights and chaos rushed the stage instead.

The curtains closed on the band, removing them from the audience's sight. Lights fell. One of the heavy metal hooks broke free and swung out across the front of the stage. Zaurus saw it coming and shouted for Mai to duck, but there wasn't time. The hook blasted him upside the head and knocked him back into the glass wall. It shattered and the shards rained down on top of Zaurus as she huddled fearfully against the stage floor.

The curtains were quickly pulled open but Mai didn't get up. Everyone had fallen silent, watching in awestruck horror. Then a few started clapping, believing it was all part of the show. Mai was bleeding, his blood branching out into a growing puddle upon the stage floor beneath his head. He was lying on his side so that the audience couldn't see his face – but I could. He was out cold.

The remaining lights flickered as I walked forward through the curtains and past the band. The smashed lights began to spark and buzz in a threatening manner, but it mattered little to me. I was beyond their reach. I only cared about approaching Mai; I made the hook that had struck him become still.

Where was Hazel now, I wondered, as some fans started to scream and Mai bled out before the crowd? Other people were still clapping. The lights continued to flicker. Such drama on the stage wasn't necessarily new for Zaurus. Many fans didn't believe Mai was actually hurt, but they'd have cheered even if they did. It was entertainment to them either way.

Zaurus refused to touch Mai. She had a fear of blood and bodily fluids in general and Mai was not the sort of person she trusted to be free of diseases. I found that rather funny, though I can't really say why – funny in a horrid sort of way. He was dying before her eyes and she was thinking of possible contamination. Self before others, always. No one ever criticized her for it.

Most realized the matter was indeed serious when the paramedics rushed onto the stage and carefully placed Mai on a stretcher. The show was over a good fifteen minutes early and Zaurus was left in a rut. She stood and waited – she *wanted* to finish the show solo – but then someone announced that she wasn't permitted to go on. The reason, which no one told the audience, was that Basil had been found dead backstage. He'd been killed by a serious blow to the head. They found the loose rope that had started the entire mess still clutched in his hand.

I thought it best not to ride in the ambulance with Mai, as there was little space and sensitive equipment with which I would likely interfere. I didn't want Mai to die – not like that. I wanted the medics to be able to properly do their jobs. I hung around The Razor instead and stared at Basil's corpse. He'd been killed by one of the sandbags, it had struck him right on the temple, but he looked as though he was only sleeping. I tried to imagine how I must have appeared. Certainly not as pleasing to the eye. I wondered if Mai had seen my corpse.

I expected to see Basil. I expected to see his spirit and have the chance to taunt or at least smirk at him, but it didn't happen. He'd already quit his body and gone off to wherever he was meant to go. He hadn't been given the chance to linger about as I had been.

Hazel was seated at Mai's bedside by the time I decided to go to the hospital. Mai was asleep, a bandage around his head and left ear, dressed in one of those ugly white and blue spotted gowns. Hazel seemed suddenly so much older in my eyes as he sat with head bowed, his concern for Mai genuine.

Over the years, Mai had become something of a brother to Hazel, a relative that he actually liked and felt loved by. When Mai hurt, Hazel also felt the ache – that was the real difference between Hazel and me. I had always taken the hurt and thrived.

They expected Mai to be fine. His ear had taken the brunt of the blow and they feared that there might be some loss of hearing – apparently a risk that already existed because of his skin disease – but considering how deadly the blow could have been that seemed a blessing. The glass hadn't cut him too deeply – overall, he'd been extremely fortunate, indeed.

The monitor next to Mai's bed made an odd bleep as I drew near. Hazel's head perked up, alarmed, and he began staring hard in the monitor's direction. He couldn't see me, I even waved to make certain of that, but he *felt* me. Whether he'd believed Mai's talk of the dead pool and its spirits at the time or not, the talk had opened his mind to the possibility and now he could feel me. I enjoyed the mix of fear and anger that was spreading across his face, but he didn't say anything. Neither of us said or did a thing for at least an hour.

There was really no calming Mai down once he woke up.

He'd been told that Basil was at the show and that the accident had been Basil's doing, but he didn't believe it. They'd been playing footage of his accident on the television near his bed and Mai had watched it. He'd seen the curtains flutter as if someone was passing through. He'd seen the flickering lights. Even Hazel couldn't convince him that I hadn't been there.

"People keep dying!" Mai shouted. "Everyone but me…it's *never* me. I'm gonna end it. I'll just fucking kill myself. Will that make you happy? Blue or Gray or whatever the hell your name is…?"

The nurses thought Mai was crazy, they even gave him a sedative to force him to quiet down and tried to phone the psych ward. Hazel talked them out of contacting a shrink, thankfully, though he was as concerned as they were. I'd been wrong when I thought that Hazel was speaking to me in Mai's apartment, he'd simply been issuing a prayer of sorts out loud. He still couldn't let himself believe I was haunting Mai. He didn't *want* to believe. I decided to convince him.

The bathroom tricks had worked so well on Mai that I decided to use them again against dear Hazel. He left Mai safely sleeping and entered the restroom across the hall with a yawn. The room was empty. I allowed Hazel to do his business in peace and then turned on one of the faucets as he zipped up his pants. I turned on another faucet as Hazel turned around to look at the sink. He was startled but he moved to turn off the water without hesitation. I fogged up the mirror and Hazel watched as I wrote the words "END IT" upon the glass. "END IT – OR I WILL."

Hazel couldn't deny it was my handwriting. He stared and trembled and then uttered a startled yelp as I suddenly wiped the message away with one quick motion. Mai's rambling theories suddenly made an awful sort of sense, his conviction that something wanted to take him away to the pool less insane. Hazel raced out of the restroom, blindly bumping into a janitor working in the hallway and nearly falling right into the bucket of dirty mop water in the process. The janitor laughed at him.

"You look like you've seen a ghost," he said.

"What?" Hazel asked with a gasp.

"You need to lay offa the coffee," the man said. "Jumpy li'l thing, you are."

Static rose up from the black walkie-talkie on the janitor's belt. He took it off and flipped through the various channels, thinking that a co-worker was simply on the wrong frequency. The static remained the same on every channel and with it came the faint sounds of music and a voice. My voice. Hazel recognized the song immediately as "Tainted."

"Never been the same since it fell in the toilet," the janitor chuckled. "Damn thing."

The man looked up to see that he was talking to himself. Hazel had already fled the area.

238

Chapter 35

"KILL HIM OR he's lost."

That's what Hazel heard over the janitor's walkie.

"Kill him to save him."

The words repeated themselves over and over inside Hazel's mind as he sat at Mai's bedside. *My* words. Grainy and distorted as the voice had been, he knew without a doubt it had been mine. Hazel believed I was there. He knew now what Mai's dead pool sounded like and believed that I'd come to take Mai back to it. He just didn't have a clue what to do about it.

To me the answer was so blatantly obvious that it was frustrating. I'd told Hazel all he needed to know, but stupid, dimwit Hazel wasn't getting it. I don't know *why* that surprised me. I couldn't tell him anything more, it simply didn't work that way. Messages from the dead can't be anything other than distorted, given the many layers and veils they have to pass through. I'd come too far to quit, though. I had to keep trying.

Hazel stayed with Mai until the hospital released him, not once mentioning what he'd seen or heard in the restroom and hallway. They emerged from the building into an onslaught of flashbulbs, screeching fans and shouting reporters all packed together so tightly that the two of them barely had room to walk. Mai hid behind dark sunglasses and an oversized black coat. He appeared extremely unsteady on his feet, shaking like a leaf before the cameras.

"He still needs rest, give him some space for God's sake!" Hazel nearly barked; when his words went ignored, he resorted to shoving anyone that happened to come too close.

"Sign this? Please? I always miss the chance to ask!" a girl cried.

A small smile crossed Mai's lips when he spotted the girl, a teenager with a round face and messy brown hair. She was one of the Rocks that had finally managed to speak out at what seemed such an inappropriate time. There was something about her youth, her shyness and sincerity that appealed to Mai. He took the CD she'd held out to him and quickly signed his name to it. It was a copy of our first album.

"You didn't like any of the others?" Mai asked playfully.

"Oh no! I mean, yeah, but…this one was the first, so…"

The girl was embarrassed, unable to speak any further. Mai simply smiled warmly and returned the CD. He'd made her day and given her a memory that would last a lifetime. He would forget her face by the time he went to bed that morning.

"I hope you're better soon," she said.

Mai's smile darkened slightly and he forced a quick nod. "Me, too," he whispered.

Dozens started crying out for autographs after that, but Hazel shoved Mai into the car and made him leave the area. Hazel had asked that Mai be given space, but Mai would never be given such a thing. He was too big, his name and image simply too marketable. He didn't have the shoulders to properly carry such weight and yet he couldn't walk away. He'd tried and he'd been lured back. He would always go back. He couldn't leave the music and couldn't seem to have the music without the fame.

"I could walk down the street unnoticed if I was dead," he murmured, well on his way to sleep.

"Then make it happen," I whispered into his ear. "Leave it all."

"I can't leave it," Mai said. "It's not even about me anymore, is it. I'm not there…"

"Who are you talking to?" Hazel asked, giving Mai a shake.

Mai opened his eyes, startled and clueless. Mai had been able to hear me while half asleep. He answered me even when unable to register that he'd heard a statement he needed to respond to. I knew how to communicate with him, then. He had no control when asleep, he'd have to listen to me. It was about planting seeds. I could plant them while Mai slept – maybe plant them in Hazel, too. It was certainly worth a try.

Chapter 36

TIFFANY HAD BOOKED Mai's solo tour months earlier, and since all of the tickets had been pre-sold and shows completely sold out, she refused to listen when he and Hazel both said he shouldn't do the shows. Medically, Mai had been cleared and was told to simply wear earplugs and to sit down if he happened to feel dizzy. No excuse stood as justifiable in the eyes of the executives backing the shows.

Hazel told Mai to back out anyway, but he couldn't. People were depending on him and his neurotic fear of disappointing others was overwhelming. Anyway, history proved that people would continue to look for him if he simply disappeared,. They would have caught up to him in Alaska, eventually, had I not beaten them to it. He had no easy escape.

I tampered with their dreams for weeks, always whispering into their ears. Mai's solution was to stop sleeping altogether. In order to cope with no sleep he once again turned to pills. It was nothing like it had been when I was with him, but it would have risen to that level eventually. One day Hazel would wake up and find Mai a wasted waif on the verge of a breakdown just as I had. That's how it goes.

No one can save someone else no matter how positive or negative their influence unless they want to be saved. Hazel realized it. He realized how someone so close could begin to so badly deteriorate without his noticing. He was too close, just as I had been, but he wouldn't repeat my mistakes. That was one thing I could like about Hazel Grantz – he could do what had to be done no matter how painful it might be. He always slept well at night. He always let me into his dreams.

For weeks, Mai toured and ran himself ragged. He did his final appearance on Gary Trevors three months into the tour and nearly burst into tears when Gary jokingly asked when he found the time to sleep.

The mishaps also continued. I had to continue my role, after all. I couldn't stop. Lights were forever falling down or flickering, windows blew open or simply cracked for no apparent reason. Mai crashed his car into a street lamp because I caused the CD player to continuously screech or fast-forward through the songs no matter what disc he tried to play and he became distracted trying to turn the thing off. Alarm clocks went off an hour early or late – if they went off at all. The list went on and on and the fans became more divided. There were believers of Mai's "curse" and those offended and annoyed by what they saw as an overdone gimmick. Mai refused to address either.

Mai finally came completely unhinged when Hazel became the victim of a falling light. It hadn't really hurt him, he'd been too quick to receive a serious blow, but the incident had scared Mai. It terrified him. Those promises Hazel had made not so long ago had proven empty. Neither of them was safe. Nothing was okay. Nothing could ever truly be over until Mai answered my call and they both knew it.

Hazel caught Mai standing over the sink in their hotel bathroom directly afterward with a razor to his wrist. They got into a fairly nasty fist fight as Hazel struggled to steal the blade away. Hazel won only because Mai was afraid he'd accidentally hurt him if he didn't submit. It really was the breaking point. Hazel and I both knew what had to be done. We were finally ready to work together.

"I can't go on like this," Mai whispered, shaking his head. "I just want it to stop. I want it to *stop.*"

"I know," Hazel said softly. "It will, I swear it will. All you have to do is take control and do what you have to do more than just reach out to it. Throw the door so far open there's no chance of it swinging back shut."

I forgot to mention that I'd discovered something else about being dead. Being liberated of one's own flesh makes it easy to borrow that of another. Influencing dreams can turn to influencing thoughts. Occupying thoughts turns to controlling the flesh. I'd started practicing it at first without even realizing it. Mind over matter, they say. The mind never dies.

I took Blue's name in order to feel like someone else. Now I could actually *be* someone else. Being dead is like being born again and again for as long as there are thoughts to occupy. This is Mai's dead pool: the place that allows me to be without flesh yet remain amongst the living. To prey amongst the sleeping minds and susceptible bodies. A place where restless souls like myself looking to be heard and recognized can find satisfaction. It's very real, both tangible and fluid, coexisting directly between the veils of physical and spirit. Souls are reunited for a dance before fluttering away. Dreams become gateways. Inspiration couples with madness. Everything is intertwined.

Did Basil pull the rope that led to his death and Mai's injury? He most certainly did: but I was the force within his veins that guided his hand. It was Hazel's finger I used to write the message on the foggy mirror in the hospital bathroom and he didn't even know it. Just like he didn't consciously know that I was lurking inside of him now. I'd played a part in other things, too. Past events like the padded room and the coffin and the football field. Time is broken here, as I said before. I probably even influenced myself a time or two as bizarre as I know that sounds.

Hazel moved without saying a word. He put the razor that he'd snatched away from Mai to his own wrist and dug the blade in, his dark eyes remaining fixed upon Mai's face.

"What are you doing?!" Mai cried, his eyes wide and immediately misting over with tears.

"It's been long enough," Hazel said. "I can't stop. I can't stop until you make it stop."

"Then *take* me!" Mai shouted, pinning Hazel's arm down so he couldn't cut himself any deeper. "You can have me. Just get it over with!"

"You have to give yourself to me," Hazel said. "I've already shown you what to do. You've seen what to do in your dreams."

Mai could see me in Hazel's eyes. The normal reddish tint had turned blue and an expectant smile far too sharp to belong to the boy crossed Hazel's lips. I'm sure Mai couldn't fully comprehend it all, but he knew enough — understood on that unspoken level on which we know all truths that can't be put into words. He knew he had to come to me, but not out of spite or fear. He had to come out of love. Love for Hazel and me and himself. It was the only chance for freedom any of us had.

"I'm coming," Mai said, stealing the razor from Hazel's hand. "Where do you want to meet me?"

"The roof."

Mai rose to his feet and walked willingly onto the elevator outside his room. He rode it up to the roof in silence, avoiding the large mirror that hung on the wall behind him. He didn't need to look upon it to know that it was completely covered with frost.

The roof of this hotel was much like the one upon which I'd believed that Mai and I had made love. It was nearly identical. Perfect. The perfect place to end it all.

A swarm of fans had gathered on the sidewalk below, a roaring sea of white and brown ants that rocked, swayed and grew excited as Mai stepped out onto the ledge to greet them. He silently stared down at them, not moving at all, and then he lit a cigarette and took a long and graceful drag off of it.

Mai walked to the corner and peered down at the water directly below. The hotel had been built on a cliff that overlooked the ocean. Endless water. An endless pool. There was nothing but endless blue all around the eastern side of the building. The distance was fairly great, but Mai didn't find it terrifying. The fans could still see him, barely, from where he stood. They were still cheering and waving their arms. Mai turned his back on all of them.

The door to the roof's stair entrance suddenly flew open and there was Hazel, holding his bleeding wrist and panting frantically. Mai looked at him with near indifference and cracked a bittersweet smile as he tossed his cigarette aside. It started to rain, the drops light but tightly packed. They fell in a near solid sheet.

"What are you doing?" Hazel asked.

"You know what I'm doing," Mai replied softly. "Go back inside."

Hazel shook his head. "Get down from there, Mai."

"I'll not wait for Blue to slash your other wrist," Mai said. "Or maybe next time it'll be your throat. Or, maybe, next time a light will fall and bash both our brains in and it'll be a joint reunion. 'Trust that this is for the best and it will be.' Blue said that to me in a dream. 'Fall and you'll live on.' Now, get yourself to a doctor, Hazel. You're a mess."

Hazel stared as if Mai was speaking another language. He was standing on the edge of one of the tallest buildings in town and speaking about falling off of it as he might discuss the color of a carpet. Hazel's mind told him that he ought to be pleading with Mai to step down, but there was something that prevented him from doing so. He'd had dreams, too. He finally understood it all.

"It's your moment, Blueski," Mai remarked, holding his arms out to his sides with his back toward the ocean view. "Let's do what we've got to do."

He looked radiant as he stared fearlessly at Hazel. Stared and saw me lurking once again within the boy's dark eyes.

Hazel smiled and quickly walked over to where Mai stood. The fans couldn't see Hazel, he was too short and the angle was wrong, but they could see that Mai appeared to be talking to *someone*. Photographers with their expensive cameras started zooming in, hoping to "eavesdrop" even from such a great distance through their lenses. They could see Mai was smiling, giving *that* smile. Hazel returned it with a smile of stone.

"Don't be afraid," Hazel said.

He put both hands upon Mai's waist and gave him a violent push. Mai fell quite quickly, his arms falling back behind him, his fingers combing the air. Hair matted down by the rain, dark and wild, eyes closed, face serene – Mai looked something like an angel on his way down to the water below.

Much like the day he had nearly tumbled over the railing of the hotel stairwell, Mai suddenly opened his eyes and stared with an intense curiosity at the darkness closing in around him. Finally he was returning to the place part of him had always yearned to return to. It felt like coming home.

This time, as he falls and stares and wonders what might be awaiting him, I'll be there to catch him.

246

Epilogue

THE BODY OF Mai Evans was never recovered, though a rescue crew searched the ocean where he'd fallen for days. He was declared dead and fans all around the world united in mourning. Candlelit vigils were held and televised. Mai's songs dominated the radio. Magazines paid one tribute after another. The albums flew off of the shelves and people who hadn't heard of Mai before or simply hadn't paid much attention decided to become new fans in order to fit in with the grieving trend.

Mai's face continues to appear on magazines, calendars, shirts, coffee mugs and key chains more than a year after his apparent death,. One of the photographers with a zooming camera had snapped a photo of Mai falling back off of the roof, slicked by the rain, with arms spread out behind him and head tilted back – the last picture ever taken. It kept Mai frozen in time, made immortal by death. Another undying beauty idolized and mourned, remembered for a legacy of grace and cigarette smoke. The picture was recently used as the cover of a compilation album and appears on a few of the shirts available for sale in the trendy music shops.

It all keeps Mai Evans, the product and the image, very much alive. Dying in the public eye turns men into gods. Icons. Posters and logos. The industry will see to it that Mai Evans continues to fall forever.

Gary Trevors delivered the eulogy at Mai's televised memorial service once hope of retrieving Mai's body had been abandoned, though the words he read sounded more like something Mai would have written himself:

"He was a wildfire that lit up the night, restless and powerful and too hungry for his own good. Like all flames, he eventually burned out – though I think we all feel his extinguished far too soon."

It seemed a touching close to the service. Hazel, Minnie, Dart and Jim all teamed up to pay their respects through an original, exclusive song. Hazel took the singing honors, though his performance seemed strangely unemotional. Afterwards, Minnie was caught selling illegally burned copies of the song on his website.

I spend my days and nights haunting a cozy little bar and nightclub called After Life, an intimate little hole in the wall with dim lighting and candles blazing on every round table. They have a house band that plays every night, a steady gig that allows a lot of freedom and earns little publicity.

Most only focus on the lead singer, an older woman with a soft, bluesy voice called Janis, but my eyes remain on the guitarist. He's a rail of a guy always dressed in jeans, some sort of oversized shirt, and black and white sneakers. He keeps his stormy gray eyes fairly hidden beneath a black knitted hat.

He's rather rugged. He sometimes doesn't bother to shave and rarely ever lifts his fair face up out of the shadows to look anyone in the eye. Whenever asked his name, he replies that it's Jeremy. Plain, simple Jeremy – though in the back of his mind, I know, he's still tempted to tell them Mai. It always rises to the tip of his tongue and then he remembers to push it away.

Mai, as in mine…

About the Author

JD PHILLIPS IS a native of Bartholomew County, Indiana. She attended IUPUC, where she majored in psychology and earned a bachelor of arts degree from Indiana University. She is currently employed by a residential treatment facility for troubled youth.

She has been writing since childhood and has had several short works published in *Literalines*, a magazine published out of IUPUC.

Her first two novels were *Dreaming While You Sleep: Book One of Footprints on the Other Side*, followed shortly thereafter by its sequel *A Beautiful Rain*. *Tainted* was her third novel, which saw its debut in September 2006 and became the first to sell internationally. It was named first runner up in the 2007 Best Books of Indiana Awards. Her fourth novel, *The Dead Pool*, was released in 2007 and received an honorable mention at the 2008 New York Book Festival. *Mad Angel* was released in July 2009.

With many other books already written and ready to go, many more are sure to follow in the days to come.

To read excerpts from JD's books and other writings, visit www.jdphillipsauthor.net.